The Dutch Winter

A Novel

By
Albert vande Steeg

Aakenbaaken & Kent

D1518205

ISBN: 978-1-958022-00-9

Dedication

To Cindy, my sweetheart, who stands by me
and blesses me.

*"I would have despaired unless I had believed that I
would see the goodness of God in the land of the living"*.
David, King of Israel

Raid

Hiding

Prologue

January 1943

The Arnhem Centrum, city square or plaza was a vibrant center of activity. Shops bustled with shoppers. Cafes and beer gardens filled with hungry thirsty people taking time to visit with friends.

The historic brick church stood open for tourists and the needy souls who need prayer and seek a blessing. The clock in the tower showed the time of day and its bell clanged on the hour and half hour. People scheduled lunch by the bell and closed businesses when it rang six times.

The clock is stopped. The bell no longer tolls. Shoppers no longer roam the streets. The Centrum is empty, cold, dreary and dark. The patches of snow by the lamp posts and in the shady side of the buildings are the only bright spots as they reflect what little light there is. Only a few windows have lights. Shadows and gloom prevail. Nazis occupy the rooms that have lights. The few people still living here get by with what has not been conscripted by Nazi Germany's soldiers. Their windows are dimly lit by candles and kerosene lamps.

This once vibrant city on the Rhine has lost hope. The future is as dark and grim as the gray sky and the soot clinging to the walls; even the Arnhem tower and the Cathedral across the square are closed and dark. Gloom surrounds the city. No one comes or goes; despair shuttered the shop doors for months.

A small group of people are huddled in the square. Clustered in a small area, they seek comfort in their closeness but also to have a view. Their husbands, fathers or in some cases, mothers or sisters are in custody of the enemy. Thirty cold, scared people hope to find comfort or warmth from each other this cold January morning. Sixty eyes look at the corner window of the fifth floor of the burnished brown brick building on the south end of the city square. Fear brings tears to their eyes. Distraught they gaze at the window hoping to see the face of the person they love.

This dirty brown brick building is composed of shops at the street level, offices on the second floor and flats and rooms to rent on the upper floors. The Nazi occupation has closed the shops, the flats are empty. Everyone fled when the Nazi SS took this building as their own.

Alida Mollengraff huddles in this small group. She holds her bicycle in a gloved hand. A scarf, she knitted covers her neck and ears. Her cheeks are rosy from the icy cold, her eyes sad and fearful. Nearly everyone holds a bike. Many rode twenty kilometers to gather here. Everyone holds a hope. A desperate hope to see the person they love one more time, but fearful that they have been shipped to concentration camps.

Some bikes have no tires, the wheels wrapped with rags or willow branches; really anything that will prevent damage to the rims. Replacement tires for bikes or cars are not available; all the rubber products have been sent to Germany for the Nazi military.

The group is silent. All eyes focused on the window. Alida comes every day. Today is the tenth day since the SS dragged her mother and father out of their home, taken away for harboring and aiding a Jewish mother and her six-year old daughter.

This non-descript building is the holding area for arrestees on their way to extermination camps or, if lucky, labor camps. With little hope, everyone wants to catch one final glimpse of their loved one trapped inside awaiting imprisonment in Germany or Poland.

Alida held on to the hope her mother might be released because she has been here ten days. Each day Alida waved to her mother when it was her turn to come to the window. Her father has not appeared since the third day. Trembling, Alida wondered if he is alive or if he has been gassed and buried in a mass grave, a grave that will never be found. Those buried there will never have a priest or pastor say prayers over their bodies commending them to eternity.

Alida rode sixteen kilometers to stand in front of this building, a long ride in the bitter cold, even worse when wind blew the snow.

2

Her face is frost bitten from riding into the wind. She has waited here for three hours, the pain in her heart is excruciating.

Her mother didn't come to the window. Sobbing she turned to go, her mother is gone. Probably gone forever.

The woman next to Alida places her arm over her shoulder offering comfort. "Ja, my Piet is not coming to the window today either."

Turning toward her Alida wraps her arms around this stranger both weeping in the bitter cold. "Gone, dying for caring about people they did not know, but could not let die just for being Jewish," She whispered. They wept on each other shoulders.

Her head bowed so the tears fall without freezing on her cheeks, Alida rode away. The tears formed tiny icicles on her scarf. "Damn them", she swore. "They must pay. Either God does something or I will!"

That is life in war; people find comfort and compassion from strangers. People contending with problems, pain and loss created by a common enemy; the Nazi regime of the Democratic Socialist Party.

Chapter 1

August 1936

Jon and Nieske hold hands, as sweethearts do. They stroll in the woods just outside Ede in the Provence of Gelderland. They are in love, have been for years. Marriage must wait till housing becomes available.

Gelderland is in the middle of The Netherlands, north south and on the east side adjoining Germany. Nederland, as the Dutch call it, was once referred to as the Low Lands. Gelderland is the only area of Holland with natural forest lands. There are no canals, no dikes and few windmills in Gelderland. This is the original part of The Netherlands, the part above sea level. The Dutch boast that God made the heavens and the earth but the Dutch created Holland. Dutch ingenuity salvaged this land from the sea, creating a nation called The Netherlands.

The late afternoon sun brings slivers of light across the path. Deep in these woods there is no air movement except for the murmur of the wind passing through the tree tops. The rustle of the leaves are background for the music of birds singing or chirping.

Their conversation is animated; her voice is urgent with desire while his is terse and modulated. They are in love, he adores her and she admires and respects him. Their feelings for each other are noticeable. Their voices are soft and considerate, their eyes shine with admiration. Jon pushes his bicycle with his right hand, his left holding Nieske's right hand.

They rode their bicycles many kilometers to meet here. She came from Bennekom and he from Otterloo. Five years they have dated, meeting in these woods and conversing in village cafe shops. Three years ago they promised eternal love to each other and began planning a life together. Their application for housing is lying on a bureaucrat's desk waiting for approval to rent or buy a house.

Housing is scarce. The provincial government controls every request for renting or leasing. Few homes are built because farmers are loath to sell land for houses and the forested land is protected from development.

The economy has struggled since the Boer War in South Africa and the rebuilding after World War I. Land is scarce, money is short but hope is eternal. Their three year wait is short when compared to friends who have waited five to six years for housing.

Jon Van Bemmel, stops. He lays his bicycle down alongside the path and lays her bicycle next to it. He is tall with dark Gallic hair trimmed short. Under the hair falling down over his forehead is a pair of bright green eyes. His eyes are steady, warm, not glaring, they show strength and determination. A deeper look reveals eyes with a glint of humor which confirm the smile lines. This humor softens his face. The lines at the corner of his eyes reflect a smiling face and the twinge of his upper lip brings character to his high cheek bones and firm chin.

Facing each other he grasps her hands. Jon has strong working hands, calloused from working the fields; plowing, cultivating and harvesting, but the power comes from feeding, milking and working cattle and sheep.

Nieske's hands too are strong but not calloused; strong because she milks her father's cows by hand and soft from doing house work. "Nieske, I have a plan," he announced. "It has been a long time coming, but things are happening so that you and I will have a home together. No more wandering in the woods and Sunday after church lunches."

Nieske looks up at him. Her heart skips a beat when she hears the hope in his voice. "What? How? Have you heard from the housing authority?"

"No, this is better than that. I have found a small farm that we can afford. It is eight hectares, large enough to raise a family and to give us our start in life together. The best part is that buying this farm does not require approval from the government, no applications, no waiting for bureaucrats. I am sick of bureaucrats and their asinine rules; go here, sign this, wait in this line, come back next week, bring this or that form; I am so done with it all.

6

I checked the waiting list; we are at least a year away from approved housing! When we buy this farm all that hassle and red-tape will be over. He smiled, his face crinkled and his eyes lit up with hope. Nieske, we can make this work! We can get married and start our family!"

"Do you have enough money? Is it a nice house? Remember, you promised we would never live in a house that is a dump! I am not settling for a worn out dump even if does mean we can get married sooner. I love you Jon, but."

Jon stopped her in the middle of her sentence before she could ask about the barns and farm.

"Whoa, slow down. Yes, the house is nice; it is a modern brick house, built ten years ago. It has a tile roof, not an old thatched roof house. There are three bedrooms, a water pump in the kitchen and one in the barn. Yes, there are barns. The cow barn holds fifteen cows, the hen house has space for three hundred chickens and the hog barn has room for eight sows and their litters. All are in good shape."

Nieske Bultan dropped Jon's hands. Doubt crept into Jon's face. He feared she would not grasp the possibilities for their future as he did. Nieske stepped into Jon's arms, not noticing his fear as laid her head on his chest. "Is it really happening, Jon? Are the years of waiting really coming to an end? This is the second best day of my life!" she sighed. "I, too, want to start our family soon."

"Sit down, I will tell you everything," Jon pulled her to a fallen tree to sit on. This was their favorite spot to get away and talk. Here they were alone sitting in their own private alcove; a natural arbor, surrounded by ferns and trees. The trees span across the space below creating a canopy with filtered sunlight. The sun rays flicker through the fluttering leaves. The warmth has dried the log where they sit. This morning's rain has washed the ferns and trees, creating this garden spot that is as bright and shiny as Jon's dreams. The breeze whispers overhead, the sun light flickers over their faces. They love this place. It is an alcove of peace and quiet, far from the noise of family and neighbors or the distractions of a café.

Jon plucks a few blueberries growing amidst the ferns. He shares them with Nieske. They savor the sweet juice as they squeeze the berries with their tongues, not biting them, just squeezing till the juice squirts filling their mouths with the wonderful flavor of forest grown berries.

Before Jon could start, Nieske's doubts returned. "Where is the money coming from, Jon? Did your mother leave you more inheritance than you said? Are your brothers and sister helping you? Have you saved enough money for the down payment? Can we afford the payments?"

A grin spreads along Jon's mouth; he realizes that she is incapable of asking a single question. Habitually she assembles her questions into groups.

She ended with, "Are you sure this will work?"

Jon grabs her hands, "I love that about you. You have so many questions and they are all good ones. I thought about what you would ask. That helped me figure this out. I am so glad you trust me to do this right. You do trust me, right?"

He does not wait for an answer, just continues, "You know I stayed home to take care of mom till she died. She had no one to take care of her when my father died. I was twelve years old then. The second oldest brother in the military and the oldest brother and my sister both had lovers. They married and left home, so it was my duty to take care of her. I was disappointed but not surprised that my mother stuck to tradition; giving my brother the family farm purely because he is the eldest. He has never helped his mother. He ticks me off. He's a taker, never giving, even to his mother."

"My sister is appreciative and generous too, she is just like mom. Mom gave her cash to help her and her husband buy the farm on the *Otterloo Ede* road. I got what was left in cash and the sheep I tended for her. The brother in the military seldom wrote and only came home once. Mom sort of wrote him off. He has not contacted any of us since he was stationed in Indonesia almost six years ago.

My little flock has grown. I have thirty-five ewes that will lamb soon. Along with that I have set aside a nice tidy sum from my job at the Wageningen's Farm Co-op."

"I am sorry Jon, but I am worried. You know my father has five of us. We are all living at home. He has no extra money and his new wife is really stingy," Nieske sighed." No help coming from there! We are on our own. I do not want to put a damper on this and do not doubt you; I just need to know it will work!"

"On our own, that is exactly what I want. I want us to be independent and not beholden to anyone, especially not your stepmother. I am thirty two years old and you are twenty seven, it is time for us to be on our own. We can do this!"

Chapter 2

Lost in their musings they hold hands. Jon thinks about the future farm, raising a family, buying more cows. Six cows and one yearling heifer come with the farm. He needs a horse or two to pull the plow and the wagon. His brother promised to give him two sows to start the hog operation and his sister is giving twenty chickens to kick start egg production.

This has been Jon's dream. He made plans like this once before, eight years ago, when he was in love with Elsie, the daughter of the farmer living two farms down the road from his mother. They had kept the romance a secret for a whole year. His mother heard about the romance through the gossip circle at church. She came home in a rage.

"What do you think you are doing?" she screamed. That family is Protestant Reformed! We do not date or marry those hard-nosed religious zealots. They have the doctrine of God's grace all messed up. No son of mine is going to marry or be one of them! Them, those" She sputtered not wanting to or knowing how to voice the name of their faith.

His mother laid out the rules. "You stop seeing that girl or move out of my house. You will have no place to live and no inheritance, your choice!"

Too young and too poor to leave home he went to see Elsie for the last time. His lip trembled as he recalled that heartbreaking meeting. She began to cry as she too related what her father had said about her dating a liberal Christian. He too ordered her to break off the relationship. Jon knew he needed to stay to help his mother and Elsie would not break her father's heart. Victims of bias and bound by tradition they wept in each other's arms before departing.

The pain and loss of that experience haunted him for years. It was ancient history since he found Nieske. He loved this woman.

Shaking his head he returned to his thoughts of the farm. They would have eggs to eat and plenty extra to sell. The cash will help the weekly budget. The hogs would both produce a litter of eight to twelve piglets. That money will grow the hog operation.

Boer (farmer) Lambertus had an early start on planting grains finding time between the rains. The crop is looking very good; they would have wheat and rye for making bread and barley for animal feeds. Hopefully there would be more than they needed, the extra he would sell at the local mill. Then he could buy an extra cow or heifer.

Smiling with hope and confidence in the future, he looked down at Nieske. He was excited; his dream of having a farm and a family was about to happen.

She was lost in her own thoughts She was excited to be marrying the man she loved and very happy to leave home. She would miss her father, two brothers, Geert who was thirteen months younger and Case the youngest of the family and two sisters Wilma and Trina who were between Geert and Case, in age. As the oldest she had managed the house and meals after her mother died. Nieske had been the woman of the house since age sixteen and now she was twenty six, almost twenty seven. A long time, she mused. She was tired of competing with her new step-mother. Reluctantly she admitted that her father was the happiest he had been in eleven years.

The Bultan family was shrinking; Geert and both sisters were marrying within a year and Case was keeping company with Altje Smeenk a farmer's daughter from nearby Wekerom.

She, Nieske, wants to marry this man who is devoted to her like he had been to his mother. She sees him as being hopelessly optimistic and expecting great things from the future. He denies being an optimist, stating he just follows his vision in pragmatic ways. He was a realist who knows it takes work and dedication to fulfill a dream.

He was a hardworking man. They might never be rich, but for sure would never be poor. This man will provide for his family and be dedicated to taking care of her, always. She trusted him with her future. Yes, life would be good.

Sighing she looked up at him; she was only five foot two and he was six foot two. "I love you Jon. I am in. When can we go see the place?" Looking down she blushed shyly and whispered, "I can hardly wait to get married." She hoped he did not misunderstand. She looked forward to the security of marriage and life with this man. Embarrassed, she thought about their love life. That would be good, too, Jon was tender and kind, sex would not be wild, just deeply satisfying.

"Tomorrow; I work until noon Saturday. I will come by your house on my way from work; we can ride to the farm together. It is on *Danmakerweg,* half a kilometer from the *Otterloo Ede weg. Boer* Lambertus is expecting us at two p.m. We will have tea with his family. Then tour the farm and discuss the business part."

"How have you kept this a secret so long?"

"Not long, three weeks ago he approached me with the idea for us to buy it. He is friends with my sister and has known our family for a long time. She told him about us, that we want to marry and start a farm. It has been real difficult keeping it secret. I did not want to get your hopes up until I could figure out if this was even possible."

Jon continued, "He, *Boer* Lambertus, has already gone to the bank. He talked to *Heer* Kammerling to see if we might qualify for the loan. He checked that out first, he didn't want to waste his time pursuing this or disappoint us. He really likes the idea that we get our start there. He respects my sister and brother-in-law; they convinced him that we will take good care of what he started. He really loves his farm and wants to make sure his creation is well taken care of. He didn't want to sell the place but he needs to move to Kampen to take care of his mother. His mother lives there on the old family farm. The farm is been in the family for five generations so they want to keep it in the family.

His father died two months ago. The hired hand is helping his mother run the place. His sister is not interested and neither is her husband. Her husband has a butcher shop that he loves and it is doing very well. So, Lambertus expects to inherit the family farm. It is larger, but older; he's pleased that he will be close to his family and his old church. He was baptized there, in the same church his family attended for four generations, so he has a spiritual connection to the town. His wife is willing to move but says that if she is giving up her nice house for the old one she wants to modernize it and make it more comfortable."

"He is selling us the cows, calves, implements and the tools. I plan to bid on one horse at the auction. The banker knows your family and my family, so the trust is there to make us the loan. He expects we can manage the farm and knows that if we work hard the debt will be manageable. Having a good name and reputation is paying off."

Their future looks bright; life is going to be great. Jon has that "happily ever after" look in his eyes. Neither one of them knew that a storm is coming. A storm named Nazism, a product of Adolf Hitler chancellor of the Democratic Socialists.

Chapter 3

Jon's business plan came together nicely. The farm is doing very well. The crops are growing; the wheat is especially tall and forming heads full of grain. The income from the milk and eggs is more than what he and Nieske estimated. The bank accepted his down payment, made the loan for the farm and cash for two horses and three cows. He was proud of his plans and enjoyed the rewards of seeing it come together. The house was mostly empty of furnishings. They have a bed to sleep on and table and chairs for eating meals. His confidence was affirmed. The farm was producing enough income to buy all the things they will need. After all, you can't have everything when starting out.

He learned economics from his father, Arie, who stressed the importance of building the barn first and then build the house. A barn will provide for a house, but a house never builds a barn. Simple business logic from a man who had schooled for only three years, and Jon understood this. For him it is not a Dutch thing; it is just good business sense.

Jon and Nieske are confident that their business plan will bring the money for the furniture they need and provide the funds for the babies they plan to have. They are doing very well with a bedroom set, kitchen table and six chairs and the antique cabinet and hutch his mother left him.

Smiling to himself he remembered how often his mother would say, "Stuff is not what makes one happy."

Tomorrow is his wedding day. The past three months have sped by. Most of his time was spent working and making plans for the farm while Nieske made the wedding plans. The pressure and stress of taking on these life changing events brought out the best in them.

They made a good team. He liked her ideas and financial acumen and she understood and supported his business plan and pragmatic outlook; it was a good partnership.

With Jon living on the farm they saw each other more often.

Their farm was only three kilometers from her father's farm, making it a short ten minute bike ride. Nieske rode over to see him every day, sometimes twice a day. She knew he was busy with the chores; weeding the rows of vegetables or later in the day feeding the animals and milking the cows. She liked to come at milking time, often pulling out the extra stool, snuggle up close to a cow and milk her while they talked.

Jon loved to hear her chatter on about the wedding plans and events of her day as they relieved the cow's heavy udders of their milk. Nieske was a good milker, the milk squirting into the pail with enough force to create a layer of foam. The cows stood peacefully for her, loving her gentle hands and kind demeanor as she talked to them.

Today Jon is sitting on the hitching rail, one foot on the ground, the other hanging comfortably. His foot sways slowly as counts his blessings and contemplates his future. The *klomp*, wooden shoe, falls off but he ignores it because he is lost in thoughts about how fortunate he is to have this woman who loves him. He feels honored to be trusted by the bank and is more than pleased to have found this farm.

"What do you mean, luck or good fortune?" his father would have said. Arie was a strong Calvinist who did not believe in luck. "Providence - that is what it is! Providence! It is God taking care of his people. No such thing as luck." Then he would scowl, drawing his forehead into wrinkles while his eyes glared intently. He was not angry, just intense about his theology.

A smile crosses Jon's face when thinking about his father. A hard working man, who loved adventure; he had not settled down to marry until he was fifty-two years old.

His nomadic life brought him to farms in almost every province from Maastricht to Friesland; where he worked the fields or tended livestock. He worked the fishing boats in the North Sea and the freighters on the Rhine to Switzerland and the Danube in Austria. He loved seeing new places, doing new things, learning new cultures and meeting interesting people. Working hard provided opportunities; he loved the challenge of new jobs and new places. For him life was an adventure to conquer and enjoy. Then he met the love of his life, bought a farm and settled down.

When he met Gerda he changed, the love bug bit him hard. He gave up his wandering, adventurous and nomadic ways and settled down. Seventeen years of marriage had produced four children and a happy contented life.

He started looking for a farm after asking Gerda to marry him. He gathered his savings from the banks he used in the various places he lived and worked. He called the loans he had with people in these scattered places. He had a nice "nest egg" when all his loans and savings were collected into one account. He bought the farm in Otterloo.

He loved the farm, enjoyed working with animals and planting crops. Watching the seeds sprout out of the soil renewed his hope in life and faith in God's plan for the future. But most of all he loved his wife and family. Arie was fond of saying, "If I had known being married was this good, I would have done it a lot sooner."

Arie loved his sons, Gerard, Bernard and Jon but doted on his daughter, Elorene. She was the apple of his eye.

Jon smiled to himself with contentment, as he thought about doing what Gerard and Elorene had done before him. They were both happy on their farms and each had two children. Now he too is making his own way, like his dad, doing it on his own merit and hard work.

His chores are done, Nieske has gone home. He sat watching the sun slip behind as a cloud's shadow envelops him. Soon it will be night and dark out. He shivers as the darkness closes in, like the darkness he experienced last night while reading the newspaper, *de Trouw*. Jon's life is doing well but the world around him is facing dark times. Fortunately the darkness will not come to Holland. Queen Wilamina declared The Netherlands an officially neutral nation.

Jon muses about this neutrality; will that make Holland safe? Is it only three years ago that the Democratic Socialist Party made

Adolf Hitler the Chancellor of Germany? As the darkness of night surrounds Jon the darkness of the future brings shivers up his back.

Hitler is using that position to travel the country giving fiery speeches. Hitler is promising a new economy with jobs for everyone and to make the world recognize the greatness of Germany. He has mesmerized the youth by offering free education, free health care and guaranteed retirements. The promise of free living has rallied the youth's support. They love their new found power, they can control elections. With zeal and delight they promoted this zealot.

The youth form brigades and organize support groups for Hitler's programs and ideals. Rowdy and boisterous young men formed the "Brown Shirts" which soon morphed into a vigilante posse. They roam the streets harassing Jews and anyone that did does openly support Hitler. Harsh treatment awaits anyone opposed to this Socialist Democratic idea of the government providing free stuff.

The Brown Shirts enforce Hitler's order to disband all political parties. Now the Nazi party is the sole political party in Germany, establishing socialism in Germany. That was 1934.

Hitler restored the military might Germany had when the Kaiser ruled. He installed a rabid nationalistic pride that excluded everything not Aryan.

A scowl crossed Jon's face as he contemplates this angry, volatile man. A man, who had no God, does not use tobacco or alcohol and eats a vegetarian diet. Hitler is his own god, loving his own intellect and power; he has no use or place for God or any spiritual power. He is a power that answers only to himself, nothing will impede his agenda. He became a monster. A monster that euthanized everyone he deemed inferior. The old and feeble were not denied health care, they were killed. The children with disabilities, either mental or physical, are used as laboratory rats, experimented with and then euthanized.

"What is this world coming to, how much evil can we handle?" Jon asked himself.

Chapter 4

Jon heard the bike as it rode up the gravel driveway. When he saw it was Nieske he jumped down from his perch. He embraced her with his muscular arms pulling her close. He smelled of sweat and cows but she snuggled close, relishing the warmth. She found comfort in the aroma of his embrace.

She was accustomed to cattle and liked the smell of cows. She liked the odor of horses better but cows were good. As a farm kid she learned to milk cows when very young. At age seven her father taught her how to squeeze milk from cows' teats. Now she and Jon milked their cows together. She set her stool close to a cow, leaned her forehead into the cow's side. Soft words and this snuggle made both she and the cow comfortable. The cows were happy to have a warm hand grasp their teats, especially on cold days.

Enjoying their embrace neither one thought about cows, milk or the farm. Their minds were focused on tomorrow's events. Both of them were dreaming of life together. Their dream is truly naïve; marriage is never as it is imagined. Jon knew that his father had found it to be far better than expected. He was confident this would be true for him too.

Tomorrow they would be man and wife, she could hardly wait. And neither could he.

Hand in hand they walked through the open barn door to the hay wagon. He boosted her up and jumped up next to her letting their feet dangle down. She sat close, tight actually; he hugged her with one arm and kissed the top of her head.

He scooted away enough to be able to look into her eyes. "How are the plans for tomorrow coming?" he quizzed. "Are we ready?"

"All set; we gather at City Hall at nine-thirty. My father, step-mother and siblings will all be there along with one of your brothers and sister. The Burgemeester of Ede will do the civil ceremony and sign the license. He and my father are good friends, they attend the same church. Then we walk to the *Oude Kerk* for the church wedding. It is only three blocks and the wedding party will walk together."

"My new suit is ready and shoes are polished. How about your dress, did the seamstress do a nice job?"

"You are going to love the dress. It is a beautiful creamy satin, you will see it when we meet at City Hall. I have a dark red carnation for me and a white one for you? My sisters are making an arrangement of flowers for me to carry; it has dark red carnations surrounded by white carnations and pink roses. I love it!"

"The wedding will be great, I am so proud of you! I just wish my dad and mom could see how blessed and happy I am. My mother was worried that I would not find the right girl. She would be so pleased and excited to be your mother-in-law."

"How is your family doing with our big day? How is your dad handling all this?" he quarried.

She did not tell him that her father was not happy with their choice of church. He thinks the Netherland's Reformed Church is the only good church; he dislikes the thought of entering the building of another denomination, even when it is reformed and Calvinistic.

Nieske persisted when arguing with her father that the church she was attending with Jon was the church to be married in. Just being in this church built in the twelfth century made her think her marriage would be as stable and permanent as those bricks. She expected they would grow old together and age well just as the church.

They too would become weathered like the bricks. The symbolism made her smile thinking of how they would look when they were old. Would they have wrinkles in the right places and still have a sparkle in their eyes? The eye is the window to the soul just like those stained glass windows in church reveal stories about God. Their eyes too would tell stories of shared hardships and the gleam of victories.

Instead Nieske told him what he wanted to hear. "He is having some sad times. I am his first daughter leaving home. But he is happy with you, he thinks you are great. But it is big adjustment when his oldest is leaving the nest. He has not said it, but I think he is sad that he does not have money to make the wedding a grand event.

My brothers and sisters are the happy ones. They are delighted to see me go. They will have more to eat and won't have me bossing them around anymore. Plus there will be only two sharing the bedroom and each will have their own bed." Nieske laughed.

Jon poked his elbow into her side, laughing he said, "You will still be sharing a bed, only with a man instead of a sister. The wedding will be grand, you will look beautiful and the carriage and horses will add a nice touch. Just being married to you is making this a wonderful event for me. The carriage from the church to our home is an especially nice touch. They both smiled as they thought about what "our home" meant.

"My brothers and sisters are happy about the rooms they share. I will be happy to still share a room, being it is with you. We will have way more fun than they do."

Changing the subject, she told him about tomorrow's plans. "Are you aware that the plan is for our guests to come here, to our home, for a combination reception/house warming party?" She added, "By the way dad is paying for the food, proof that he is happy for us. You have to pay for the church; he is rigid about not supporting other denominations."

"Here? The party is here? The place is a mess, I have not had spent much time cleaning. I was waiting for you to make it a home."

Frustration and a hint of anxiety crept into his voice. All of them are coming? How long are they going to stay, who is going to prepare and set out the food?" He muttered, angry with himself for not being happy for her. He looked down at the ground, not wanting to see her disappointment.

"Nieske chortled, "I know just what to expect. You men all want a sparkling clean house but have no idea how to do that; well my friends are coming early to dust, wash and arrange this house. They will bring flowers and doilies and table clothes. I got it covered dear."

Relieved, Jon smiled, jumped down and hugged her.

Chapter 5

Dutch weddings are secular events. People of faith solemnize the marriage with a church service. Jon likes this separation of church and government. The municipal process is legally binding while spiritual blessing brings God into the union; Jon saw this as the best of both worlds. The legal aspect is at city hall and the religious part is at a church or synagogue. The legal requirements mandated by law. The religious part dictated by whatever faith the couple adhered to. The civil event is in the ante room at city hall with the Burgemeester officiating, as required by Dutch law.

The ceremony in the *Oude Kerk* is cool and efficient. The Calvinistic church rules make this a serious event. The ceremony is seen as a binding contract made in the presence of God. The predominate color of suits and dresses is black. Jon commented, "this is not a funeral; it is the beginning of life. Why is it so dreary?"

Jon and Nieske want the ceremony to bring God's blessing on the couple and joy to the family they create. The *dominee* is committed to church traditions and rules. He pronounces threats of divine punishment if any of these rules are violated. Jon preferred encouragement, guidance and elements of joy and excitement. Jon sees God as a coach, teaching and guiding. This *dominee* preaches a God that reminds him of his drill sergeant at boot camp.

Jon shrugs saying, "*Ja*, let him carry on if it makes him happy. I just want God to witness our commitment."

The reception/house warming party was a pleasant break from religious piety. Riding in the carriage was exciting. The carriage pulled by a team of dapple gray mares added pizzazz and pleasure to the journey home. Nieske was embarrassed by the attention they received riding the in the carriage, so she snuggled close to Jon.

Sitting behind the lace curtains they were out of view and all alone; alone enough to embrace and kiss. They kissed for the first time as husband and wife. The *dominee* did not allow kissing or displays of affection in his church. Clinging to him she felt complete and happy. Six years of dating had finally come to an end, tonight she would become a wife.

Chapter 6

Two hundred people attended the party counting the children. Uncles, aunts and cousins accounted for over half the crowd. The other guests were neighbors, friends, co-workers, Jon's former employer and their banker. It was a fun family festive affair.

It was warm enough for the children to play outside or in the feed area of the cow barn. Children were not allowed to mingle with the adults after age three.

The men sat in the parlor smoking cigars or pipes while the women fussed over food and drinks in the kitchen. The room was filled with smoke and man talk. Conversation ranged from business, to world events and ribald humor about wedding nights.

The ladies drank *citron* a fruity low alcohol drink while the men drank *Jenever*, a Dutch gin, or single malt scotch.

Jon and Nieske stood in the parlor doorway for the toast. Everyone shouted *Proost*! It was a wonderful time. Jon liked the mix of traditions along with freedom to do and act as one pleased. After all this was their wedding, they could do as they pleased.

Jon's brothers failed to attend the ceremony and reception. Jon knew Bernard could not attend because he was a soldier stationed in Indonesia. Gerard skipping the event disappointed Jon but was not a surprise. Jon had expected his brother to be a "no show." He reneged on his promise to provide two sows for the farm as a wedding gift. Gerard was known for his empty bravado and failure to keep promises.

Heer Kamerling draped an arm on Jon's shoulder, "I came to see how the money I lent is being used and check on how well you are taking care of the farm."

Jon knew this was more truth than fiction. He responded with, "Let's take a walk to the barns for a look; you can see if your investment is safe."

Herr Kamerling, trusted his ability to judge character. He knew that character is worth far more than numbers on a bank statement. He replied, "I know you are the right man. It was not so much a loan as an investment in people that I trust."

His wedding gift proved his confidence. He gave two beautiful brocade living room chairs made of carved dark cherry wood with padded arm rests and stuffed button seats. "I heard your living room was empty so my wife and I decided to do something about that."

Others must have had the same idea and planned things together. When the party was over the living room was furnished with a divan, four chairs, two tables with candle lamps, an area rug three meters square and several wall hangings. The rug was Persian and fit the area between the furniture.

Chapter 7

Three days later, Nieske was relaxing on one of those chairs meditating on her life and the blessings she had. She sighed with happiness and whispered, "thank you, Lord" as she arose and started on her work, cleaning, dusting and thinking about what to make for Jon's lunch.

Their honeymoon was a short two night stay in Rotterdam. Dairy farmers do not stay away many days, but it was a great time being together. Sleeping together was a new experience; both had maintained virginity for this night. They stumbled through the night being shy and embarrassed, but in the morning, rejoiced in seeing each other.

Jon discovered that the room had a *douche,* shower, over the bathtub. "Come on let's try this out," he called to Nieske. Having only bathed in metal tub set next to the kitchen stove he had to figure out how this worked. This was really nice, much more fun than a bath tub." Someday we will have a shower," he promised. Doing a shower together was an unexpected joy and luxury. After breakfast they walked hand in hand to tour the harbor and Hollsum Gardens.

The harbor was fascinating; they counted the flags of the countries and tried to read the names on the ships. Rotterdam was home to the busiest seaport in the world, even more than New York. Jon thought about all these exotic places and dreamed of visiting some of them. Nieske was dreaming about the nice things these ships brought from places like India, Indonesia, Suriname and America.

She recognized the places that provided the spices she used in her kitchen. Her favorites were white pepper and cloves that came from the Dutch East Indies. She loved to use them to enrich the flavor of ham and sausages. Nutmeg she used in meat balls to hide the flavor of the oats or barley used to extend the meat. The aroma of a Dutch kitchen is as wonderful as it is unique, when the south sea spices accompany the wholesome Dutch staples, like sour kraut, endive and cheeses.

Hand in hand they walk and smile at each other and embrace when they thought no one was looking. Married life was fun. They ignored the stares of strangers watching this couple do the honeymoon dance.

Hollsum Gardens enthralled them. They loved the orderly, sculpted shrubbery admired the craft of the gardener and enjoyed the late summer flowers. They would have loved to visit the Keukenhoff Gardens but it was the wrong time of the year. Spring was long gone; the only flowers left were asters, roses, some nasturtiums and geraniums. The second reason for the short honeymoon was preparing for harvest.

Harvest time! Nieske jumped up and hurried to the kitchen; she was late making lunch. Soon Jon and his two helpers would be at the door hungry enough to devour everything she had made and then some.

They were mowing the rye today; tomorrow they would cut the barley and next week the wheat. Mowing with a scythe is back breaking work. The men are in rhythm as they artfully stroke the scythe's blade laying a swath of grain bearing stalks into a neat windrow. Watching the three of them cutting the cereal grasses fascinated her. They are in a staggered pattern; Jon beginning at the left side of the field. When he is five feet into mowing, the next man started and the third man follows suit. They maintain this pattern so the razor sharp scythe stays a safe distance from the others.

Jon's strokes are smooth and steady. The lead man sets the pace; it is a shame to be a laggard. In that staggered row they work across the field, one swath at a time, each stroke of the scythe smooth and precise.

Tomorrow they will use a different scythe. The barley has a cradle to catch the swath of grass and lay it in a neat pile ready to tie into a sheaf.

This is back stretching and shoulder aching work. Both feet on the ground, slightly bent at the waist, swiveling at the hips they swing the scythe. The scythe blade would leave two inch stubble.

These guys pride themselves in having a field look even on top when the grain is gone, like barbers in the field.

She heard the men coming across the gravel drive and the clatter of the *klompen* as they took them off in the barn area before coming into the house. Their backs are wet with sweat even though the temperature is in the mid forties. They worked without a coat, just a long sleeved cotton shirt. They take off their blue denim coats, hanging them on a fence post at the end of the field.

The cow barn was attached to the house and the chicken barn was at the back of the cow barn. This arrangement worked well in the low lands when winter is often bitterly cold. The cow barn provides warmth to the house and keeps the farmer from being in the snow or the cold north winds. Across from the cows are three horse stables and between the animals and the house was the toilet room, with two holes. It is a pit toilet that gets cleaned out in the spring along with the cow manure.

The aroma of cows, horses and hay are acceptable but chickens are too noisy and stinky. Pigs are the worst, of course, so they had a separate barn set ten meters back. The hogs could handle the cold winters better than cows and chickens and they did not have babies during the coldest months.

The best smells came from the hay stored above the cows, creating a sense of warmth and comfort as it cures before being fed during the long winter.

"Brrr" came from all three men as they took off their denim jackets. "It is only 8 degrees (centigrade) out there" mumbled Jaap.

"Good working weather, keeps you moving," retorted Jon.

"Spoken like a slave driver, or a man paying by the hour."

"Aw, come on, who is the fastest man out there? You are, so nobody is pushing you, I am having a dickens of a time keeping ahead of you. When we go back out, you will lead, okay?"

Nieske butted in, "You guys are not working nearly hard enough if you have the energy to joke around and pester each other. Put some food on your plate and enjoy."

They wolfed down three sandwiches of homemade rye or

mixed grain wheat breads. Each sandwich had two thick hand cut slices of bread, a layer of pork fat or homemade Gouda or Edam cheese, a sausage or a sandwich with homemade jam. This was the dessert sandwich, usually saved to savor at the end of lunch. All washed down with two glasses of cold water drawn from the kitchen pump. Leaning back in their chairs they sigh with contentment.

"Feed us like that again and we will be back tomorrow; in fact we may never leave," threatened Jaap.

"Come back tomorrow and I will have chicken soup along with the sandwiches," promised Nieske.

"Deal, see you tomorrow," and they walked out to finish the day's work.

Nine hours a day they worked with Jon and then go home to milk their cows before eating supper and resting. Each man falling exhausted into a chair or bed happy with his days work.

Jon and Nieske ate a light supper and retired to the sitting room. Jon picked up the newspaper. The article on the second page startled him. "Nieske, listen to this."

He read the news report about events in Germany, Italy and America. The entire world was concerned about this mad man in Germany. The story related his climb to power and how he gained control over the political parties, labor unions and business. Hitler had confiscated guns and was now killing politicians who opposed him.

Jon fretted about the hopelessness of being a citizen in Germany, and for that matter of Holland. Both nations had removed firearms from the citizenry. There was no protection against tyranny. Those who dared to oppose Hitler or the Third Reich were summarily shot. No trial, no help, no protection.

The choice appeared simple. Support and salute Hitler or die. No amount of power or money was enough to protect one from this zealot Nazi.

Jon shuddered, wondering how this situation had all started with the Democratic Socialist Party, called Nazism.

The article ended with the fact that Germany had withdrawn from The League of Nations.

The League of Nations was President Wilson's dream of bringing unity and peace to the entire world. With Germany dropping out there was no international clout left to persuade the man.

Hitler despised the League of Nations. He saw it as a confederation of blacks, Jews and weak people, everything his Aryan ideology despised. He would never allow them to have influence over Germany.

Chapter 8

Summer 1939

Nieske and Jon ride their bikes to Ede to do some shopping for items not grown on the farm. She plans to shop for spices at the Indonesian import store, and then go to the market for rice, breakfast Rusk, and the yeast for making bread. She has plenty of staples, home grown vegetables and fruits in her pantry. She does dream of having enough money left to treat themselves to an orange or banana.

He rides along, enjoying her company. Telling her, "You are my favorite person to be with." He cleaned up and tagged along. His chores are done till evening when the cows need milking, chickens and hogs need feeding. The next few hours the farm does not need attention. Happily they ride side by side to the Centrum.

Riding past their field he looks with pleasure on the grains growing tall, the newly formed heads of kernels swaying gently in the breeze. Rain came regularly this summer; he is expecting a good crop. The vegetables look great too, at least as well as can be determined by looking at the tops. When the tops are lush and full of color you know the carrots, beets, turnips and rutabagas are doing well under the ground.

Both have a child on their bike. Jon has the oldest, a boy named Arie, riding on a seat mounted on the bar between his seat and the handlebars. Nieske has the second son, named Evert, riding in the basket mounted in front of her handlebars.

The family has grown in the three years of marriage and the farm has prospered too. Jon made two extra payments on the loan and added space to the hog barn so they now have twelve sows and a boar. Jon is happy to have his own boar. He no longer needs to hire a boar to breed the sows. He hated or dreaded the hassle of handling these huge aggressive males. Herding them on the road was nearly impossible and getting them up the ramp onto the wagon was extremely difficult. He bought his boar after the one charged him and knocked him butt over tea kettle.

"How do you stop a six hundred pound pig from going where he wants and doing what he likes? That is why I got one, he stays in his pen and I bring the sow to him." He explained, and then added. "When the boar is tired the sow will gladly leave the pen and return to her place."

The boys are his pride, the first born is named after his father and the second is named after Nieske's father, following the Dutch tradition of honoring parents. Breaking family tradition is not good. Feelings are hurt when a baby is given the name of distant relative or no relative at all. Too often relationships become estranged and family feuds begin. Better to live in peace.

He hopes the next child will be a girl. She will receive Nieske's mother's name. Ah, tradition he thought, "Some traditions are good but the restrictions and expectations are burdensome and a real pain as he shifted his weight on the seat."

They ride side by side while on *Danmakerweg* where. Bikes and horse drawn wagons are the only traffic on this country road. When they were on the *Otterlosweg* to Ede there might be a few cars or an occasional truck. Here the only the sound is bike tires on gravel and birds singing. Holding hands as they pedal, they are at peace with the world and happy together.

Chapter 9

The Centrum is bustling with shoppers. Dutifully Jon followed his wife from grocery marts to the household store and the drapery shop. Here on *Grote-straat* the shops are all lined up offering specific items. The kitchen store stocks pots and pans and dishes but no glass ware. The same is true in hardware stores; a store will carry hammers and axes but not saws and planes. The stores complemented each other but did not compete by carrying what others were selling.

Nieske saw the concern on Jon's face; grinning at his discomfort she said, "don't pout, I am just looking honey. I am not buying anything, so don't worry."

Nieske browsed the shop and Jon went outside to converse with a friend from church. They were classmates through sixth grade before leaving to work on the family farm. Now they sat on the bench in front of the window watching the shoppers. Their wives would find them here.

"Have you been keeping up with the news from Germany?" asked Bas.

"*Ja*, I read the paper when we get one, haven't picked one up today yet."

"That is all old news; the radio has the latest happenings. Oh, that is right; you do not have electricity on the farm. Your news is always a day late. You don't have a phone either, do you?"

"Anyway, it seems that Hitler is more passionate and weirder by the day. I would not want to be a Jew living in Berlin or anywhere in Germany or Austria."

"What is he doing now? Last month he ordered Jews to wear a Star of David on their coat and place a star in the window of all Jewish shops. Now what?"

"He ordered all able bodied men older than eighteen to report for military training. They serve for six months, three months in basic training and three months in specialties. Yesterday, he called up these men to report for active duty. He has assembled the largest army in Europe. They must have been manufacturing tanks and trucks in some secret place; they are very well-equipped. The whole world is watching these goose-stepping fanatics and waiting, wondering what he is up to."

"*Donder*, that is scary" muttered Jon. "What do you think is going to happen?" Jon did not swear much so he used less offensive words like "*donder*" which means thunder, when something ominous was about to occur.

"My wife's cousin lives in Dusseldorf; she keeps us informed from a German citizen's view. She really liked Hitler when he became Chancellor. In fact, she shook his hand when he visited there for the opening of a new factory. She thought he was great!

He brought Germany from weakness to strength from a nation that was scorned to one demanding respect. He created a country every German can be proud of; even the Prussians are feeling proud again. My cousin did not wash her hand for several days; she was that excited to have touched the Fuehrer. Now she fears him and hates what he is doing. My wife and I visited her; Germany is a prosperous place," informed Bas.

"What does she think now that he is called the Fuhrer?"

"She is worried. What once was a growing and prosperous environment with happy people has become oppressive and freedoms are curtailed. Hitler says it important to give up some freedoms. He says giving up freedom is 'for the common good.' She thinks the loss of freedoms is just his lust for power and his hatred for anything not Fascist."

When Nieske arrived the conversation ended and Bas wandered off to find his wife. "Nice to see you, see you Sunday."

"What were you and Bas talking about? You look worried. What's up?"

"Another multiple question," Jon chuckled looking down into her face that was wrinkled with concern.

With the packages in one arm, he grabbed her hand and steered her to the cafe next door. "Let's have a cup of tea before we go home and we can talk about what Bas told me is happening in

Germany."

Sitting at the courtyard table she ordered a cup of tea and an apple tart and he ordered a beer and fries with mayonnaise to dip them in.

"Find anything in that shop that we need?"

"I promised you that I was only looking but they do have a nice coffee pot and the canning jars are on sale. If we have more children I will need to can more meat, vegetables and fruit."

Jon's mind jumped on those words of needing more canned food. He was not thinking about having more children to feed. The events in Germany made him anxious and fearful; his heart beat faster as he thought about what the future might hold.

"We have room on the bikes; go buy as many jars as we can carry home."

"What is wrong? You sound so angry or uptight. What is this sudden urgency of buying a lot of canning jars? I am not pregnant and the boys are not eating huge quantities yet. This is about what Bas said, isn't it?"

Setting down his beer, Jon told her the latest events in Germany. He explained what Hitler was doing to Jews and Gypsies. He told how Hitler was gathering his army at various locations in the country, nearly a third of the army is in the north with the rest divided into the east and the west. Why would he do this? None of Germany's neighbors had a large military. Germany was not in danger from its neighbors.

Sure the world was upset about how he is treating Jews and outlawed other political parties. Nobody was going to attack Germany. Besides Holland had made a proclamation of neutrality and Belgium was considering doing the same.

Since Germany is safe from aggression what is Hitler planning to do with those tanks, artillery, trucks and light armor? *De gek*, madman, is he going to do what the Prussians tried twenty some years ago? Does he think he will succeed?

Being very pragmatic, Jon was thinking ahead. When war comes food becomes scarce. The invaders take it and the civilian population struggles to survive. If Holland is invaded he wanted to have lots of food stored away. If nothing happened they could can less food and eat the stockpile until life was back to normal.

After explaining his thinking to Nieske, he outlined his plan. "We can afford to butcher an extra hog from each of the next two litters and that cow with three teats is not producing enough milk to pay for her keep, so when she calves we will butcher her. We will preserve as much as we have jars for; the rest we sell."

"Where are we going to store this food? No sense do all this work and have it snatched from us by the enemy, I'll be damned if you think I am preparing food for them!"

"How about I make a cave or cellar behind our cellar, it will be cool enough and it can be hidden behind the stone wall. They will never find it when the stones are mortared in place. We will not need to access it once the food is there. It will be good until we need it."

"Are you sure we need to do this? It is a lot of work."

Chapter 10

September 1939

Jon jumped off the wagon before it stopped and rushed into the house. The horses stood still waiting. He was anxious to tell Nieske what he learned at the mill. He was there to have his harvest of rye ground into flour. Rye flour to make the heavy pumpernickel bread he loved to eat with a slice of cheese, butter or pork fat. The blends of rye and wheat are used for sandwiches or to eat with split pea soup, his favorite.

In a few weeks the barley and the wheat would be harvested, brought to the mill where the barley would be bagged in burlap and wheat in cloth. The miller stored what Jon wanted to keep and sold the rest. This time Jon asked for one hundred fifty kilos to be processed soon or traded for the equal amount now.

"What's up Jon? That is a lot of flour, way more than you normally take home?

"I am filling the pantry, there is a dark cloud coming from the east. And it is not rain!

Nieske was scrubbing a pot at the kitchen sink when she saw Jon riding up the drive. Seeing the intense expression on his face she straightened up, dried her hands and went to meet him at the door.

"What happened didn't you plan to leave all the grain at the mill? There are two sacks on the wagon."

Jon did not answer; he just looked at her with a blank stare. Frowning she watched his face, "What happened, is the miller ill or what?"

He plopped down into a chair, "there is trouble in the world! Germany invaded Poland yesterday! *Donder!* I wish we had electricity so we could have a radio and hear the news right away," he grumbled.

Nieske's face paled. "It is starting isn't it?"

"I am afraid so, no one stepped up to help Poland; the whole damn world is afraid of Hitler. His military is too great, everyone is afraid of him. So who is going to stop him? Diplomats scream and threaten but their noise has no power and no effect. Many of them are hoping that Poland is all Hitler wants. The rest of Europe is ready to cede Poland to Germany, hoping Hitler will stop there. It's as if those "Stanleys" are of no account, let them be murdered. The politicians have my brother, Gerard's attitude. He says, 'it is better them then me'. It is so wrong; we are out brother's keeper. That is God's plan. We are in this world together."

Nieske's jaw clenched in fear, her face showed the turmoil of feeling helpless. She was barely six years old when World War I swept over the Netherlands, but she remembered the terror she had of soldiers and uniforms. Instantly the memory of those years rushed over her. The terror of war wrenched her stomach and the fear and hunger she felt back then hit her like a ton of bricks. She looked at Jon for assurance; assurance that things would not get that bad again. She was not too concerned for herself; this time she was hoping her boys would not have to suffer as she did.

"Jon, the other countries must do something. Britain and France must get other nations to help real soon and not wait like they did in 1914. Who will Germany invade next, us or Belgium or both? We are just little countries. If no one helps Poland then we will not get any help either."

Trying to control his own doubts and fears Jon replied, "It will be Holland and Belgium, we both have good sea ports. Our ports are open all winter and we don't have to contend with the ice of the North Sea. They know that Rotterdam is the best seaport in the world. The airbase at Ockenberg and Ypenberg will give them easy access to attack England. If they control Rotterdam and those air fields they will be able to control all of west Europe's shipping. Plus, if they want to capture Britain this makes it very easy. England needs to help us just to protect their country and people."

"That is why I brought the sacks of flour," he continued. My plan is to harvest the wheat and barley as soon as possible and take as much home as we can stash. If, I mean when, the Germans get here they will take the grains from the warehouses and leave Holland short of food. We will store our own flour."

Reaching out to hold hands they looked deeply into each other's eyes, he trying to reassure her, and she looking for hope. Her fingers felt his calloused farmer hands, looking for assurance that his strength would help her. This helped her but he knew this was beyond what he could do. He would do and plan what he could. They would be short of cash, but hopefully have food.

"It is going to take God's hands not mine to survive what is coming," he said. Then he bowed his head and talked to God about his fears, doubts and the dread of war. He pleaded with God to change the hearts of the aggressors, to bring sense to a convoluted world.

As good Calvinists are wont to do, he ended his prayer with, "But Lord, we trust you and know that this evil is great, so we place our welfare in your hands knowing you will see us through the coming holocaust. Amen"

Little did he know that that is exactly what was coming, a holocaust. The big question Jon and Nieske had was how this would change the world and how drastically will it alter their life and the future for the family.

That night Jon was awakened by the stirring of his bed and by the moans coming from the other side. Sleeping on a feather bed creates a nest for each person which does not transmit tossing and turning. Nieske's tossing and turning woke him. He knew something was amiss; really amiss.

He rolled onto his back, kept his breathing the same and waited. He knew she worried much more than he did. He figured that made them a good match as they evaluated things together. He was calm and assured her and she sharpened his senses and awareness.

The moaning stopped, but only briefly. With a loud shriek Nieske shot straight up into a sitting position. Shocked he bolted and sat up. She began to cry and leaned over onto his shoulder.

Sobbing, she told him, "I was not sure so did not tell you but I missed my period for two months now and think I am pregnant."

With hope and fear he hugged her, "That's great honey!"

"No, it is not great. I just lost the baby. Please help me up and clean up the mess." She sobbed onto his shoulder. "Damn, Germans" she muttered.

Jon wrapped her in his arms to comfort her, assuring her that all would be well. Meanwhile he cussed himself for having brought the news of the invasion to her without handling it gently and with less fear. But then he realized he had no idea she was bearing their third child and that Hitler's actions would frighten and upset her this much. War was not declared and no move made against Holland, but war did seem to be coming and coming soon.

"Was it a boy or a girl?" he mused. A tear formed in each of his eyes as he sorrowed over what for them would be the first casualty of war.

Chapter 11

Klaas Van Bemmel sat at his kitchen table surrounded by his family. He is home on his farm, in Pease, Minnesota. His brow furrowed by deep thought. It is the time of year when he has time to think about world events.

It is late November; harvesting is all done. Corn cribs are full, the hay loft is stuffed to the rafters and the manure pit emptied. The manure and old bedding was spread out on the corn field to decay under the coming snow. The farm is ready for winter.

He loves this time of year, especially when the crops are plentiful and the harvest completed without injuries or serious mechanical problems. Thanksgiving is his favorite time of the year; this year he is very thankful. He loves being thankful, even in poor harvest years he has reasons to be thankful. He counts his blessings and is pleased that his neighbors are also blessed.

America is a great nation, abundantly blessed. Seeing these blessings and experiencing gratitude creates an aura of peace that affects everyone. The family is at peace with each other and guests feel the peace when entering this home.

Over the front door is a sign, "Family and Friends gather here." They do gather here, basking in the warmth of caring people.

He enjoys this relaxed period of time farmers have during the winter. The only work required are the standard chores of milking the cows then feeding them and the few chickens. He collects the eggs while the chickens are off the nest eating. A true farmer, he does these chores before breakfast knowing the animals depend on him for food and life. He takes care of them first before going to the house to warm up and enjoy his own breakfast.

There is nothing like fresh eggs in a bacon and cheese omelet or scrambled eggs with an English muffin, to start the morning. He wolfed down his breakfast then sat back to drink a few cups of coffee and talk with Trina, *Trientje*, in Dutch. They often talked about the "old days" of living in Holland. They miss family but are delighted to have made the move to America and have no desire to go back.

After breakfast and after the sun has taken the bite out of the cold he heads to the equipment barn. He spends a few leisurely hours working on the implements and tractors. On really cold days he fires up the potbelly stove to heat the corner of barn where he is working. Mostly the stove was used to warm up the tools or his hands after lying on the cold floor working under the equipment. He takes frequent breaks to warm his numb fingers, wrapping them around the coffee mug sitting on top of the stove. He knows the importance of having the equipment ready before hauling away the winter's accumulation of manure and straw bedding and preparing the fields for spring disking and planting.

For a thankful man he sometimes comes dangerously close to losing his temper if equipment breaks down or was not ready for the planting and harvesting. Planting on time is crucial to having a good harvest. When the soil was warm enough and the weather was perfect, it is time to get at it. Rain or winds could delay getting on the fields, which is unavoidable. Being prepared is vital and he knows it is your own responsibility. Late planting makes for late harvest and late harvest means worrying about early snow or muddy fields.

Supper is the light meal of the day. A hearty breakfast after chores and dinner at noon or near noon to see them through the hard work of the day made having a light supper a pleasure and a nice ending to a busy day. Supper time is when the family shoves back their chairs, stretch out the legs, sigh with contentment and talk together. Everyone at the table is given opportunity to talk about his ideas, problems or tell a joke and then discuss events.

Today had not been a busy day; at least he did not work very hard. Instead of working on his equipment he drove into town in his model T to pick up some parts for the cultivator and stop by the co-op creamery for his milk check.

Few checks are mailed; the dairy farmers like to come in to chat with the manager or other farmers. In the busy seasons the checks are mailed; when the checks lay in the office for two weeks.

"Well, I might as well see how the guys are doing," he mused to himself. So he stopped in at the Family Café. The café provides a large round table available for the farmers to sit near the front window. There they discuss crops, herbicides, pesticides, world events and share the gossip they accuse their wives of spreading.

The radio was on when he entered. "Hi Joe, hi Bill, Jack," he said and then stopped as he realized that no one was talking, all ears and attention is on the radio. It was a strange sight, fully grown men with eyes focused on the radio, watching the radio as if it a live person. The news reporter was talking, indicating the regular program was interrupted.

Europe was big in the news lately. Klaas was not sure what to make of the mess over there. Is it Hitler or are all Germans going Fascist? Those Nazi party members and Brown Shirts were doing crazy things, beating up people who they thought were weak or more helpless than them. They loved bullying Jews and anyone suspected of not supporting the Socialist Democratic Party. They paraded around with that silly looking goose-step. Nuts to them. He knew lots of German immigrants, none of them were like that crazy bunch in Berlin. German immigrants were like the other immigrant farmers; hard working with little time or interest in messing with other people's lives.

Today's news was not about Nazi antics; it was about the military. German troops entered Poland and nothing was being done about it. Politicians and newsmen gave opinions and some political rhetoric, but no help and no plans to help. Germany had split its army into three divisions with the north division moving into Poland. What were the other divisions going to do?

Who was going to be invaded next? That was the question. It was not a question of if, but who and when. It looked like Hitler was on the move, other invasions are imminent.

That is what he is thinking about at the supper table. His sons Arie, Jon and Wim had pushed back from the table too. Their stomachs satisfied, it is time for the family to discuss the day and use the opportunity to talk about events in their lives and make plans for tomorrow. School studies were always a topic; mom and dad checked on how the boys were doing with their studies.

Tonight Klaas spoke first. He did not ask about school or talk about the parts he bought or what he had repaired or replaced on a tractor or other implement. Not this time.

A scowl crossed his face, his brow is deeply creased; everyone is paying attention. "The Germans are making a move," he stated. "Looks like they may invade Holland and also Belgium; hope our Dutch family will be okay."

"How big is the Dutch army?" asked Arie. "Will they have a chance against the Krauts?"

"Hold on, we do not use derogatory names even if we do not like them and I have good German friends who may never be referred to with names like that." Klaas waited for Arie to accede to the correction before replying.

"Yes, Dad, sorry."

"No, the Dutch army may be good and the air force is excellent but they are both small, they have the will to protect the country but have little chance of success. Five days maybe ten and they will be forced to surrender. The best they can and should do is to hold the Nazi's back until the Queen and Parliament can clean house and get the royal family and leaders out of the country."

"Can you check on your uncles or other family, to see how they are? Asked Wim (Willem).

"My only family there is cousins. My last uncle, who you are named after, Wim, died some time ago, not long after your uncle Evert. They do not have phones on their farms yet, so the only contact is by mail and that takes a month to get there. I think I will write Jon and ask how things are. It is time to check on him. Haven't heard from him after he got married, must be busy making a family," he chuckled.

"You better write today," advised Trina. "Once the Germans take over the country it will be impossible to get mail in or out."

Chapter 12

Minnesota, May 10, 1940

Klaas pulled into the Allis Chalmers dealer on Main Street to buy parts for his tractor. He's doing routine maintenance to be trouble free into harvest time next year. He uses the McCormick and the Allis Chalmers tractors to plant and cultivate. The Allis Chalmers does harvest duties harvesting corn for silage.

He harvests his own silage, chopping the corn and filling the silo. The grain corn is harvested by his friend, Fritz Hounderjager.

Fritz owns two combines. He harvests corn and wheat for farmers in two counties. This works well; Fritz makes a nice living and the farmers do not need to buy expensive combines. In return Klaas harvests Fritz's silage.

Today, Klaas needs head gaskets, as the ones he installed last December decided to leak. He also wants spark plugs and plug wires; the old wires are cracked from two years of exposure to the sun and engine heat. He checked his list to see if he remembered everything he needs. Jon slapped his thigh, Oh yeah; I need grease for the wheel bearings and oil. He has enough transmission oil but needs hydraulic oils.

He does the routine maintenance faithfully every winter, he will pack the bearings, change the engine oil, fill the power take off and hydraulic oils, and check the transmission, fuel pumps and water pumps.

"Busy day here," he mused. He counted four trucks and two cars are parked in front and two trucks alongside the store.

The whole county was muddy from last night's rain. Klaas stomps his feet, dislodging the dried mud off his shoes, before walking in. The counter is busy; both clerks are taking orders while listening in on the conversation going on with the farmers waiting their turn. The sales crew loved to interact with the local farmers when they shop. It is similar to being in the barber shop, a friendly place where gossip and news is discussed. Today was different; only one person was talking; Klaas notices that everyone is listening to what Fritz said.

"Interesting," thought Klaas. Fritz is the only German here and he is surrounded by Dutchmen and a lone Swede. Most of these men are immigrants, only one Dutchman is a second generation immigrant like Fritz.

This is Pease, Minnesota, a quiet farm town in Mille Lacs County. It was not founded by the Dutch but they took it over after Benjamin Soule moved away because his lumber mill burned down. Now it is a Dutch town, not far from Princeton.

Fritz had a slight accent as his family spoke Deutsch at home and he had not learned much English before attending first grade.

The conversation is interesting as it is in Yankee-Dutch or German-English.

Each sentence is liberally sprinkled with a few ethnic words. That is okay as even the English only speakers, working as clerks, understand what is said. And if they did not understand each word the meaning was passed on with the hand motions or by the response from the others.

"America must remain neutral, this time," stated Fritz. "Germany will not make the same mistake as last time. They will be careful with what they do because they need America to stay out of this conflict."

Braam Koster jumped on this opinion with his own view point. "That is easy to say when it is not your country being invaded and your family shot!"

Several farmers quickly try to cool Braam down. They know him to be a firebrand; if they let him speak his opinions this conversation will become a fierce argument. "Wait a minute, Braam," said Egbert. "When you and I became citizens of the United States we made an oath to protect this country against all others. Our allegiance is to America, not Holland."

"Sure, you are right, but I have family in Doorn, Driebergen and Apeldoorn. The troops are gathering just east of there. My family will be overrun or killed within the next day or two, so I am really concerned and right now really ticked off at Germany." "Nothing against you, Fritz," he says looking Fritz in the eye, "but I hate that ego-maniac, Adolf Hitler."

"Ja," I understand. My family in Germany does not like Hitler or any of those socialist radicals. They are afraid too. My cousin was picked up a month ago and never heard from again. My uncle thinks it was the result of an argument he had with the police. Those Police and the Gestapo make people disappear never to be heard from again; no trace, no records, no corpse, nothing. If someone does ask questions they too disappear or lose their job or their business is shut down."

"I suspect many are wondering what they got themselves into when they elected Adolf. He promised honor, dignity, jobs and respect for Germany. Those things did happen and the whole nation was happy. But now the country is oppressed and fearful. They must obey him or die. I am afraid for the people there and afraid for us and the world!"

All the guys nod in agreement. They like Fritz and are relieved that he, too, does not like Hitler. Fritz is a good guy, respectful, considerate and a great worker who always takes good care of his clients.

Chapter 13

Klaas put his hand on his Fritz's shoulder, "It is going to be tough for a while, my friend. Some of us Dutchmen are a little tense and will shoot off our mouths. Please do not take it personal. They are venting their fear for family, it is not about you."

"Thanks Klaas, I expect some troubles. I hate what is happening there too. I'll try to stay level headed and realize we have to work together and help each other through good and bad times. It is good we are in Minnesota; we will survive. We are now Americans, right?"

With that Klaas ordered his parts, thanked the clerks and left.

Outside several men were gathered around the tailgate of the new 38 Dodge pickup owned by the largest farmer in the county, Dick Groothuis.

Braam was still upset and ranting. "America should get involved soon, later will be too late," he spouted. "I do not care what Fritz thinks or what the Fuehrer says. Germany will damage America or attack us when they are ready. We must beat him to the punch and kick their butt."

"You may very well be right, Braam, but there is nothing we can do here in Minnesota. And we sure as heck should not let it divide good neighbors against each other. There is no sense in bringing this war to Minnesota and you best not screw with Fritz," ordered Dick Groothuis. "After all we are Americans, people who come from everywhere."

"Come on, it is noon, let's get some lunch," said Dick, "I am buying."

Seven farmers and Fritz gathered around the table at the Family Café at the corner of 1st Street and Central. All ordered coffee and the special of the day, Swiss steak and mashed potatoes. That is what the man paying was eating so the others followed suit. They understood the axiom that it is impolite to order something that costs more than the host is having so it was safe and a complement to the host to order the same dish.

Dinner was finished; they pushed back from the table with the third refill. The music on the radio stopped. As one they all look up at the radio, coffee cup in hand. They know when the program is interrupted some special news is coming. Anxiously they wait.

"Germany has crossed their border and is invading the Netherlands! No shots have been fired as the Dutch army is six kilometers from the border dug into the hills and forest there. More news as we get it."

"Bombers headed for Holland!" shouted the announcer. "Stay tuned as more information comes in."

Braam slammed his fist onto the table. The plates and silverware bounced and clattered. He rose to his feet, his face red with rage. "That is it!" he shouted. "I am going back to fight those damned Nazis!" He stormed out, forgetting to thank Dick for lunch.

Chapter 14

May 10, 1940

The German Army crossed the Maas River into the Netherlands ignoring the Dutch government's official proclamation to be recognized as a neutral nation. Their hope was crushed. The Dutch only chance of survival or to stay out of the war was to be accepted as neutral. Hitler had other plans for his Aryan neighbors.

The Nazi western army launched a three pronged assault. In one coordinated strike they entered Belgium and Luxembourg and invaded The Netherlands.

The ground troops and tanks moved across the borders as the Luftwaffe launched aerial attacks. The first objective was to invade the capital city of The Hague, neutralize the government and capture the legislative leaders. The second objective was to capture the airfields at Ockenberg and Ypenberg, neutralizing the Dutch Air Force. With no air support the Dutch ground troops would be defenseless. The third objective is to control shipping by capturing Rotterdam.

The two airfields are critical to the Luftwaffe's plan. Immobilize the air force to protect Nazi troops from bombs. The Luftwaffe planned to use the captured aircraft and the bases to launch attacks on Great Britain, just a short distance across the channel. The attacks launched from Ockenberg and Ypenberg would give little if any notice to London of incoming aircraft. London will have no time to prepare for a defense or launch counter the attacks.

The Nazis planned to seize the government buildings and Parliament leadership, thus forcing the Queen to surrender. Then Hitler planned to set up a puppet government under his control and direction. The Prime Minister and the Queen would be captured. A puppet government with the queen as figurative head was his first choice. Hitler's plan would succeed with or without the Queen and Prime Minister.

The Dutch fought with inferior weapons and no air support. Only their intense grit and determination slowed the German attack. They managed to stall the invasion for a few days, ruining Hitler's plan. The government leaders fled and the invaders took heavy losses the first day.

The Nazis failed to capture most of the Dutch transport and military planes. When the battle became hopeless the Dutch destroyed its own planes. Losing is bad enough for the Dutch. Aiding the enemy was never going happen.

Chapter 15

Fear wracked Jon and Nieske's hearts when they heard the news of the invasion. They gathered their small family at the kitchen table. Together they prayed for the royal House of Orange, asking God to help Queen Wilhelmina escape. Then they asked for mercy on their nation.

Arie and Evert saw their mom's face turn pale and angst shone in her eyes, they began to cry in fright.

Jon remembers the misery of life during the first big war. He was ten years old when it started. That war was bad, the Kaiser had been ruthless, but this Hitler was cruel and inhumane. "The *klootzak (Scrotum)* was demonic" said Jon.

Despair visited them, they feel helpless, which is exactly what they are. They are powerless to stop what is happening; there is no way to escape. Nieske knew they would have to ride this out and hope to somehow survive. She is pleased to have stored several hundred liter jars with food in the secret cellar and had several fifty kilo sacks of rye and wheat flour stashed in the barn under hay.

A glow of pride came to her face as she looked at Jon. "Thanks for thinking ahead and planning for the future. I love you, Jon."

Jon took her hands into his rough calloused hands, he stroked her hand. She loved how these thick-skinned hands could be so gentle and tender when he touched her. He smiles in spite of his fears, his angst hidden from his brood and wife.

"I love you, too, honey. God will take care of us. Remember what we read this morning in Psalm 27? *'If God is for us whom shall we fear?'* We will survive this and Hitler will fall. God is not going to let that evil, depraved system rule Europe."

"Are you sure? This war looks a lot like the events prophesied, in the Bible, about the days before the world ends."

On May 12 the Mayor, *Burgemeester,* of Rotterdam received a phone call from Berlin. He must surrender the city and its port or the city would be bombed. Hitler would bomb the residential area, kill citizens but leave the harbor intact. The *Burgemeester* hesitated because when Rotterdam is in German hands they would have the best seaport in Europe to launch their navy and receive cargo.

Two days later Rotterdam was bombed. Twenty five hundred houses destroyed and thousands of citizens killed. The enemy waged war against helpless civilians. This is not collateral damage; this is coercion. The section bombed was selected to instill fear into the Dutch government.

The *Luftwaffe* was careful to preserve the military post, navy yards and the port. They would be used by the invader to launch attacks and provide protection from invasion by Allied troops.

The *Burgemeester* signed the surrender document knowing this was the only means to save lives. Unfortunately, the surrender document was received too late for Germany to cancel the Luftwaffe's attack.

Utrecht is next. "Surrender or your people will die."

Five days after the invasion began and one day after Rotterdam was bombed the nation of the Netherlands surrendered. It was a difficult decision to make. Would less people die if they surrendered or would they just die from different means? Surrender to the Nazi did not guarantee peace and safety.

Chapter 16

On May 12, 1940, the queen realized that Holland could not stop the mighty army and Luftwaffe of Germany and help was not coming. She sent crown Princess Juliana and her family to safety. The British destroyer Codrington took Juliana and her husband Prince Bernard to exile in Ottawa, Canada.

The next day the Queen also escaped. She was a widow and departed the Netherlands, May 13, 1940; transported to London on the British destroyer HMS Hereward.

Hitler raged. His plan to use the queen as the face of the puppet government had been thwarted.

May 15, 1940 General Winkelman formally surrendered the Dutch Army to Germany. The Dutch soldiers were taken to internment camps where their weapons and uniforms were confiscated. The soldiers were counseled to adhere to German law and given copies of the rules of the occupation and released.

Hitler had a fondness for the Dutch; he saw them as part of the great Aryan race. Therefore he did not send the Dutch soldiers to POW camps or Concentration camps. His plan was to gain favor with the Dutch military to help set up a puppet government. This puppet regime would introduce the NSB political party as the sole power in politics. The *NationaalSocialistischeBeweging* or National Socialist Party was a minority party before the war. Now it was the only political party permitted.

Referred to as the NSB; it was fascist and authoritarian. It removed individual freedoms or rights. These freedoms were taken away "for the common good" according to Adolf Hitler.

Hitler's plan was for the Dutch to see the benefits of uniting with the Third Reich. His hope was that when the Dutch understood his system they would desire to incorporate the Netherlands into the Greater Germanic Reich. After all, they were Aryan and the queen's daughter, Juliana, was married to a German prince. It all made sense to Adolf, but the Dutch did not see his logic. They refused to become Democratic Socialist!

The Dutch are fiercely independent; having carved most of the country from the sea they are not about to give up their creation to a Fascist. They may have a queen but the people ruled themselves.

The drone of planes filled the sky. A quick look verified they were German. Most everyone headed into basements or secure areas of their house, the curious ones noticed they were not Luftwaffe bombers of the past few days; these were smaller planes that flew very low and slow. The plane's hatches opened filling the sky with leaflets. This act occurred over every major city in The Netherlands.

Not expecting anything good from German planes Dutchmen hesitated to pick up these leaflets. The propaganda written in bold red and black said; *"Welcome to the Greater German Reich."* It proposed that every Dutchman is invited to become part of this great political and economic system. Joining all Germanics as one nation would increase the economy and prestige of every Dutchman. They were instructed to sign up at the local government centers that would soon be set up. They should encourage or pressure the elected officials to join the NSB. Only through the NSB would there be career advancement. The NSB would bring unity and prosperity for all Aryan peoples.

Queen Wilhelmina, the Prime Minister and much of Parliament escaped to England. Surrendering was not an option to consider. When she was presented with the Nazi proposal, she replied to the request of a puppet government with a resounding, *"gebeuren nooit,"* never going to happen. She crumpled the letter and threw it on the floor.

She fired Prime Minister Geer, who wanted to cooperate with Germany and Hitler's plan for a puppet government. She replaced him with Pieter S. Gerbrandy who set up the Dutch government in exile.

The government in exile was based in London, giving Hitler double incentive to bomb London, thus subduing two nations.

Chapter 17

Jon and Nieske put their boys to bed, prayed with them and over them. Their heart's desire was that the boys learned reliance on God. Then they sought God's blessing for Holland during this time of uncertainty and fear of the future. Rising from their knees they went to their own bedroom where they huddled in trepidation. Hoping for the best they tossed and turned far into the night.

Two weeks later Jon looked up from weeding the row crops to the sound of a truck on the gravel road. It slowed down as it neared his farm. As the truck turned into his drive he spotted the Swastika on the door.

In sheer panic, he dropped his hoe and ran to the house; he needed to be there with his wife and family. His mind screamed as he ran. "No, no, they cannot come on my farm, we have done nothing! Why are they coming here?"

As he rounded the corner of his barn he sees the truck has stopped and soldiers jumping out from the canvass covered rear. He ignored them and ran into the house where Nieske was staring out the kitchen window. Her face paled as the blood drained from her face, her jaw open in awe. She froze in fear. The boys are oblivious to what is happening and continued playing with the empty thread spools.

There was a loud rap on the door. *"Komen je buiten"* (come outside) ordered the sergeant. With dread, Jon picked up Arie and Nieske picked up Evert, they walked out the door. Facing them was a line of twenty German soldiers standing erect with their eyes on the sergeant; each held a rifle across his chest.

Are they about to be shot? What for? Why? Jon stepped in front of his wife. The sergeant and a private stepped up, neither had a rifle, the sergeant did have a pistol strapped on his side. He nodded to the private.

The private moved up one step and spoke in Dutch, "This is Sergeant Essen," introducing the man with the chevron. "We are taking over this farm in the name of the Fuehrer. "Hiel Hitler" This

59

is an honor for you. You will be a host for the army of the Third Reich. You will not be harmed as long as you obey our orders. The men will sleep in the barns and the sergeant will sleep in the house, *verstaan?"* (Understand)?

A platoon of Nazi soldiers has just taken over the farm.

Chapter 18

Braam Koster stepped off the SS Veendam, the same ship he traveled on to America. It seemed ages ago that he boarded the ship to go to America, but it's only five years. He was anxious for two reasons. Just being here in Rotterdam brought a tingle to his spine. Getting through immigration and customs might be tricky. He was ready for the coming interrogation; confidant with his story of why he was coming to Holland during the occupation. He was excited to begin this new chapter of life. A chapter where he would help in the fight for freedom for the country he still loved. This was bigger than him. This was patriotism for his heritage and the people he loved. His home was in Minnesota but his heart was here with memories and values.

He realized there would be danger, but it was worth it. He was ready. He knew he must make the right contact. Joining the resistance could be tricky. Trust must be established to survive; he needed to be with the right people. He came to help not to die. With the right team much can be accomplished. Contacting the wrong people or venturing into the wrong place could be a fatal error. Dying was not on his mind; he fully expected to live and succeed. His friends in Minnesota told him he was brash, but he just felt confidant. He was confident in the cause, and in the need. He was confident in his ability to serve the cause and his heart said that righteousness wins over evil.

Maybe he was a little crazy to fight for freedom in Holland and then not stay. He wanted freedom for his native country but planned to return to America. He loved America but this needed to be done first. It was his duty to pay a debt to the nation of his birth. When the war was won, he would settle down, marry a good farm girl and have a family. "Ja," he said to himself, "it is the right thing to do, and it's my payment for my heritage. Doing the right thing is always important and my children will be proud of me."

He expected problems with his return. How much of a problem he did not know. He had memorized a story to explain why he was here at a time when most people were trying to leave. He had kept his Dutch passport and planned on using it for entry. His American passport was in his suitcase.

He had a stack of twenty dollar bills and all the Dutch Guilders he could get from friends and the bank. All together he had nine hundred eight dollars, some of it donated by supporters. The dollars he secreted in the lining of his jacket, those Minnesota winter coats gave lots of padding to hide currency in. Not wanting it all in one place he hid some in his socks and some in his suitcase. He hoped none of it would be discovered but if it was he was sure most of it would pass through customs.

The customs desk was occupied by a Dutchman, with two Nazis standing near nearby. One was in uniform and the other in a suit with a vest and tie, both Germans were armed.

Alert but calm, Braam strode to the counter, presented his Netherland's passport and waited. He had been watching and listening while those before him had been interviewed. He chose his place in line after a family with four children, hoping they would take a lot of time, making the officers anxious to expedite the process and thereby relieve him of too much attention.

He handed his passport to the Dutch agent. "Good morning," he smiled.

"Why are you coming to Nederland now?" demanded the German in plain clothes as he snatched the passport before it could be stamped. He scowled as he looked up at Braam's six foot two frame, just an average Dutchman but still several inches taller than this Nazi.

"To see my mother, she is old and not well."

"Now is a fine time to think of that, you have been gone, how long? Five years?"

"Ja, it has been long but work is hard and does not pay as much as I hoped, so saving up enough to come took almost all my money."

He smiled, "if she had gotten sick before now I probably couldn't have come."

"Take this man to the interview room," the plain clothes Nazi ordered.

The uniformed man took Braam by the arm. "This way," he said leading him toward a room off to the side.

As they walked Braam took the man's hand off his arm, "No problem, I will do as you say. Do not to treat me like a prisoner or a child."

The suit took the seat behind the desk, facing the door. Braam was given the chair with his back to the door. This was to intimidate and create the idea of no escape from this windowless room. The soldier posted himself at the door. Now there was no escape.

Looking around the room Braam saw that the walls were painted a dismal dingy green with nothing on the walls. The desk was equally bare; on it there was only a phone and a pad of paper. This was typical for an interrogation room; intimidating those being interviewed with the cold efficient look, no comfort, no warmth, and no hope. The weak or fearful would hopefully confess to avoid confinement in a similar cell in jail.

"Stay cool, just calmly answer them. They don't know shit," he thought. A smile would be too much, so he calmly looked at the civilian, noted his name tag said Franz Holder, and said, "Herr Holder, what would you like to know?"

"Herr Koster, please explain your presence here during this time of, err, for lack of better word, adjustment."

Braam looked into those pale green Aryan eyes and saw nothing but coldness. He had almost sputtered about the term "adjustment" wanting to say, it is a damn war you idiot!" But he kept his calm and related his story; a story he had gone over many times on the journey. Now it spilled out naturally, just as if it was true.

"I promised my mother I would come to see her in two years and as you see it has been over four years. It was difficult getting enough money together to make the trip, but I made it. I came now because Holland is occupied and not at war, so while there is peace

I came. I am not a danger to you, I came because she is not well, and she is sixty six years old. In a month, I will return to America."

"That is all that there is to this, just a nice humanitarian visit? You are such a good son, aren't you?" sneered Holder.

"Yes, I am a good son. If you must know I hope to bring her to America with me. Friends in Minnesota have offered to pay her fare. I did not take enough money to do this as I was fearful of what might happen once I arrived. I will send for her fare when she is well enough to travel and when her travel documents are ready."

"Please empty your pockets and open your wallet, place it all on the desk."

Braam turned each pocket inside out as he emptied them; the little pile contained a pocket knife, one hundred forty dollars' worth of Dollars and Guilders, a handkerchief and a wallet with several photos. Some photos of the Minnesota farm and two of his mother.

Holder glanced at the pile, noted it was insignificant and said. "Put it back." Looking up he continued in a more pleasant voice, "Tell me about life in America, is it as good as I hear and read?"

"Yes and no, life is hard there, one must work hard and be smart to get ahead. It is good because no one tells you what to do or not to do, taxes are low and everyone has the freedom to be and do as they desire. You may live where you want and buy or sell as you are able, there is endless opportunity."

"Are there German immigrants in the area you live?"

"Ah, you want political information, I know nothing political."

"Not political, I just am interested in knowing how the German families feel about the Father land. Do they miss it?"

"The town just a few miles over, sorry, it is about 7 kilometers from us is mostly German and a small group of Poles and Swedes. Everyone gets along and trusts each other in business. Some talk with fondness of "back home" but mostly because of family they have left behind."

"What do they say of the Fuehrer? And his plans for the Greater German Reich?"

Braam hoped he could make some political impact, but he

must be careful in this answer. "The farmers I know are too happy to be in America to care about what is going on in Europe. Most just hope America will not get involved. There is a small group that is excited about the Fuehrer and another group about the same size that hates him and what he is doing. They especially are upset with the program to eliminate the handicapped kids and the Jews."

"Must be old fashioned Lutherans," he huffed. "When will they learn to despise those 'Christ killers' for what they are? Jews are worthless parasites, the world will be better without them."

Looking up he changed the topic, "If the German people do not want to come home to join the effort, will they have enough influence to stop America from entering the war?"

"So, this is political question time. I do not know, probably not. Let me tell you what I do know and that is anyone who makes the Americans mad is going to pay dearly. They love freedom and hate oppression with a passion. They do not give a toot about 'the greater good' or Democratic Socialism."

"Humpp," muttered Holder. He stood up and motioned toward the door. "You are free to go, take good care of your mother, if you want a visa for her come see me. As for you, you must keep your passport with you and go to City Hall in Apeldoorn. There the Commandant will issue your identification papers and permits for travel. Keep those with you at all times as you will be checked often. And remember that the curfew is to be off the streets between 8 pm and 7 am. "

Braam gathered his bags, which had all been collected and placed just outside the door. Smiling with relief he walked to the train station.

He exchanged some dollars to guilders and purchased a one way ticket to Ede.

Alida Mollengraff was waiting for him at the station. She would go with him to Apeldoorn to see his mother and get the ID papers, just in case Holder checked on his story. Then they would meet with a group in Veenendaal to be introduced to the resistance members in Gelderland.

The underground group expected his arrival. Alida had told them about Braam's history and heritage. He had mailed a few letters from a P.O. Box under an alias. He shared his vision in these letters, writing them in a code he and Alida knew. The two letters he received during the time he procured his visa and arranged his finances had been opened and resealed so he knew mail was being censored.

Alida was a childhood friend; they had attended the same youth group in the Christian Reformed Church. She and her family attended the Reformed Church but that was not an issue to either set of parents. At age seventeen his adventurous mind took him to a new life in America. Now he was back. Their friendship picked up just as if he had not been gone. This was good. Alida was single and as cute as he remembered.

Chapter 19

Jon watched the soldiers unload the truck; there was nothing else he could do. His face remained stoic, his eyes glazed with intensity; his heart raged and his stomach filled with bile as he watched the soldiers take over his farm. His heart skipped a beat as helplessness overcame him. Forlornly he watched the German soldiers walk across his pasture with shovels resting on their shoulders as if they were rifles. They had no need for rifles; the closest enemy was across the channel in England.

With total disregard for preserving the livestock's food they dug three holes. With great precision they made the holes a foot deep with perfectly level bottoms. They stacked the soil around the perimeter making the hole two feet deep.

It sickened Jon to see that beautiful red clover dug up and piled on the perimeter of the hole forming a low bunker. His cows and horses had less to eat due to these huge holes and the damage caused by these men ruining his pasture. These holes became home to anti-aircraft guns, cases of ammunition and three soldiers.

Jon looked at the guns next to his hog barn; Three 2cm Flak30 *Flugabwehrkanone* (antiaircraft canons) that shoot 20milemeter bullets at the rate of 120 rounds a minute. Jon shivered.

Four soldiers dug and piled the sod as a barrier to water filling the holes. Others stood guard and watched as the mechanics prepared the guns for placement. Six more soldiers sat on the truck or leaned on the barn wall watching, their rifles in hand. Jon realized these guards were there to keep an eye on Jon. They watched his movements and calculated his facial expressions to see if he was thinking about attacking them.

Jon stood there for an hour, quietly watching the enemy. Jon spat in disgust; what was he going to do, hit them with a shovel or stick them with a pitchfork? He would like to but he had a wife and two boys he loved more than he hated these soldiers.

The guns arrived right after the soldiers; one gun on a trailer and two on the truck. There was a driver, a mechanic and two guards. Now all of them were busy as they prepared the guns for what would be their home for several years.

Jon had just inherited twenty extra mouths to feed. He realized the gravity of this when the driver went to the chicken coop, pulled out his Luger and shot four chickens off their roost. His rider plucked them and roasted them on an open fire. The troops smiled and smacked their lips as they ate the chickens, supplementing their daily rations.

Nieske ran out of the house when she heard the gun shots, hoping that Jon was alright. She was afraid that he might have said or done something to rile the Nazis. The boys were in the house and safe, but she was afraid they had shot Jon. When she saw the chickens being carried out of the barn she lost her composure. "*Stommerik*" (blockhead), she yelled at them. "Don't you know that when the chickens are gone the eggs will be gone too?"

They laughed at her, which infuriated her even more. Before she could say any more or attack them with her broom Jon grabbed her and pulled her into the barn. "Easy, woman, don't get yourself shot over some chickens What will Arie and Evert do without a mom?"

Standing there in the cow barn in the area where the feed was stored and where the manger for the cow feed was he saw the fury in her eyes. He wrapped her in his arms pulling her to him, calming her rage. Slowly she quieted down, but then she began to sob. "I can't handle this Jon. They will destroy the farm, destroy our lives, and probably kill us. Our children will live in fear; it is too much!"

She sank to her knees; slipping down and out of his arms she laid her head on the sacks of potatoes piled along the wall. "They will shoot us with the same smugness as he shot those chickens. They are brutal, they are beasts," she sobbed.

Jon pulled another sack down, sat on it and cradled Nieske onto his lap. Silently, they sat clinging to each other, each lost in their thoughts and fears.

Jon was the first to recover. Stroking her hair, he murmured softly to her, "Come dear, we need to stay calm and careful with what we say and do. I will always be with you and protect you, and God will not forsake us."

"Just because God is here does not mean we will not die or be killed. Look what happened in Rotterdam and De Hague. Thousands of people died in their houses. They never knew what hit them when those bombs came. Geert's house was only a block away. Besides that we have more problems. I hate them! They kill women and children just to intimidate us."

"What do you mean more problems? What is worse than war and occupation? Or looking at swastikas, and having the enemy in my own house taking our livestock and food supplies?"

"Yes, besides all that I am pregnant too. What am I going to do with another baby? Another mouth to feed, another person to be responsible for, another person to worry about, I cannot do this. I do not want this war; I do not want this baby. How am I going to raise a baby with soldiers and guns and a war going on? No more sex until the war is over, I just can't do this!" She screamed. Sobbing in grief and fear, she ran into the house.

These things ran through his mind as he watched them dig. Discouraged he muttered to himself, "They will probably kill and eat the cows anyway so we won't need this pasture or the hay."

He was concerned about the hay in the loft; would it be ruined or burned by a negligent smoker? Nineteen men were sleeping in the loft while the sergeant slept in the house. The sergeant commandeered the bedroom nearest the door nearest the stairs which gave him access to the barn and pit toilet.

Jon leaned against the corner of his barn as he watched the fifty caliber guns being set into the hole. They were leveled and blocked. Now the guns would withstand the recoil when fired.

War. "Damnable war and damn the egotistical men who start wars!" He muttered to himself.

Jon turned and walked back to the cow barn. He eyed the newly arrived munitions truck parked between the hog barn and cow barn. He realized that his family was in greater danger than he imagined. The truck was hidden from the road and its canvass top was nearly the same color as the hog barn roof. The truck would be difficult to spot with surveillance planes.

Should, and he had no doubt Germany's foes would arrive. Holland was occupied but he was certain that sometime England, France and others would come to drive them back into Germany.

If only America would come like they did in the first Great War. Then Canada would join too giving England and France the help they needed.

After all, these guns were not offensive weapons they were placed here for defense. They are the defense against the inevitable counter attacks of the Allies. The Allies would come, "hopefully soon" he prayed.

When the liberator's planes come they will bomb these guns and strafe the German troops and blow up this munitions truck. When the munitions exploded his house and barn would disappear, leaving a hole in the ground with only a vapor rising from the explosion of the fuel and ammunition.

"May God help us," He prayed.

Chapter 20

Seven men and three women are riding their bikes, all have the same destination. It is evening; the sun is a deep red as it sets. The riders disappear into the long shadows of the trees, and then reappear in the bright sun. It is peaceful and they do not attract attention. None are riding together nor are they coming from the same direction. Braam is coming from the east, whistling as he peddles. Alida is a few minutes behind him. She is more intent and business like. All of them appear natural as one by one they approach the bicycle repair shop. They go around back parking behind the building.

This is the organizational meeting of the local Resistance. They spaced their arrival three to five minutes apart and quickly move their bikes into the storage area of the shop. Marinus (Mies) Sukkel greets them at the back door to his shop. Everyone is directed to his kitchen where a pot of tea is brewing and a plate of ginger cookies sits in the middle of the table. The cookies are shaped like windmills; these and almond/sugar cookies are his favorites.

Like many small businesses the shop is part of the house, a show room or sales floor next to the living quarters of the house, but under the same roof. The shop is closed for the day. Here they can safely meet away from customers, sitting as friends sharing tea. They need to appear normal and not raise attention when they arrive or when they go.

They are acutely aware of the need for caution as you never know whose eyes are watching. Alida keeps her eyes open, viewing the windows of the houses she passes. She watches to see if someone might be watching from behind the lace curtains. Their lives depend on secrecy. The SS has made it profitable for informers to aid the Occupation Forces.

Informants get special privileges like curfew passes, coupons for restricted or difficult to get items. Some cash payments are made or wealth is shared when art or jewelry is seized from those arrested and taken away to camps.

The Nazi presence is at a minimum in this small town. In reality it is an unincorporated village. There are no municipal buildings, police station or town square. The shopping and business district is just two blocks in length with a few side-streets where the bakery, the butcher and cobbler sit along the bicycle shop. All are closed for the day.

The Nazi forces are camped just outside of town at the first farm. This farm is owned by Floris Osten. Herr Osten is a gruff, dour man who tolerates little interference in his life. Not a good place for the Nazi, they will be busy keeping an eye on him. Having them watching Floris gives Marinus the freedom to work and meet his team without drawing any attention.

When the last rider arrived and the tea is poured the meeting is called to order. First item of business is everyone introducing themselves and stating what they hope to accomplish. All of them already know each other or know about each other. Braam was the sole new face. Mies knew that this exchange of names and goals would help him establish who the workers are and more important it would determine the level of trust they have in each other.

Mies stood up. "Friends, citizens, we are all patriots. The love we have for our country and our citizens has brought us here. We have an enemy we hate and who demeans us. What are we going to do? What is the focus of this group?" he asked. He looked each person in the eye as he went around the group, making this a personal question, as they responded.

Jan spoke first. "I would love to go out every night and sneak up on the sentries and slit their throats, kill the *"moffen"* until they give up and go home."

Mies nodded with understanding, "they will keep coming, there are more of them then of us, besides the revenge they exact will be more than we can bear."

Pieter stood, "I propose that we focus on gathering intelligence, then smuggle that information to the Queen and government in London."

Alida was next, "let's set up safe houses for Jews and those

72

young men who need to hide to avoid being shipped to Germany to work in the factories. We cannot overcome the enemy until help arrives, but we can prevent patriots' deaths and Jews being sent to extermination camps!"

Chapter 21

"Onderduikers" is what they were called. That is to duck under or go underground. These mostly unmarried men and women between the ages of eighteen and twenty five with a smattering of middle aged married join cadres in their area.

Many of these young men opt to be an *Onderduiker* when faced with the demand to join the *Arbeitjeinsatz* or "work force" set up by the Nazi occupation. Those men were the ones called or conscripted by the SS to report to work and aid the occupation forces. Mostly they were city dwellers, where the SS had access to municipal records and therefore knew where these men live, knew their ages and what they do for a living.

The *Arbeitjeinsatz* workers do the labor to develop the airfields for the *Luftwaffe* to use in their assault on England or be shipped to Germany to work in factories making military equipment. No patriot would volunteer for this, nor would they willingly report for this work. Germany was getting free labor but this conscription of laborers also created resistance and enlarged the cells of *"Onderduikers"*.

The SS would post an announcement in the Centrum or City Square and placed posters at the corner of every city block. These announcements set a date and time for the able bodied men to report to the Square for assignment.

Those who did not report for this work assignment were hunted down, brought to the Square and summarily shot. When the news of these shootings spread across the nation it increased the number of men hiding or joining the Resistance. The strong patriots joined the Resistance, fled or went into hiding. The others reported for work assignments, many of those were never heard from again.

The young men who do not report for duty need hiding places or safe passage or transport to a safe locale. They disappeared from life, joining the resistance or working on a farm, where farmers would claim them as sons. With forged documents they could assume a new name and a new role. This was possible as the municipality or *"graafschap" (county)*; data was often not as detailed as city records. Or they just hid in basements or cellars close to home.

The unofficial leader of the Dutch Resistance in Utrecht was Anton Groendyk. He was a great patriot and not to be confused with Anton Mussert who led the NSB and collaborated with the Nazi regime.

Chapter 22

At forty Mies was the oldest of this group. Mies was elected the leader. He had leadership skills and military savvy, having served as sergeant in the army when posted in the Dutch East Indies.

The group's semi-official goal of the movement was to cause trouble and hindrance to the occupation forces. After that it was about protecting the *Onderduikers* and the Jews. Those priorities and just how much help for Jews was left to local groups to decide. The intelligence gathered was routed through sub groups, located in ten Provinces.

Marinus had contacts in Dieren, Barnesveld, Nijmegen, Bennekom, and Ede and of course Utrecht. With advice from other groups they chose to focus on rescuing Jews, helping the *Onderduikers* and gathering of intelligence. Any force used would be carefully analyzed to prevent the backlash the Gestapo would bring.

They all knew of the assassination of the Fascist leader, General Seyffardt, in Scheveningen by the local Resistance. The Gestapo responded to this assassination with speed and great ferocity. The Gestapo rounded up two hundred fifty men, took them to the Centrum, lined them up and shot them in front of their wives, families and citizens. The bodies laying on the street for three days as a reminder to the populace to comply with the Occupation Authority and to have second thoughts about killing German soldiers, especially generals.

Alida and Braam proposed that the group be more active. "We could poison their food, or capture messengers. That would be easy, they ride bikes between cities, we could pick them off and steal the message and guns," coaxed Braam.

Alida chimed in, "Both my mom and dad have been interrogated and threatened for suspicion of smuggling Jews. The interrogation was rough, they were beaten and had a gun stuck into their mouths; I want to make those vermin pay!"

"Who will they line up and shoot if you do this? The van

Bemmel's and your parents will all likely be killed if you take out the messenger from that platoon. Do not do something rash, think it through. Better yet, do not act on your own. If you do something at an opportune time at least use our common judgment to guide you."

"We should do what we can to obtain ammunition and guns. Then when help comes and fighting happens locally we can pitch in and make sure the *"moofen"* pay for what they have done to us."

Braam Koster was anxious to do more than gather intelligence. So he volunteered to set up routes and means to move Jews and men to safety. He made contact with several farmers in Bennekom, Barneveld and Ede to loan wagons or trucks with hay or produce to hide people under. He volunteered to be the driver, thriving on the risk.

Jon van Bemmel became his close friend and helper. Jon was willing to drive his own wagon, but Nieske and Braam convinced him this was too risky.

"Are you nuts?" Braam glared at Jon. "You have twenty soldiers on your farm most days. "What are you going to tell them when you go away with a wagon load and come back with the same load? They will figure it out real quick, and then?"

"I'll just need to have an empty wagon on the way back, simple."

Nieske's father, Evert Bultan, was one of the stops for the underground route in the movement of Jews. His farm was on the outskirts of Bennekom and on a dead end road so there was little traffic and no Nazi or Gestapo patrols in the area.

Braam and Alida rode off together; they must hurry to be at Bultan's before curfew. The conversation was light as they rebuilt the relationship they had before he left for America. Alida was in love with him and had been crushed when he chose to immigrate and leave her behind.

Braam had liked her but he was blind to her feelings. His heart was set on exploring the world, or at least America and he did not need a woman to take care of or to hinder his roaming.

Chapter 23

1941

Four in the morning Nieske woke up Jon. "The baby, I think it is coming. I feel pressure and the contractions have started. Quick, go get the midwife." Then she groaned as another contraction rolled through.

"*Donder*" thought Jon. "Here it is mid-January, it is freezing hard and I have to ride to Ede, I will be frozen stiff and may never thaw out."

He rolled out of the feather tic bed. He sat on the bed's edge as he lit the candle on the bedside table. He pulled on pants over his long johns, put on two pairs of socks and two shirts, the top one flannel. He hurried down stairs. Then he ran back up the stairs, and knocked on the first bedroom door.

Jon knew he could be arrested or shot if found riding his bike this time of the night. He needed papers, authorization to be out on the street. "Come on, wake up," he muttered.

He knocked again, this time with more urgency. "Probably had too much schnapps last night, but that is too bad, I need those papers!"

The door jerked open, the sergeant was standing there in his long johns, pistol in hand. "What?" Before he could finish his sentence Jon told him he needed papers to authorize him to go into the city and papers for the midwife to come out with him.

"I do not have proper forms or seal to stamp a document; those are only available at the government center. You should have gotten them several weeks ago." He grumbled.

"Babies come on their own schedule, you know that. You have three."

"All right," he grumped. I'll write an explanation and sign my name; most of the men in and around Ede know me by now." Then he went back into his room, lit a candle and wrote the note.

"Take my bike," he suggested, "it has better tires than yours."

Jon was grateful that not all the soldiers were in agreement with fascism or supported Hitler's Nazi party. The older ones were understanding and considerate. Not so the young ones; they carried a chip on their shoulder from the indoctrination Democratic Socialism taught in the schools since Hitler became Chancellor. They thought highly of themselves and had disdain for everything not German or Aryan.

"Danke," "I will be back soon."

Another groan, emanated from his room, this one louder than the last one, he hurried even faster down the stairs and out the door. Pulling his wool cap down over his ears, he peddled with urgency the three kilometers to the midwife's house.

He waited for her so they could ride back together; it was good security to do this. Women were known to be accosted and raped when alone on the streets.

No one stopped them so they hurried through the lightly falling snow as fast as they could and not slip on the ice; now hidden under a thin layer of new snow.

As they wheeled into the drive a soldier stepped out with his rifle pointed at them. "Halt" he ordered.

Jon pulled his cap off his ears and face so the soldier could recognize him. He lowered his rifle. "What are you doing out this time of night?" Then seeing Jon was on the Sergeants bike he raised the rifle again. "You stole the bike; you will be in big trouble."

"No, no, I did not steal the bike, Sgt. Essen gave me permission so I could get the midwife, Nieske is having our baby."

"Good Lord, you better hurry, sorry," he said as he stepped back to let them pass.

Before they walked in the door the midwife began giving orders. "You heat some water while I go check on the *Juffrouw*, (Mrs.)" instructed the midwife as she took off her coat and gloves.

"Bring the water when it is very warm, oh, and some towels, diapers or whatever is clean. With some soap, got it?" She glared at him hoping he was not like so many men who get flustered and forget what they have been told. "Got it?"

This was the third baby she was delivering here so she figured Jon knew what to do. He did know what to do as ten minutes later he came into the room with a bowl containing the water, and the towels draped over his arms, the bar of soap on a dish in his other hand.

Half an hour later the midwife placed her hand on Nieske's stomach, "*drukken*, (push)," she ordered.

With a loud groan the baby's head came into view. The midwife quickly placed both hands on the head and gently pulled.

"Plunk," he came out. "It is a boy. Oh my, three boys in a row. You are a blessed man, Jon."

He was not paying any attention to what was said as he gently cradled Nieske's head, telling her everything was fine. "The boy has all the fingers, toes and looks good. Listen to him he has good lungs too!" He exclaimed.

After cleaning up the baby, the midwife wrapped him in a blanket and gave him to Nieske. She did not reach out for the baby so Jon took his new son and held him. Looking at his new son he was smitten with how awesome birth was; how great a blessing this was from God to have a healthy boy. Sure he looked rugged and not cute at all. He laughed to himself, every mother thinks her baby is beautiful but every father knows they are not cute at all for at least a week.

Holding the baby out to Nieske he says, "You better take him I think he is hungry already. I have nothing to feed him," he joked.

His mother took him and began to nurse her new son, and then she began to cry. "I don't know what to say or do. What have we done bringing a baby into this cruel and evil world? Jon, you know that any day we could all be killed and this baby has no chance. I am afraid for him and for me; promise me no more babies while the war lasts."

"*Het kompt wel goed, schat,*" "Everything will be alright, dear," he whispered in her ear.

"I hope so; I will need your help with this one."

"What do you want to name him? It is your turn."

"These are troubled times, so I thought about naming him after a great uncle, Herve' van den Born. He fled France during the Roman Catholic persecution of the Huguenots. He and my great aunt, Everdina, came to Holland and settled near Renkum. This boy will need to be resilient like him."

"That is good, an honorable name for an honorable son."

"I can tell everyone the good news at church Sunday and the next thing you know the family will all hear about it."

"Or you can tell Braam, he has a better grapevine than anybody we know," commented Nieske.

"Hush woman or we will all be in trouble, these walls have ears," he whispered.

So Herve' was born into a hostile world; a world of war, of hunger and fear; a world that did not need another mouth to feed or a life to look after. His mother never completely adjusted to the responsibility; she resented the intrusion into her already overloaded fearful life. She knew in her heart that she could never love this one as much as she wanted to and he needed. Take care of him, yes, but be delighted to have him would never happen.

Chapter 24

Alida Mollengraff jumped off her bike at the rear of the bakery; she pushed it into the storage area, closed the door and strode into the kitchen. She rode her bike to Ede every day for work which made it easy for her when she had messages to pick up or deliver. She did not arouse suspicion as it was common for her to make bakery deliveries to homes and businesses during the day and after work. When she had bread or pastries and a delivery slip she could peddle anywhere. No one suspected her when she stopped in Bennekom to meet her main contact on the way home.

She also worked at the Fabric Shop on *Arthurbann* four days and the bakery, *Hubert's Bakkerij*, just around the corner on *Cornelius Straat* one and a half days.

The bakery job was on Friday and Saturday mornings. She delivered pastries, bread, cookies, rolls and other baked goods on her way home the other four days. These deliveries made her courier service for the resistance appear as routine work when she made her stops. Hubert made sure she always carried a loaf of bread or some bakery item along with the message.

Today she noticed the head baker, Hans, short for Johannas, was engrossed with kneading bread dough. His hands covered with flour as he worked the dough with intensity. He looked up when he heard the door close. Seeing her he looked around to see who might be watching. He said nothing; looking up at her he rolled his eyes to the left.

That was the signal that there was a message for her. Sometimes it was just news, other times it was information to pass along.

Alida went to the rear of the kitchen where the aprons and towels were stored. She walked a little slower to give Hans time to place the dough into the pan where it would wait for the yeast to work and raise the dough before placing it into the oven.

As she put on her apron, Hans came to stand next to her. "Good morning, aren't we bright and chipper this morning." He put on hand on her shoulder while with the other hand he slipped a note into her apron pocket. Then he quickly moved away, wiping his hands as he went to the restroom.

Alida went to the front counter to wait on customers. There were fewer customers this morning than last Friday she noted. When Hubert came to the cash drawer she mentioned the slow customer traffic.

"*Ja*, it has been going down a little each month. The Gestapo is putting fear into people. They do not like being interrogated and hassled for being on the street. It is a good thing the deliveries are up or I would have to let you go," He grumbled.

Fear crossed Alida's face as she thought of losing her job. She needed the income but her greater fear was losing the means to deliver covert messages. "Do you think they will ease up with time as they get to know the regulars and local residents and our clients?"

"No, they are typical *moofen* that like to push their weight around and delight in making people afraid. I am afraid it will only get worse, not better. But that is good for you. The housewives like the delivery service instead of venturing out themselves."

"*Varken, (Pigs)*"

"Hush, do not be so bold. The pressure they put on us has created the atmosphere for many of our citizens to become collaborators. It is damned scary now. Who can we trust?" He voice was a mere whisper, so only she could hear.

The Dutch are religious about taking a break at precisely ten in the morning and a tea break at precisely three in the afternoon. Sipping her coffee Alida slipped out the note to read it.

"In your deliveries tonight take the loaf of dark rye bread, there will be only one, and give it the man you will meet at the corner of *Arnhemsweg* and *Op de Berg*. He will ask you for pumpernickel. Your response is to tell him this bread is better."

She finished her cherry tart washing it down with her last swallow of the dark rich coffee she loved. She tore up the note and then spilled coffee on it and threw it in the trash.

That evening she met Braam for a beer at the Amstel Garden bar and cafe. She related what her instructions had been on the message and that she had completed the assignment.

"Why are you telling me this? Is something wrong?"

"Something just did not feel right; it is just an eerie feeling. Nothing was said or done any different from other drops but something was strange."

"Did he say something or do something?"

"No, he was normal. He was a new contact though. I am not sure if I was followed or if it was him. I did not see anyone following me and did not see anyone watching him either. It was just strange to pass a loaf of bread with a code and nothing was exchanged. I expected to be handed a secret message. Maybe there was something inside the loaf. What do you think?"

"You are just getting nervous; calm down. Just to be sure, the next time you make a drop, take a ride around the block or go from where you are supposed to go and after a block or two turn around. Then without making it obvious check out who is there or who turns around, too."

"Okay, there are a lot of shop windows I can use to see who is in the area, or if someone is following me. But this drop was at the corner of a residential street and the woods, it was just an odd place for a drop."

The next week she made two deliveries after work and one on Saturday afternoon. Sometimes Hans would bring bread or tarts to the fabric shop for her to drop off, always leaving the address with each basket. She knew that most of these were regular customers; the soft white breads often went to Nazi sympathizers or collaborators, who seemed to have more money and less fear. She despised these people who would betray their own countrymen or kinfolk. She wanted to spit on their breads or tarts, but feared being found out. "*Waaderloos afval*" (worthless trash), she muttered to herself. She had worse names for them but would not demean herself to utter them.

Chapter 25

Braam was whistling as he rode his bike toward Bennekom. He was headed to Evert Bultan's house for supper. Food was always good there. It may not be the best cut of meat or choicest vegetables but they were always superbly prepared. Frau Bultan knew how to turn mediocre food into a feast. But what made him happiest was that Alida was coming too. He was growing fond of this daring woman. Besides having guts she was pretty too and the sparkle in her eyes mesmerized him; it had been great to reconnect with her.

He was not sure if she knew he was becoming infatuated with her but he suspected she did. This gal did not miss much. She had great intuition. Smiling, he began to whistle a tune as he pedaled along the gravel country road. He began to wonder if Bultan might have any refugee Jews at supper. He often had one or more staying on the farm while they waited for documents or new identification papers while awaiting the next leg of the underground journey.

Braam wondered who printed up those identification papers, documents and travel permits. "Best not to know too much," he muttered. "What you don't know you cannot tell."

Just then he saw Alida coming from the other direction. His heart skipped a beat. "You are in love, duffus." He smiled to himself, admitting what he had known for weeks. Maybe it was time to talk to her about this.

"No, not now," he muttered, "We need to wait for this ugly war to be over and see if we survive, then he would tell her."

He saw her turning right onto *Albertlaan*. This road was lined with oak trees and blueberry bushes along the ditch banks. As she slowed for the turn he saw two men jump out of the roadside brush. They grabbed her, threw her onto the ground and bound her hands behind her back.

Braam was hidden in the shadows of the huge oak trees and was far enough away to not be seen. Obviously they had not seen him or heard him whistling. He moved deeper into the shadows and slowed down. He watched one man lift Alida and hold her while the other one searched her pockets. Finding nothing on her he searched her handbag, and the package she had in the basket behind her seat.

Braam could not hear what was said but it appeared that they found what they were looking for as the search stopped and they looked at what was taken from her basket.

Fear gripped him as he realized that they had found a message or package she was delivering. That means these men knew something about the group and now they would know more. All of the group's lives, his and Albert Bultan's for sure, were now in danger as well as members of other groups. Alida was surely going to be interrogated, tortured and then shot.

He had little doubt that the fierce and cruel treatment would eventually wring some information from her. The interrogators would eventually pull off her finger nails, then break her fingers, one at a time or burn her with cigarettes until she broke down and give up names. This would lead to arrests and assassinations of the group members. Mies would be tortured and interrogated too and then shot. Plus it would cut off an escape route for Jews.

Braam knew he had to do something and do it quickly.

Chapter 26

At Braam's feet lay a meter long branch of sturdy oak. His hands trembled, not with fear but rage as he quickly he picked it up placed it across his handle bars and took out his pocket knife. The blade was three inches long and sharp enough to shave with. He kept his knife sharp knowing that it might someday be his only weapon of defense. Now he was happy to have it and would use it to defend Alida.

Calmly and focused he rode to where these men were now forcing Alida onto her bike. One was holding her bike while the other man got two bikes out of the brush. As one mounted his bike the other man was pushing Alida's bike into motion before getting on his bike. Braam rode toward them, trying to appear casual.

Surprised to see a rider coming toward them the first one looked up, but it was too late. The oak cudgel caught him full under the chin, snapping his neck. Braam jumped off his bike, dropping it where it landed. The second man let go of Alida's bike; she and her bike fell to the ground. She lay partially under her bike as it tangled with her kidnapper's bike. Before the man could dismount, Braam brought the cudgel back, swinging it down. The make-shift club came down hard on this man's arm, breaking his wrist.

Braam realized these were not soldiers or trained fighters, for the man instantly grabbed his arm in reaction to the pain. Taking advantage of this Braam swung his knife up in a swipe motion severing the man's windpipe and aorta.

Panting he stood there looking at what he had done. Alida meanwhile got herself untangled from the two bikes, hers and the dead man's. She staggered over to stand next to him. With wide eyes and gasping for breath they looked down at the two dead men.

"Ptew," she spit on them. "Damned traitors."

Braam nodded, "They are not even Gestapo, they are Hollanders hoping to make points and get a reward for turning you in."

As her hands were being untied, Braam asked, "What are we

going to do now; does anyone know that they were going after you?"

"Who knows if anyone sent them; for sure somebody snitched on me. I bet this is related to that weird drop I made last week. But that doesn't mean anyone knew what they were up to tonight. They could be trying to show the NSB or Gestapo that they are a valuable asset and useful to them; maybe hoping to get a reward."

"Like what? I am not a big catch and neither are you."

"They might get more ration cards or coupons. Most likely they expect the Nazi to win this war and they want to be on the winning side."

"Come on we are wasting time. Let's bring these guys further up this road and we can drop them there, then the suspicion will not focus on this road or point to Evert."

Alida held the bike while Braam hung both men across the bars and together they pushed the loaded and unloaded bikes to a spot where the ditch along the road had water two feet deep. There they dumped the men and the bikes. They wiped their hands in the wet grass, cleaned off the knife and threw the club away.

Only then did they stop moving. Now they hugged each other. "You saved my life! How can I ever thank you enough? She sobbed into his shoulder. Finally, she had time to allow the emotions to sweep over her. Both stood there momentarily, the adrenalin rush was fading, while relief surged through their hearts and minds.

"Just hugging me is reward enough," mumbled Braam.

She stepped back, looked up into his face; smiling she laid her head back on his chest. She sighed, confidant that he loved her. Why else would he have done such a brave and dangerous thing? Well, besides being a patriot?

"Come we have to get out of here before someone comes by," ordered Braam when he snapped out or his revere.

"Where?" she asks.

"We will go to Evert's house, have supper and tell him what happened. He will need to be aware that informants might know stuff. He will cover for us and say we came for supper and that he knows nothing about what happened."

"That is good; we have to go there because Hubert and Hans knew I was going here for supper."

"Do we go into hiding? Or shall we just act as if nothing has happened? What do you think, Braam?"

"We have no choice, continue with life as usual, and take our chances. If we hide we will be seen as guilty and they will hunt us down. What we did makes it seem that it could be anyone who killed them; it is good we took their wallets and watches, that way it looks like a robbery. Hope, hope."

Chapter 27

The table was set and the food was in the oven keeping warm when Braam and Alida walked into the kitchen. The aroma met them at the door, refreshing Braam's hunger.

Evert met them and rushed them into the kitchen. "What happened? Your clothes are dirty, shoes are muddy and you have fear in your eyes?"

"Two collaborators tried to take Alida," blurted Braam.

Alida broke in, "*Ja*, but Braam came along just in time and rescued me."

"Are we safe? Were they alone? Where are they? Does anyone know you are here?"

Martha, Evert's wife, was listening and watching this exchange. "Come; let's clean you up quickly, just in case someone comes here and finds you like this. You will not have good enough answers if you are questioned. Then sit, we will eat and you can tell us all about it."

Calmly she wet some towels and began wiping the dirt and grass off Alida, while Braam took off his shoes. Standing at the kitchen sink he began his tale while washing the mud off the shoes. Finished with the shoes, he placed them by the stove to dry.

Martha took a sponge to wipe away the dirt and grass, then wiped up as much moisture as possible with a dish towel. When she finished wiping Alida's dress, she began on Braam's pants.

Abruptly she stopped, looking up she asked, "Someone was hurt bad, weren't they? There is blood on your sleeve. I see it is not your blood. Quick take your shirt off, I will wash it. You can wear one of Evert's shirts and trade next time we see you."

Dressed and calm they sat at the table waiting for Evert Bultan to say grace. In this house it was forbidden to eat or even take a small sample until a prayer was said. "We always have time to be grateful and thank God for his blessing," he intoned, "after all we are not heathens."

He did keep his prayer under three minutes, which was short

compared to some of his ten minute prayers. Evert only prayed at meals at his own home; anywhere else someone else would pray. His friends and family had learned his lengthy prayers allowed the food to get cold. They might be poetic prayers that told tales of the beauty of nature and enumerated the small joys of the day. God might enjoy those prayers but the family was bored and hungry.

Alida was known to say, "I am more thankful when the food is warm, so God is happy with my short prayers."

Martha scooped mashed potatoes onto each plate from the pot sitting in the middle of the table. Food was not passed around the table. It was all in the center in the pots or pans it was prepared in. The only bowls were the gravy bowl and the butter dish.

As she ladled the food, she looked at Braam, "Okay, get on with the story, what happened, how did blood get on your shirt and where did the mud come from, were you in the ditch? It hasn't rained in days."

Alida just looked at her food; it was one of her favorite meals, pork roast, apple sauce, mashed potatoes with gravy and peas for vegetables, Pumpernickel bread with homemade butter to go with it all. Her stomach was still in knots, too tense to regain her desire for food.

Her voice broke with the fresh rush of emotion as she recalled her brush with death; she blurted out her story.

"I was just turning onto your road when two men jumped out of the bushes and grabbed me. Braam saw it happening, but they did not see him coming."

Smiling she looked at Braam with that "you are my hero" look. "He clubbed one of them and when the other attacked him he cut him with his knife. They are both dead."

"That is the short version of a big event."

All eyes look at Braam in disbelief or amazement. "What did you do with these guys?" asked Martha.

"That is when we got mud on us. We loaded them on their bikes and took them further up the road past your road where we dumped them and the bikes in the ditch. No one will see them until

94

tomorrow. We took their wallets and watch to make it look like a robbery."

"You have those items on you?" Let's take a look at who they are, then we will burn them in the stove and the watches will be buried. You cannot be found with any evidence!"

Opening the wallets they took the money and divided it amongst themselves; it was not much. Twenty guilders total from two wallets. The identification cards did not have photos, just name and address.

"Menno," said Alida looking at the ID card, "I think that is the name of this man who comes to tea with Karl. Karl is the man who ices our cakes and decorates the tarts with cream."

They sat back in their chairs, thinking.

"What now?" asked Evert? "Karl deserves or needs to die but we cannot kill all the collaborators. Fully twenty percent of this country is either sympatric to Germany or have sold out to them. He is going to know something went wrong when Menno does not show up and later is found dead. He will connect you to this."

"They are rather secretive when they are together. It seems that they work together, how else would Menno know where I was if Karl had not told him. Only two people in the bakery knew where I was going tonight, Hubert and Karl."

The reality hits Braam on why Alida had been spooked with the rye bread delivery. These guys had checked her out to see if she really was a courier and had proved it with the phony drop. Then they waited till they knew for certain another drop was being made. Braam concluded his thoughts with, "Here we are. Tonight was planned to capture you and get information on who you are working with."

"I will take care of Karl tonight, before he can go to the Gestapo. We do not have much choice. Hopefully the Gestapo is not involved yet and we will be alright. If they are involved they would have simply arrested you. We are in deep trouble no matter what we do but if Karl is eliminated we have a chance."

Braam mumbled under his breath, "I knew it would come to

something like this when I left Minnesota."

"Maybe this is God's providence, you coming here to help just for a time like this. I agree, your idea is the best plan. Not just best it is the only option we have."

"Three in one night, may God have mercy."

"It is God's mercy to us that you are here to protect Alida and these innocent people," said Evert as he pointed to the cellar. There are two Jews hiding here, waiting for the opportunity to travel to France and then to England. Besides saving Alida, whose life is worth more than all of those NSB scum combined. You saved our entire group and who knows how many others. We are grateful."

They burned the wallets and hid the watches. After Evert replaced the brick covering the hiding place he handed Braam a pistol. "You may need this tonight."

Braam looked at Alida, "Do you know where this traitor lives?"

"Yes, it is three streets from the bakery. His house is the oldest house on the street, it stands alone. The others are joined with no lot lines and no side yard gardens. His has plants around the entire house. It is *Steenstraat* number 16."

There were anxious looks and pats on the back when Braam and Alida left. No words were spoken. Each one was lost in their thoughts and fears; it was a heavy load they carried.

Braam had forgotten his plans for talking about love. Anger and hatred for traitors and the danger his friends were in consumed his thoughts.

~~~

Eleven thirty that night there was a knock at the door of 16 *Steenstraat*. It was not the front door; it was the back door by the garden. This is the door for family, friends and those familiar to the house. He waits for a minute to see if a light comes on or hears footsteps before knocking again. No lights come on no lamps or candles, nothing. Three softer raps and Braam hears footsteps coming down the stairs.

"Who is it?"

"Menno,"

The door latch is heard sliding and the door opens. "How did it.......?

"Boom," Karl did not finish his question before falling backward into the kitchen with a hole between his eyes.

By the time he hit the floor, Braam was pedaling away on his bike. He disappeared into the darkness of the side street.

Chapter 28

December 1941

Nieske went to the barn to be with Jon while he is helping a cow deliver its calf. The calf's nose was the first to appear. This is not how it was supposed to be. Normal births have the front feet appear first. When the nose or head comes first it means front feet are bent at the knees; with the legs pointing back into the uterus. This position creates a blockage instead of streamlining the body.

The cow dropped to her knees and rolled onto her side. She stretched out and laid her head down on the straw. Panting and moaning she labors, foam formed around her mouth as she pushed.

Jon soaped up his hands and arms to provide lubrication and to help kill germs, and then reached into the vagina. He must push the calf's head back, and then find the front feet. Finding the feet he unfolds them to where they will come out first. The calf's head is now resting in between its legs. In this position the calf is pointed out with the feet leading the way for the head and the body. When the front legs come first they provide a place to grip the calf and help pull as the cow pushes.

The cow moans softly and grunts as Jon moves the calf into position. He is careful to not damage her uterus. A broken uterus would allow bacteria to enter the body cavity and cause infections. Infections could kill her or cause her to become unable to have future calves.

Her contractions become intense, her groans are louder as she trashed in anguish. Jon calmly talks to the laboring mother, assuring her that he is helping and soon it would be done.

Turning to the three soldiers watching this procedure he said, "Dutch cows are smart; they understand, see how calm she is now?"

"You think German cows are not smart?"

"I don't know about German cows, just that this one knows me. If you talk to her in German she will not understand, maybe

German cows understand Dutch too."

"You are scoffing at us, watch yourself, warned one of them. The others laughed, "He is just talking; do not take it serious. Leave him alone; after all he provides most of our food."

"You are right, in a few weeks this calf will make a great meal; nice tender veal cutlets. I will cook them myself," he declared. Then turning to Jon, "Make sure that calf lives," he warned.

"Ah ha, got them" laughed Jon as he pulled first one and then two small hooves out. Giving a firm but gentle tug the legs straightened out.

As if she knew that all was ready the mother gave a huge grunt when the next contraction came. Out popped the head. When the contraction came Jon gently pulled until the calf slithered out on the straw bedding.

With a huge sigh the mother rose to her feet, turned to nuzzle her baby. Satisfied that it was alive she began licking it clean, beginning with its nose.

"How does a cow know to clean her baby's nose first?" mused Jon. Soon the calf was clean, the hair shiny and dry, no longer covered with birthing lubricant.

The soldiers wandered off, but Jon and Nieske stood together admiring the scene. She was in awe of how a cow instinctively cares for her calf, first cleaning her baby's nose so it would not inhale liquids, then cleaning the birthing fluids off before nudging it to stand. Only after licking her calf clean does she take a long drink of water to refresh herself. Within a few minutes the calf was standing on spread eagle legs, wobbling but not falling down.

Chapter 29

"Jon, I want to go see my father, he hears news before we do. I think something big is happening or about to happen. I think it is good news," she whispered, not wanting any ears to hear her.

Jon looked around and seeing that the soldiers had gone out, replied "Someday we will have electricity too and a phone, maybe. Your father has the radio so go see him. Remind him that the radio will get him killed if they find it."

"He is very careful; he keeps it in the wood pile and only takes it out early in the morning before curfew is over while soldiers are getting up for breakfast."

Jon turned to watch the calf nuzzle up to his mother and searched for her teat; finding it he began to suckle, drinking warm colostrum milk, the perfect food. The mother made a low moo and munched on the sweet clover hay.

"Ja, so life begins," sighed Jon

Nieske, came back to the barn, "I am taking Arie and Evert with me, keep an eye on Herve'. I cannot take them all."

Three hours later Jon went to the house holding Herve' in his arms. Herve' was almost walking now; he was taking steps and walking along side whatever he could hang onto for support. Jon wanted to see if supper was getting ready; he had not seen Nieske coming home but hoped she was back. He worried about her when she was gone. It was not unheard of to have women abducted by soldiers and raped. "May God curse the *moofen!*"

That was one reason to take children along. Women with children were safer from rape and were not suspected of being couriers for the resistance.

Just then Nieske rode up; she smiled and waved as she approached. Setting Herve' down Jon helped unload Arie from the back of the bike and Evert from his seat on the bar going from the seat to the handlebars.

Taking a quick look to see where the soldiers were, she grabbed Jon by the arm. "The war will be over soon, the Americans have joined the war."

"Really? They said they wanted to be neutral."

"Neutral did not work for them. Yesterday the Japanese bombed the American navy and Germany declared war on America. If they want to or not the 'Free States' are now in the war."

"It was inevitable; they have been providing aid to England and France for some time already. Glad they are in; there is hope for us now."

"Sure but they are a long way away, the Atlantic is a huge ocean."

"But the Japanese only bombed the Pacific Fleet; the American's have a fleet on this side, too."

"Hope, *ja*, hope is what we have been praying for. Hope was dim when Hitler secured most of Europe"

"I wonder if Hitler made a mistake getting America involved. They are very patriotic and love their independence. They will never concede to the Fuhrer."

"*Ja*, but Hitler has them fighting a war on both sides of their country, which may spread them too thin to win against two enemies. He hopes Japan will keep them away from Europe."

"Can the Americans get enough planes, tanks and guns to help us while they fight Japan?"

"This is God's answer to our prayers, I am sure of it!"

Hope dimmed the next few weeks as the news broadcast said the Americans were going to enter the war by freeing North Africa first., When Italy and Germany were defeated there the Axis would be weakened and improve the ability to land troops in Europe. Meanwhile the Dutch despaired and waited helplessly.

Chapter 30

More bad news came when Braam visited. "The Japanese have conquered the island of Java. They have captured the capitol, Batavia. The Dutch East Indies is now controlled by the Japanese."

"My brother is stationed on Java," moaned Jon. He and his family will be prisoners of war! Will he be captured or killed? Will I ever hear from them again?"

The pressure in Holland increased as the Gestapo realized that the Dutch had access to news far faster than they should have. Isolating the citizens from the world was part of the plan to bring compliance and sway the populace to join Germany's goals for a United Germanic State.

Notices were placed and broadcasts made that all radios were to be brought to the Centrum on the day designated for each city or village. Immediately those who were brave enough hid their radios or brought an extra radio or an old broken radio. At the Centrum the Nazi gave them a receipt to prove they had turned in their radio. They needed this receipt for when the soldiers came to do house searches. Those who kept a radio made sure no one knew. Even the children, friends and especially neighbors were not trusted to keep this a secret.

Three weeks went by before Nieske heard the news, her cousin had been arrested. A radio had been found hidden in the hay stack. The soldiers had also gone along the entire stack of hay with pitchforks. They stabbed the forks into the hay every few feet hoping to stab anyone or anything that might be hidden in the hay.

"Somebody snitched on him!" cried Nieske. "Who, who would do such a despicable deed? Good thing the Jew he was hiding was gone."

"Does the family know who might be the rat? If not, we can ask Braam or his friends to check on it."

"Braam could go. His mother lives in Apeldoorn, just a few blocks from my cousin's family. Nobody would suspect anything if he asked a few questions."

"Questions are one thing but if you want Braam to rescue Piet that is not going to happen. Likely Piet and all the others caught with radios or forbidden goods are in jail cells with guards. Or they are on the train to a camp. Maybe the only justice will be if the traitor is discovered and taken care of."

"That will not bring my cousin back," moaned Nieske.

The next day at ten in the morning the air raid alarm was sounded in Apeldoorn. When people came out to see what was going on they heard the gunfire; a volley of shots, maybe twenty or thirty guns being fired at roughly the same time.

Twenty three young men and one thirty year old woman were executed in front of City Hall. Piet was one of them.

Braam held Nieske as she wept.

Chapter 31

The German army spread out; occupying or conquering territories in Africa, Greece, all of Western Europe, the Balkans and making an assault on Russia. Needing to keep a large occupational army in Holland is not fitting into Hitler's plan. By now Holland should have joined the Great German Reich.

The Dutch might be Germanic but they love their independence, so they did not accept Hitler's invitation to join the Reich. Asking the Dutch to cooperate after bombing their citizens did not sit well, raising anger and resistance instead of compliance. Hitler was going to find out that making a Dutchman angry is not a good idea. They can be stubborn as mules and obstinate as a rock.

Across all of Holland the Gestapo laid siege to cities and villages. Every month new locales in provinces and cities or new towns were occupied by soldiers. The invaders rounded up unmarried but able bodied young men to work in the German factories making war supplies.

"It is like a cattle drive out west," Braam commented. "Round them up, put them in the cattle cars, packed so tight they cannot move and ship them to slaughter."

The train cars were packed so tight the riders could not sit or find a place to relieve themselves. Soon the train's cars reeked with urine and feces. Thus all human dignity is removed from those headed to the labor camps, making them submissive and compliant.

By bringing in conscripted labor Hitler freed up able bodied German and Austrian men for the battle fields.

The hunt for Jews also increased. The Gestapo confiscated the records in City Halls, using them to locate and identify Jews or mixed Jewish-Dutch. The Dutch had no idea that their fastidious record keeping would actually aid the enemy and not the citizens for whose benefit the information was gathered.

Systematically, the troops would go to the residence listed in the municipal records to arrest Jews. When a house was vacant because the occupants fled it brought trouble. Friends and neighbors were interrogated and threatened for information. Consequently most escapes were done secretly; no goodbyes to friends or well wishes to neighbors, just disappearing into the night.

By 1942 nearly sixty thousand Jews had been arrested and deported. Life for them was scary and everyone lived on edge until they could find a safe escape.

Who would be arrested next? Who are the informers? Whom could you trust? Informants are everywhere.

Informants were the weak, cowardly or greedy; trading information and Jewish lives for favors and personal gain. Thinking they had picked the winning side in this conflict they sold out their neighbors, family and country for personal security. They were hated like the rats they are.

Braam's nephew Kees Weeda was arrested too. Braam knew that Kees had a network of hiding places for Jews in *Zwolle*. Someone informed on him and he was picked up along with seven Jews. All of them were sent to Dachau.

Chapter 32

The organ prelude opened the service at the *Oude Kerk*. Evert Bultan's pastor, Pieter van de Broek rose from his chair, grabbed the sides of the lectern in his aged and gnarly hands. He was sixty three years old and endured many hard years farming during the First World War. Now he preached God's word during a second war. This war had all the signs of being worse than the first one. His voice was strong. His gnarled hands shook the lectern but his voice did not waver. It was strong and not afraid.

Pastors in the churches supported the resistance. They might not be active in working the underground but they encouraged and preached the "righteous cause of protecting Jews and opposing Hitler."

The *Hervormde, Gerifermeerde, Lutheren and Catholic churches* had a few pastors or priests who were pacifist. They were careful to avoid Nazi attention but others were vocal in their opposition to the Third Reich.

Dominee (Reverend) van de Broek read from the Bible, in Psalm 83, *"O my God, make them like the whirling dust; like the chaff before the wind. Like a fire that burns the forests, and like a flame that sets mountains on fire, so pursue them with Thy tempest, and terrify them with Thy storm. Fill their faces with dishonor, that they may seek Thy name, O Lord. Let them be ashamed and dismayed forever; and let them be humiliated and perish,"* his voice thundering.

"This is my prayer for the Third Reich!" he roared.

"It is our duty as Christians to stand for justice, it is our duty to stand for righteousness, it is our duty to stand with our Queen, it is our duty to stand up and be counted in resisting the evil that has invaded our beloved land."

"We are not pawns that fall before conquerors, we are not weak and we are not afraid." He boomed. "God is on the side of the righteous. We may be a small nation but we will not and must not allow our hearts and minds to yield allegiance to evil, no matter what his strength. We are people of God, we are strong, we are The

Dutch!"

Thus he encouraged them to stay strong, not to be intimidated by the power and might of the aggressor. He advised them to help the Resistance and most of all the help the Jewish people.

"We cannot fight them, we cannot kill them but we will not help them. Help those in need; protect the Jews for they are God's chosen peoples.

Those are deeds of the righteous. Do not yield to evil, do not become informers or help them in anyway. God will send informers to hell! Where they deserve to be!" he thundered, slamming his fist on the lectern. His Bible bounded up and his glass of water fell over, but he continued his condemnation of evil.

He concluded his message with a reading from Psalm 20, "*I know that the Lord saves His anointed; he will answer him from His holy heaven, with the saving strength of His right hand. Some boast in chariots and some in horses, but we boast in the name of the Lord, our God. They have bowed down and fallen; but we have risen and stood upright.*" With those words he comforted and assured his congregation to fight evil and trust God to see them through the trials.

Word passed throughout the Resistance groups that assassination of German troops or leaders was fruitless; a wasted act of revenge. The backlash is always devastating. The focus shifted to locating and terminating informers and traitors, sabotaging what they could.

Chapter 33

The occupation forces took what foods they wanted leaving less and less food for the Dutch. There was no famine yet, but everyone was acutely aware to eliminate waste; no food was thrown away, not even scraps. They used to wipe the plate clean with a piece of bread, now they licked the plate clean, savoring it to the last drop or fragment.

The German led occupational forces created a coupon system for purchasing food. Jews were not provided coupons but Dutch families were given coupons correlating with the number of family members.

The Resistance dug in deeper, becoming more secretive and setting up secure lines of communications. Their contacts were in France, Belgium, England and even a few in Germany.

There was no perfectly safe place for Jews to escape to. Life was treacherous, finding a travel route was not easy and getting across the channel to England and from there to America was nearly impossible. France was no longer a safe haven as they too had Jews being shipped off to concentration camps for annihilation.

David Cohen was a blond haired blue-eyed Jew. Only his name would identify him as a Jew. He did not match any of the physical characteristics Hitler used to describe Jews. With no Jewish nose, facial features or olive hued skin he looked more Aryan then Adolf.

David went to his friends in the resistance for help as he knew the enemy would come for him when the SS found his name on the City of Utrecht's records.

New identification was printed up for him by the Resistance. A secreted press was used to give him his new identity. His new name was David Slagter. He left Utrecht. He placed his jewelry business into the hands of his manager. He fled to Ede. There he rented a room in a boarding house.

Every morning Herr Slagter came down to breakfast dressed in his suit carrying his briefcase. After breakfast he walked to the train station to ride to some city on the pretense of going about his business.

No one asked him what he did and he did not say. Secrets are best kept by not talking. For three and a half years he followed this routine.

The only variation to this schedule was when he would assist the Resistance fighters. Then he would simply stay away for a few days and return as normal. He and Mies Sukkel became fast friends. Mies became a father figure for David, helping him and giving him guidance. They met for tea or a beer once or twice each month.

Those Jews, who could not blend in found hiding places in barns, behind false walls in houses, under the floors. Others were constantly on the move, keeping a day ahead of the pursuit, trusting their lives to the goodness of people they did not know and who did not know them. Patriots, Christians, and those who hate tyranny worked together protecting the helpless from bigotry and death.

The watch shop owned by the Ten Booms, in Haarlem, was such a place where Jews were hidden in secret places. Geert Bultan's house in De Hague had a hiding place. He installed a trap door in the kitchen floor. Within five seconds up to three people could drop down into the space under the house and his wife Dena would cover the access with a rug in front of the sink. Geert built concrete walls to form ten foot by ten foot area. A pipe hidden in a garden shrub provided air, making it safe and difficult to find. It was only four feet tall but large enough to hold three adults sitting or lying down.

Braam's family too had hiding places. His family fought in the underground for centuries; they fought Napoleon when he occupied the Netherlands and more recently the Spanish during Spain's occupation of Holland.

Braam's grandfather built the house in Apeldoorn. At one end of the upstairs hall way there was a bookcase; at the other end of the hall was a closet. Behind the bookcase and the back wall of the closet was access into rooms in the attic. They were not large rooms but they were eight by ten and six by nine. Food was always stored in each of these rooms and the rain gutter had been modified and built into the roof so that it could be opened to collect rain water to drink.

The book shelves were built as one unit that rotated on a round pole. Under a shelf was a board that served as a pin to latch and lock the unit in place. One pin was installed on each side, one at the bottom shelf and the other at the middle shelf. For the closet there was a drawer that pulled out to grant access.

Braam used these places twice when he was suspected of anti-German activity.

His mother was often heard saying, "Be strong, do not fear, God is on the side of the righteous!" She was proud of her son, the adventurer coming home to help.

Today they were drinking tea and enjoying an *Amsterdamer*, almond butter cookie.

"Have you submitted your application to immigrate to the Free States, mom?"

"No dear, I picked up the forms and filled them out, but they require medical reports that I need to get before bringing them in."

"When you do, be sure to get a receipt to prove you applied. I am afraid someone will check with you to verify my story. Having my klompen in the back porch and clothes in the closet may not be enough to keep them from snooping into my activities."

"Where do you go when you are away, who are you working with?"

"*Modder*" (Mother) you know better than ask that. Just like I do not ask who occupies the *schuilplaats* (hiding place), you do not want to know who I am with."

"How are you getting along with food? Do you have enough?"

"I get a little help from friends but we get by, right now I am feeding three extra for a few days, so times are tough. Not like that café on the corner of *Dorpsstraat* and *Blokkenweg* where the Germans eat. They seem to always have plenty of good things. Damn *Moffen*!

"But the righteous are going hungry" muttered Braam.

Chapter 34

Gerard van Bemmel married a city girl; the daughter of the hardware store proprietor, Cor de Bakker. He fell in love with Hilda when he went to the store with his father to buy handles for a pitchfork and axe.

Now they are happily married with two children and one on the way. His family is about to grow. Hilda's sister lives in Harlem with her three children, the last one, Tuis, was born in November, 1940. With the war dragging on and food becoming very scarce the family made a difficult decision.

Unable to feed them all, Eva had brought Tuis to the Gerard van Bemmel's farm. She rode onto the farm with her three year old on the seat in front of her and a valise containing his clothes on the rear of the bike.

She was tired from the hour plus bike ride and emotionally worn out from struggling with what she was about to do.

Hilda invited her sister in. Eva hugged Hilda instead of doing the three cheek kiss greeting. "What is wrong, Eva? Why are you here and why are you alone?" Then motioning to sit at the kitchen table they sat looking into each other faces, sister to sister.

"I cannot do it anymore." Eva hung her head. My life has been a mess ever since the war began and plummeted from there when Tuis was born."

"So? All of us are suffering, but we make do and hang on." Then she noticed the valise sitting just inside the door.

Shocked, Hilda looked into Eva's eyes. "You brought Tuis here because you hope Gerard and I will take care of him, right?"

Eva bowed he head into her cupped hands, hiding her eyes, sobbing she mumbled, "Yes, we need someone who will love him and care for him. Henk is not happy about this, in fact he is angry with me, so he made me do this by myself."

"I do not understand. Why Tuis? He is a great little boy, polite, kind and obedient."

"That is how you see him. At home he is different. I did not want a baby, but got pregnant anyway. We should never have brought a child into this war, it is not fair to him and not fair to me either."

Compassion flooded out of Hilda. Compassion for the torment her sister was going through and compassion for this little boy who needed to be loved and wanted.

"Eva, look at me! Of course we will help. Food is better in the country. I was not so sure I wanted to marry a farmer, but it has been good and now we at least have food and not much exposure to the Germans."

We will take care of and love Tuis, he can stay as long as you like; Gerard will agree too, I know his heart. For sure Tuis can stay till the war is over."

Hilda went to Eva, Eva rose and there they stood weeping in each other's arms. Eva wiped her tears with her forearm.

"When the war is over, you say? What makes you think the Germans will ever leave? It is hopeless; they will kill us or starve us and occupy Holland for generations."

So Tuis joined many other children born during the war, loved but not wanted. Hundreds of families, mostly the mothers, were haunted with the dilemma of how to love a child that through no guilt of his own placed an unbearable burden on parents and the other children.

Each family member dealt with the anxiety of war in their own way. Each of them knowing that death is possible on any given day and not quite knowing how to deal with the constant fears, threats, and the lack of food. Each day is a balancing act dealing with hunger and providing for the children.

Hilda looked at Tuis where he sat on the floor playing with a top. His brow was wrinkled with determination as he tried to make it spin for more than a few turns. She scooped him up in her arms, hugging him to her breast.

"Would you like to stay with me for a little while? Your cousins would love to have you stay and play with them. She whispered and then kissed him on the forehead.

"Ja *tante* (aunt)" he said. "I Iike the farm. Can I stay?"

"As long as you like, Tuis. Next week we will go visit your other uncle and aunt. We will see *Om* Jon and *Tante* Nieske. You may play with Herve', that will be fun. *Tante* Nieske is a great cook."

Eva rose, "I have a long sad ride to make, so I better get going."

Hilda put Tuis down, and rose to hug her sister-in-law.

They both wept with sorrow and pain.

Chapter 35

Braam was irate. His rage grew daily as the Nazi took more food and hunger became an everyday pain. The Nazi troops were greedy and wasteful and enjoyed seeing the Dutch suffer. He brought his frustration to the next resistance meeting. An argument ensued, not heated but serious. Several were content with what they had accomplished; some even made friends with German soldiers, saying that many of the soldiers were only doing what they were told or forced to do.

"I get a loaf of hard-tac almost every day from one of them," reported Sam. "I try to get along with them, it helps feed my family."

Sam worked as the trash collector at canals. The troops were familiar with his duties of removing the collection of debris at the grates by the bridges and the sluice gates. He was no threat, so they shared food with him.

"Why are we here?" asked Braam of the group. "Just because one of us gets food from the enemy that does not feed the rest of our families or save our Jewish friends, does it? What the hell is wrong with you? He shouted! "Are we getting soft or feeling sorry for the invaders?

Are you forgetting what the Democratic Socialist Party did in March? Students must sign allegiance to the Third Reich if they want to attend a university. The invaders are our enemy no matter how nice some of them are. We are losing freedoms every day, It is our people that are going without food, they are suffering, and we must help them!"

The entire group affirmed they hated what was being done to Jews and as patriots it was their duty to resist the occupational forces. No one had the right to govern or control the Netherlands other than the Dutch. Doing a few things was not enough. Becoming soft and content was not okay. They needed to do as much as possible. For Braam and Alida that meant doing more!

~~~

"In the attic of the apartment building where I live," stated Alida, "is a printing press, it has been hidden there for over a year. We should use it to print food coupons and the permits and identification papers that will allow us to be on the streets after curfew. We can print new identification papers for those being sought by the SS. David Slager will help us."

"Where are you proposing this press be set up? First of all, how are we going to get it out of there? The flat below you is occupied by a member of the NSB, which is why it is hidden," stated "Mies" Sukkel.

"How about doing some raids on a German armory or raid a camp? We could use some guns and ammo?" suggested Braam.

"That is a good way to get killed!" retorted Sam

"Getting killed is always a part of standing up for your country; besides we could be killed for doing nothing. If I die I want it to be while I am doing something!" exclaimed Braam.

Mies tried to calm them down. He knew about Braam's role in saving Alida and taking out the collaborators, but the group did not know these facts and keeping it secret was best for everybody. Mies knew how much bravery and guts it took; however not everyone here had those survival instincts and it was best they not know what happened to prevent loose lips from talking under interrogation.

"Alright, each of you comes to the next meeting with a plan or ideas to accomplish whatever your goal is," requested Mies. "We will do the best idea or plan."

Alida and Braam left together again. This time they discussed what they could do about getting food coupons.

"They print those in the press room behind City Hall. How about getting some for free from a worker?"

"Which worker? Most of them are sympathetic to the Nazi or belong to the NSB. Plus the head of the printing room is Nazi. Besides how many could a sympathetic worker give us?"

"Okay, what if we rob the place?" suggested Braam.

Alida's eyes sparkled at this challenge. She rose to the

challenge knowing that she and Braam would love this adventure more than any other member of the group. "How many would it take?"

"I think four should be enough; one to drive an auto, one to hold a gun on the workers and two to fill bags or boxes with the coupons."

"Let's do it. My brother will drive and my uncle will help load the coupons. At the next meeting we will show them what we did."

Braam looked at her with a question in his eyes. "Shouldn't we wait for the group's approval?"

But seeing the gleam in her eye and the excitement in her voice he knew this was as good as done. Over a cup of tea they made the initial plans.

Chapter 36

Alida and Braam spent three days on surveillance. Friday was the target date. A daylight attack was planned; it would be when the workers finished their afternoon tea. The workers would be tired and be thinking about going home. Plus the Nazi boss would be thinking about the weekend he had planned with his Dutch girlfriend.

Braam and Alida hated those romantic relationships. They despised the women who exchanged sex for favors or food coupons. Alida and Braam would rather die of starvation than cohabit with the enemy.

Friday noon three men and a woman ate lunch at the Greek café. They all wanted a beer with the lunch. "Just to calm the nerves," suggested Dik.

Alida held Dik's hand. "It is better to be clear headed." She whispered. "Stay cool, it will work just as we planned, they are not expecting anything like this."

"Come on eat something, it will keep you strong and steady. I am having a *uitsmijter,* an open face ham and egg sandwich, I love those things and if this war goes on much longer we won't have them anymore."

"Sounds good to me, Dik," said Braam

"I'll share one with Alida," said her uncle.

At precisely five to three Braam went in the front door of City Hall. It was windy and blustery. Everyone on the street pulled up their collars and pulled caps down over the ears. He looked just as everyone else when he pushed open the door. He headed directly toward the press room, pointing with his right hand while looking at the receptionist. She nodded as if she understood his intent. His left hand was in his pocket gripping the pistol he borrowed from Bultan.

The lady at the information desk smiled and waved him through the door. At the same time the other entered the unlocked delivery door.

Braam pushed the door to the printing room, bumping into the Nazi overseer. The Nazi looked at Braam missing Braam's co-conspirators coming in the rear door. Perfect timing.

"What the ...." Was as far as the overseer got, he stopped when he felt the jab into his side. He knew it was a gun, just below the fifth rib, that would blow a hole in his heart.

"Don't move and don't say anything; you might live to see tomorrow."

Dik tied the overseer up and took his pistol and carbine; actually it was a British Sten that he was carrying on the sling.

Holding the Sten gun Dik swept it around the room. "Everybody against that wall!" he shouted pointing at the wall with the bulletin board. There he could keep an eye on them so no one could crawl off to sound an alarm.

Quickly four burlap grain sacks were filled with coupons and taken out the back door. Braam grabbed a box of coupons on his way out. "Do not shout, and do not come out or you are dead!" He hurried out to the waiting car. The trunk was full so he closed the lid and he took the box into the front seat with him.

Dik made two quick right turns and a left, they headed out of town. No shots, no sirens, nothing but silence until Alida gave out a cheer, they all laughed as the tension left them. Exhilarated and joyful they clapped each other on the back! They had pulled it off and lots of Resistance workers and Jews would now be able to get food and a decent meal.

Chapter 37

Spring 1944

Dominee (Reverend) Rolf Achterberg strode to the pulpit at the Oude Kerk in Ede. The congregation finished singing Psalm 91; they keep their eyes focused on the preacher while taking their seat on the oak pews. The organist slid off his bench and went to sit with his family. It was time for the sermon.

Rolf is not a firebrand although he does participate in aiding the underground movement. He often attends meetings of Marinus Sukkel's and sometimes meets with the group in Utrecht. He is trustworthy and serves them as the unofficial chaplain. He sees himself as the spiritual guide, encourager and prayer warrior; not an activist or doer. He prays for each person in the cadre every day. His first hour of the day was on his knees by his desk chair.

The occupation is dragging on; the battles are in far off places, Tunisia, Libya, Ethiopia, Russia and Italy. Bombers fly overhead from England on their way to bomb German targets. At home in Holland the people are weary. The Onderduikers are doing what they can but life is hard. As food becomes harder and harder to get, desperation increases. Those who had coupons would find store shelves short of stock. The coupons were near worthless for getting their allotment.

Jews and resistors are hunted and arrested. The *onderduikers* are summarily shot but the Jews are shipped off to Mauthausen-Gusen every week. Those arrested in Gelderland were taken to Arnhem. There they wait, locked up on the fifth floor at the corner of the Centrum, near the river across from the Arnhem tower.

Rolf realizes that his sermons preaching resistance and sabotage had galvanized many people to action. Everybody is doing their part, but it seems that God is slow in answering their prayers and their hard work. His congregation knows that when you pray for God to do something you did not just sit by and wait; doing nothing. They understand that when you ask God for something, God expects the person who prays to do his part. Being willing to be part of the answer is the correct method of prayer. "You have hands and feet, use them!" is what Rolf taught.

Rolf had taught them well. He would say, "When you pray for someone to be free from loneliness or are in need of food or help, maybe God would like it you go visit or you bring food or help in time of need. After all we are Jesus' hands and feet. *Jatoch*? (Yes, surely) Be an answer to your prayer," he encouraged.

On the other hand he understood fear. Just two days ago a couple had gotten married at City Hall then the couple and the entourage had walked the three blocks to his church for the religious ceremony seeking God's blessing on their marriage.

When the church ceremony was over the wedding party and guests walked out to the courtyard. There they mingled to visit and congratulate the couple. The groom was kissing his bride for the first time when a German army truck loaded with soldiers careened around the corner and skidded to a stop.

Before the soldiers were off the truck the Dutch men scattered running in every direction. Fearing capture and detention they left the women standing there with the bride, even the groom ran away. None, especially the groom, wanted to spend the next years of life working in German factories.

The women froze in surprise as the soldiers rushed past them into the open church. That is when the crowd heard the sound of the airplane. Looking up they saw the bomber, accompanied with two fighters, flying over. The soldiers ditched the truck in fear of being bombed or shot by the British. They came for refuge in the church, not to arrest anyone.

It was a scary time for all. The husbands and the groom did not return till late that night, sneaking in after curfew. Caution was safest, not knowing if they were pursued or sought.

It was slow work to sabotage or resist. Rolf was privy to much of what was happening. He knew that Hans Eleveld worked as lens crafter in Utrecht. The local German commander brought damaged binoculars, scopes and other items for repair to Han's shop.

Hans was careful to fix what stayed local but the periscope that came from the U-boat and the microscopes and binoculars that were shipped out of town mysteriously had missing prisms or lens that did not match. These items were more useless now than when they arrived. He knew that without a return address or other identifying names these sabotaged items would not be traced back to his shop. Slowly, a little at a time, the resistance chipped away at attaining freedom.

Rolf knew that the printing press Alida found had been set up in that attic. The NSB couple had moved away when given a job at the party headquarters in Amsterdam.

The man in charge of allocating houses and apartments quickly called Mies to find a tenant who was cooperating with or a member of the Resistance. Mies asked Braam if he and Alida would like to get married and move in to secure the operation of the press. Braam was not ready, not having made plans beyond survival and getting back to Minnesota. Alida wanted to wait for the war to be over. Neither one desired to become a widow.

Another couple, Dien and Jacob leaped at the opportunity. Now the building was safe for the press to be set up.

Chapter 38

David Slager set up the press, make the adjustments to how much ink was used and taught the team to operate it.

David promised to help a few days a month. With his keen eye for detail, learned from making jewelry, the press published perfect documents. Working evenings and weekends they produced realistic identification papers. Next they perfected authentic looking German travel papers and passports and food coupons.

They duplicated official papers that gave a person's name and what privileges they had for moving about the city or countryside. These papers exempted them from curfew and permitted travel outside their own locale.

Now, standing at the lectern Rolf is going to encourage his flock. He opened his Bible to the book of Psalms. Every pastor used the Psalms for comfort and encouragement. It is a great book that takes the reader through the lows and the pinnacles of life, the dark dreadful things of life and the glory God promises.

He read from Psalm 91, *"He who dwells in the shelter of the Most High will abide in the shadow of the Almighty. I will say to the Lord, 'my refuge and my fortress', my God in whom I trust!"* and Psalm 27, *"The Lord is my light and my salvation; whom shall I fear? The Lord is the defense of my life; whom shall I dread?"*

He boomed, "That is our God, he is for us, with perseverance we wait upon the Lord and do what we can while we wait. We are God's people, we are Hollanders, and we will overcome! Like it says in Revelations, *'The enemy will not overcome they will come to the fate God has prepared for them. Let me read a few verses that will make this real for you."*

He then turned the pages of his Bible to Psalm 37.

With a strong voice and with deep emotion he started to read at verse 35, *"I have seen a violent, wicked man spreading himself like a luxuriant tree in its native soil. Then he passed away and lo he was no more; I sought for him but he could not be found. Mark the blameless man and behold the upright; for the man of peace will have posterity. But the transgressor will be altogether destroyed; the posterity of the wicked will be cut off. But the salvation of the righteous is from the Lord; He is their strength in the time of trouble. And the Lord helps them, and delivers them; He delivers them from the wicked, and saves them, because they take refuge in Him."*

"My friends trust in God, do not give up hope! Our liberty is coming and it is coming soon!"

Then he prayed the final prayer of the service and dismissed them, not knowing that God was indeed actively working to bring freedom and liberty.

Chapter 39

June 6, 1944

Jon is in his field planting rows of cabbage, both red and white. Next he will weed his beets, carrots, turnips, rutabagas, and potatoes. He pushes the drill (planter) with his eye focused on the fence post at the other end of the field. His furrows are perfectly straight, not a waiver in them. He keeps his farm neat, orderly and efficient. Someday the Nazis will be gone and the entire farm will be orderly, meanwhile he does what he can.

He looks up when hears the sound of a truck speeding south on his road. He figures this is a military truck as the only traffic on this country road was horses and wagons or bikes. Dutch trucks are driven slowly to keep the Nazis calm. This truck was coming fast. He stopped planting. He is anxious as he looks toward his house to see what the great haste is.

The driver locks the brakes, sending dust and gravel flying as he slews into the drive. Fear grabs Jon's heart; he drops the seeding drill and runs for the house.

Something out of the ordinary is happening. None of the occupiers have moved this fast or been in such a hurry. Jon wants to make sure that his family is safe. Sweating in fear he ran faster.

The truck is stopped half way between his house and the hog barn. The driver is standing next to the truck. Whoever is with him is out of sight. Jon hopes he is in the barn and not the house, Jon runs on. The cow barn door swing open as soldiers pour out of the barn, each carrying his rifle, with a pack on their backs and another sack in their hands.

As Jon turns the corner of the hog barn he sees fourteen soldiers climb into the rear of the truck. The canvass flaps are open and Jon sees that the truck is full of soldiers. The benches along the sides are full of soldiers and the area in middle is filled with packs and gear. The driver slams the truck into gear tromps on the gas and sprays gravel as he speeds of in a cloud of dust.

Jon slowed as he approached the sergeant, who is standing by himself at the front corner. This sergeant, Ger Hults, was friendlier than the past leaders of the troops, so Jon walked up to him. "What was that about, what's happening?"

Ger had a grim look about him. Jon was not sure if it was anger, frustration or fear. Sgt. Hults turned to face Jon. "The unbelievable has happened; the Americans have invaded France. All available troops are on the way to stop their advance before more come."

"Where?"

"Some beaches in northern France; they have thousands of ships and aircraft. It is bloody, as you Dutch say, *"Vervloeken"* (cursed) mess and my men are going there to die!" he responded tersely and with a bitter edge in his voice.

Jon's face lit up, with hope, which he quickly brought under control in front of his enemy. "Are all of you going?"

"No, I am staying along with six men to man the guns in case the Americans come. We are the lucky ones; those fourteen guys are going to a hell of a fight."

"From what I hear the ships keep coming with more soldiers. They swarmed the beach like ants. So far they have overrun the bunkers and pill boxes faster then we can shoot them. It is a gory, bloody mess, must be a hundred thousand dead on the beaches and more dying every minute."

"Our troops are trapped in bunkers and pill boxes, what was intended to provide safety from bullets has become a coffin. The Americans that get past the bullets get on top of the bunker and then throw grenades inside. When the guns stop they use flame throwers that burn any survivors. They are not taking prisoner, everyone dies. Those who are not killed by the grenades are burned or cooked with no place to run. It is a desperate struggle of survival."

Jon saw a tear form in Ger's eyes, but he quickly turned away to wipe it off.

"Is the Gestapo going to France too?"

"No, those bastards do not go anywhere near a fight. They just love to push people who cannot hurt them and shoot people who have no guns or protection. They act tough but are not brave, bullies is what they are, cowards!" And spat on the ground in disgust.

Looking up he asked Jon, "Have they given you problems?"

"No, not directly, they did stop Nieske two weeks ago when she was in Ede, but that was not too scary. She had Evert with her so they did not touch her."

"Lucky for her, some of those guys are pretty nasty, did they interrogate her?"

"Ja, they asked her some questions, just feeling her out to see if she knows any *Onderduikers*. Nasty they are, just last month they shot her cousin for having a radio."

"Keep your nose clean, no radios, no Jews and no *Onderduikers* and you will be left alone."

"That is what you say, but we have to keep feeding you and sacrifice our health for you guys. That's not easy to take."

A ripple of fear crossed Jon's face as he realized he had just insulted the enemy. He hoped nothing would come of this.

Ger looked at him, "Yeah, this war is a bitch, isn't it? I hate it too." And he turned and walked away.

Chapter 40

June 13, 1944

Deep in the hills outside Vienna, Austria was a gypsum mine. Gypsum is no longer its main product. The mine is now a huge factory. Enough gypsum is mined to make the mine appear active. A new weapon is being developed there.

Mining created three huge caverns. They are two kilometers deep in the mountain and have hundreds of feet of mountain above them. A spring provides potable water. Electrical lines provide lights along the tunnel and power the equipment.

Here in the depths of the earth, far from prying eyes and safe from bombs is a complex weapons factory. Here engineers and scientists are creating the next level of warfare. A self propelled bomb, a rocket. A concept only thought about in Space Gordon comics has become a reality.

Here the Nazi regime is developing the VI and later the VII rockets. These rockets are capable of bombing London and the British airfields. They fly too fast to be spotted by radar and early warning systems to alert the Brits.

The rocket's guidance system and fuel needs are not perfect but useable enough that Hitler moved up the time table for using it. Hitler cursed himself and his engineers for being a year late in the development.

Now that the Allies have a beachhead in France he must speed up the use of rockets. He needs these rockets to replace airplanes. Fighter pilots are dying every day, replacing them will come to an end soon. To set back the Allies he must destroy Britain. British airfields are the staging ground for the Allies bombing raids and assembling troops before sending them to France. Hitler is desperate to destroy them.

He needs these rockets to change the tide of the war. The war is no longer going as he planned. The tide of war has shifted. Africa is no longer his, the eastern front is suffering huge loses to the Russian. He calls them "Ivans" in retaliation of the Russians calling Germans "Fritzs." The urgency is overcoming and changing his plans. Hitler is desperate; he must regain the tide of war to his favor.

Chapter 41

A screaming sound pierced the sky. It came from the east and faded away into the west. "What is that?" asks Nieske, trembling with fear.

The family is at the breakfast table, eating *havermal* (oatmeal) mixed with milk and a spoon of molasses. A second scream came. They have never heard this before, not quite a scream something like screech or whine followed by a whoosh. It too faded into the west.

Jon ran outside to see what is happening, but Nieske grabbed the three boys and crawled under the stairway. This was the safest place next to the bearing wall and a large header beam went across under it to the barn. Should the house collapse this might create a void in the debris to survive in until help came. If it came.

As Jon came out the door, he saw the soldiers running to their guns, but Gerben (Ger) stood beside the munitions truck.

"What was that?"

Just then a third and fourth scream pierced the calm spring day.

"The Fuhrer is using his new weapon."

"Weapon? It screams and cannot be seen?"

"It is the VI rocket; it flies at over 4000 kilometers per hour, (3000 miles per hour). It carries a bomb that explodes when it falls to the ground."

"*Allemachtig* (Almighty)! How does it fly that fast? Where is it going and coming from? Will it fall on us?"

"It is scary because it is not very accurate yet; just over half get to where they are supposed to go. These are coming from Germany. All of them are aimed at London. The sites are moved every day. The Fuhrer is trying to pressure England to stop sending troops to France and to keep the Americans from assembling its troops and supplies in England. Plus he wants to destroy England's airfields and bombers."

Every day the rockets came, no longer scary. A few did fall

near the coast of the Netherlands. Most of the forty percent that missed London fell into the sea.

Meanwhile the news said the troops, now properly called the Allies, were approaching Paris. The Americans and the Canadians were making the difference for turning this war around. Freedom was looking possible!

Chapter 42

The Onderduikers became more aggressive when half the occupation troops left for France. But Heinrich Himmler responded with force. Suspected resistance members were shot without question or inquiry.

The group in Veenendal sent two men to check out the guns at Van Bemmel's farm. Braam was not one of them, although he drew the map of the area. Plans were made to destroy the guns.

They would approach from the footpath that followed the property line on the south. It offered good cover with the trees on one side and the tall grasses that grew on the banks of the ditch on the other side. They would avoid the house or barns to not rouse the chickens or other farm animals. They did not want to bring danger to their friends Jon and Nieske.

They found the guard sound asleep, sitting against a fence post with his helmet on his lap. They spotted him when the moon light reflected off the bayonet.

Silently, Sjoerd, the team leader, gestured his partner to take the guard out. With a nod his partner crawled up behind the guard. He got up on one knee, covered the guard's mouth with one hand and swiped his knife across the throat severing the windpipe and aorta. He was gone before the gurgles rose from the severed windpipe.

Wiping his blade in the grass they slither to the first gun. Quietly two sticks of dynamite were placed under the first gun, and then two more under the second gun.

They froze, flattening themselves when they heard a soldier coming from the barn. Shit, it must be shift change of the guards and it is one a.m. a strange time to change guards.

Not having time to load the third gun they lit the fuse on gun two, hurried to gun one and lit that fuse. They crawl away as fast as possible. The fuse was long enough to provide about forty five seconds to clear the area. They had planned to run but now were crawling on elbows and knees.

They watched the new guard approach the dead one, "Hey, Efron," they heard him call the guard's name. There was no response, so he bent to see what was wrong. As the new man bent over, the men quickly crawled under a barb wire fence, went through the ditch and started running down the footpath.

The new guard saw that Efron was dead; he also saw the team coming from under the fence. Firing one round into the air to alert the others he then went down on one knee and carefully fired the second shot. The bullet hit Sjoerd just as he cleared the fence; the bullet hit him before his second step. The rest of the team disappeared into the trees.

Two explosions broke the night air as two anti-aircraft guns lifted out of their holes and broke up as the ammo stored with them exploded.

Three soldiers approached Sjoerd, when close they fired one more shot into his leg to see if he would react. No movement, not a twitch, so they approached him. One used his foot to roll him over hoping to find him alive so they could interrogate him.

Seeing his eyes were open they pointed a rifle in his face. "Who are you? What is your outfit?" they asked.

A smile went across his face as his eyes closed, breathing his last breath he gargled as blood came out of his nose and mouth. But his face was at peace, as if he had been blessed by an angel.

Searching his pockets they found identification papers. The address was in Sneek, Friesland. This man was a long way from home, if that truly was his address. They did a complete check but nothing was found to contradict his identification. Further searching revealed other items from Friesland indicating he was not a local.

This would make it extremely difficult to find someone who knew him or would be able to provide information about the Resistance group he worked with and had planned this.

~~~

Nieske and Jon went to her father's house two days later. There they met Braam.

"What did you think you were doing? You have put us in grave danger. They suspect us for being involved in this. They have interrogated us, threatened us and now they watch everything we do, follow us everywhere we go. Life has gotten ten times more difficult."

"We needed to take the opportunity. It is good that you did not know or they would really have been tough on you" retorted Braam.

"Sure that is easy to say, as long as they do not catch you, but meanwhile we pay the price every day; they act like it is our fault and that we planned this."

"Calm down" ordered Heer Bultan. "Everybody pays during a war, we cannot choose our pain. Are you still with us, Jon?"

"Yes, of course, damn them!"

Chapter 43

Sept 8 1944

Ten new soldiers arrived at the Van Bemmel farm. Young inexperienced kids. Fresh out of basic training, which had been shortened to four weeks due to the pressing needs in the field. No battlefield duties, just raw recruits. They were brash and cocky, full of the bravado of youth.

They were mere teenagers who had outgrown being Brown Shirt cadets. They had been tough and rough when parading the streets back home where they had police support and the populace was afraid of them. In their home town they harassed anyone they thought was not fascist. They could destroy Jewish business; poke fun of those who disliked the harshness of fascism or gang up to beat them up in an alley.

Now they are soldiers, not ready for battle. They are only fifteen and sixteen years old. Sgt. Ger is not pleased with this bunch of hooligans. They were unruly, loud mouthed and cruel. He was not the only sergeant to get new troops; these young men were sent everywhere to replace the occupation forces. The seasoned soldiers were transferred to the front lines in the east fighting Russia or the west fighting the Allies.

Even worse was the shortage of food. Shipments from Germany were sporadic so the soldiers lived off the land.

When food was available, in the city, it was severely rationed. The allotted amount per person dropped from 1500 calories per day to 500 calories.

Ger came to Nieske while she was washing clothes in the kitchen sink. Usually she heated the water on her stove then poured it into the metal tub and rinsed in the sink.

Ger set down the pail of coal he brought with him, placing it next to the stove. "Want me to put some in, or are you finished?"

"Ja, just a little more, one more pot of water will be enough to wash the diapers and then warm the soup."

141

He put the pail down and stood there with his hands in front, fidgeting and shuffling his feet.

"What is wrong, Ger? You look worried?

"I am worried; I am tired of this war and tired of what we are doing to Holland. You people are just like us. Why are we killing and hurting the Dutch? And this new bunch of troops is driving me crazy!"

A high pitched whine streaked through the sky. Nieske and Ger stood frozen, their conversation interrupted, then another a few seconds behind it.

Nieske's eyes widened with alarm. "What was that? It is not a VI." She shuddered.

"That is the new and improved version of the VI. Hitler has developed a rocket that is bigger, faster and has a bigger bomb than the VI, this one is called the VII."

Hearing this Jon asked, "Is it more accurate than the old one? Is it going to fall short too and kill us?"

"I do not know. It is supposed to be better and more accurate. It is fueled by nitrogen and liquid oxygen. It was developed and built inside mountains. No one knew what was being made or even that something was being made. They have more speed than the VI. They are so fast that they cannot be shot down by planes or artillery. At least that is what we are told."

"The plan is to bring them to Holland and Belgium to be closer to the targets in England. The portable launchers are setting up at Ockenberg and Ypenberg airfields just outside The Hague. There they can hide them in the woods and bring them onto the airfields when ready to send a barrage on London."

Ger moved to stand in front of Nieske, looking intently into her eyes he blurted "I want out of this war. I hate what is happening. The Allies are in France, summer is gone; this winter is going to be really tough. The Russians are advancing in the eastern front. We are retreating; the country side in France and Russia are strewn with dead bodies of my countrymen. This is not a war I want to die in! Please help me, I want to go home."

"What can we do? We have nothing."

"Nieske, you and Jon have been good to us, treated us like humans while we ruin your farm, eat your chickens, eggs, calves and hogs. It is going to get worse, these new kids are terrible. They will harm you take what they want and destroy whatever they do not like. They run on fascist energy doing what pleases them. Power exhilarates them. They love it when people cower and show fear."

"You remember that two months ago I took five days leave? I went home to see my family and get away from all of this" he waved his hands indicating the whole region.

"When I arrived at home I found things worse than I expected. My cousin is commander of a unit guarding the children's hospital just outside Koln. They do horrible experiments on handicapped boys and girls. They treat them as monkeys or animals. When an experiment fails or the children die they incinerate them like trash."

"I was aghast at what I discovered. My family is afraid to say or do anything. My cousin thinks this is perfectly good to do. He has lost all moral feeling he approves of this massacre and desecration of humanity. He laughed at me for caring about those helpless kids."

"Animals, animals that is what the Fuehrer has turned us into; amoral animals that do his bidding."

"I want to go home, be with my wife and kids. I need to save them from this depravity. I will not be able to control these hoodlums and I cannot stand by watching it either."

"I will tell you everything I know if you will help me escape. They will kill me if they catch me but if you provide enough food for me I can travel without being seen long enough to get behind the lines."

"Hitler is getting more and more desperate, he will send rockets to destroy London and air fields at High Wycombe until he runs out of bombs or England caves. He knows that he must stop England and the Allied bases there or he will lose the western front too."

Nieske looked at Jon; he nodded his head in approval for helping this man desert. Neither of them wanted to use the term but that is what it was, they just wished more would follow him.

"Okay, tomorrow I will bring a man here for supper. When your men are bedded down, come here and you will tell him what he needs to know. While you are doing that Nieske will fill your backpack and rucksack with food; water you will find along the way. When he is satisfied, you may take the packs and disappear.

We must make sure the troops do not know we assisted you."

"Deal, see you after eight."

Chapter 44

Marinus Sukkel arrived at six, a half hour after sunset. It was the start of a very dark night. A perfect night for treachery; the coming rain storm covered the moon and stars. Tomorrow was going to be wet.

He leaned his bike against the wall, next to the kitchen door. The door opened before he could knock, Jon brought him to the kitchen. Arie, Evert and Herve' are seated at the table, "can we eat now, I am hungry," moaned Herve?'

"You are always hungry! Stop complaining, everybody is hungry," growled Jon.

"Say hello to Uncle Mies," ordered Nieske as she carried the pot from the stove.

"Hello uncle Mies," they muttered in unison. "Can we eat now?"

The meal was a simple meal, potatoes with Rutabagas and a small chunk of salted pork. All of this stirred in one pot with the pork resting on top. Nieske set it down in the middle of the table. She cut the pork into small bite size pieces, one ounce for the adults and half that for the kids. She ladled portions to everyone's plate. Food was scarce in the country too but it was not governed by ration coupons, they ate what was not confiscated.

"Do you trust this man?" asked Marinus. "This could be a set up to capture me?"

"*Ja*, I think he is sincere, but before he comes in I will take a walk around. I will check the barns and see where the soldiers are. If anything is out of normal I will start whistling one of the Psalms as I walk back to the house."

"I hope these new kids do not act crazy when they discover Ger is missing. They have already searched the house for hidden foods and radios. Sgt. Ger told them the place has been searched four times already. Idiots, how am I supposed to listen to a radio with no electricity?"

Nieske chimed in too. They recounted all the livestock too; they know exactly how many chickens we have, how many pigs and what size they are. They even counted the jars of canned foods. Then they took the boys aside to question them. They asked where mommy hides the food jars and where daddy has his secret hiding places. First they act like friends. Then when the boys say nothing they threaten the boys, scaring them until they cry."

"I am afraid they will ration our food too, already we eat less and do not waste; but as you heard, the kids are hungry all the time. The whole family is losing weight."

As Nieske and the kids cleared the table, Jon went outside to check on the animals. Mies took out his pipe, sat back in his chair to enjoy his smoke. He had his back to the wall and had moved his chair near the living room door. He was careful to locate escape routes everywhere he went. He figured that if things went wrong he could dive out the front window and disappear into the dark.

Ten minutes later Jon returned. "All looks well and Ger is coming right behind me. When he is here I will stand outside the door and smoke a cigarette, same warning."

They heard a knock and Ger walked in, a pack in each hand and his rifle slung across his shoulder. Seeing both hands full and the Luger in the holster, Marinus relaxed. His left hand was under his shirt and his right hand holding his pipe. He looked cool and relaxed.

Ger looked at Mies and realized that this man may have a smile and seem relaxed but he would be a dead man if he made a wrong move. He would have been shot long before he could get his Luger out or get the rifle down.

Both men smiled, they had read each other well. Both are pleased that things are as promised and expected. Real men facing each other; no trust between them until they proved themselves, each one knowing a wrong move means death.

Jon and Nieske left, she went to the kitchen and he to stand outside the door and keep watch. She filled Ger's packs with sandwiches, three apples and two pears. Jon stepped out to stand watch; he hand-rolled a cigarette lit it up and looked up at the sky then carefully eyed the barns where the soldiers were housed. He leaned against the wall, put one foot back and up against the wall. He took a long pull on the cigarette, acting like he was there for some fresh air while smoking.

Two hours later a lone figure slipped out the living room window with a back pack and a ruck-sack. He moved to the shadows of the trees and disappeared.

A few minutes later Marinus rode off north bound on his bike, knowing the other had gone south and sometime later would head east toward home. Mies said a short prayer for Ger, hoping he would be safe on the journey and at home. Ger had a job to do when he got home, he had to silence his cousin or he would be arrested.

Mies could hardly contain his excitement for the things he had learned of the Nazi plans.

Chapter 45

Utrecht

Astrid Bultan sat on her front steps watching people on the street when two Nazi soldiers approached, one soldier while the other sat down next to Astrid. He offered her a piece of salted black licorice. Speaking perfect Dutch, not the local dialect and without any accent, he asked if her father was home.

Astrid refused the candy, even though it was one of her favorites. She scooted away and started to get up. She was terrified of Nazi soldiers. She overheard the stories her mom, dad and Grandpa told of kidnappings, assassinations and taking of the food. Her parents hated the Nazis and feared them, she feared them too.

She had her own reason to not like them. It was the Nazi's fault her school was shut down for lack of teachers. The first grade teacher was a Jew and had fled; the fifth grade teacher was arrested and shot for suspected anti Nazi acts. That is why she was home this October morning.

She hated being locked up in her house; she loved school and loved to learn. Now she could not study. Morosely she sat outside in the cold air watching the world go by. It was a dark and somber day in spite of the occasional streaks of sunshine when the clouds drifted by.

It was because of these soldiers and not just these two; she saw all Nazi soldiers as the same. It was their fault that she was wearing her warmest dress and two pairs of socks in her best shoes. These swastika wearing soldiers are the reasons for the four valises standing just inside the front door.

They are packed with clothing, toiletries, family photos and important documents. All sitting ready for the time they would need to flee; ready to go in a moment's notice. She did not know when they would flee their home but her mother's fear convinced her the time was soon.

Now this man wanted to talk nice, but Astrid knew he is not nice, she smelled his phoniness. She hates him and everything he represents. He and others just like him have ruined her city, school and home.

She ignored his question, besides she does not know where her father is. Her mother and father instructed her and her little brother to not talk to Nazis. When pressed for an answer they were instructed to say their father was on his milk route.

She felt the soldier's hand on her shoulder pushing her back down. "Where is your father?"

Terror gripped her chest she bent over putting her head between her knees. She began to cry.

The hand on her shoulder squeezed harder. She winched in pain and began to sob in terror. "You must tell me where your father is." demanded the soldier.

Astrid looked up, and then shouted in her fear, "He is on his milk route or at the creamery getting his milk!"

Her mother, Dena, heard the shout and realized that Astrid was shouting in fear. Quickly she peered out the lace curtain of her window to see who or what frightened Astrid.

Keeping the children unaware of the hiding place and other things forbidden by the Nazi regime was about to pay off. Quickly she ran to the bedroom for Geert.

He grabbed a blanket and sweater while she moved the rug in front of the sink, pulled up the boards for Geert to slide down into the darkness.

Dena was washing her pots when the knock came on the door. Dena Bultan went to the door with soapy water dripping from her hands. She opened the door and saw Astrid with the Nazis behind her.

"We have come for your husband, Geert. He is needed at *Westerbork* labor camp, where is he?"

Dread filled her heart upon hearing the name of the dreaded labor camp the Nazi had set up in the Netherlands. No one ever returned from *Westerbork*. The laborers worked hard with little food

150

until they were too weak to work. The weak and sick are sent by train to Germany. Herded into open cattle cars, the lucky died in route, the survivors gassed in the death camp. Dena did not want her man to be on a train ride to certain death.

"He is not here," she replied as she dried her trembling hands, "he should be at the creamery or visiting farms to find enough milk and eggs for his customers."

Shoving her aside both soldiers entered the house.

Vrouw Bultan went back to scrubbing the pots, only now she was nervous and scrubbed harder and faster, happy that they thought she had been at the sink working and not knowing she has hid her man, and that he is hiding under her feet.

The soldiers took out their pistols and went room to room. They looked under the beds, in the closets and even checked the cupboards. They knocked on the walls, pushed on shelving hoping to find hollow sounds indicating a hiding place.

When they went out back they discovered Geert's bike.

"What is his bike doing here? He is not on his route, where are you hiding him?" he thundered.

Walking to stand inches away from her, he threatened her with detention and shipping to a camp if she did not tell.

"You have looked everywhere; you know he is not here. He must have gone with someone else. All I know is that he said he was going to find milk."

Shaking in her shoes, with soapy water dripping from her hands, she mustered up the courage to be defiant. Defiance would make them think she was truthful. "Now get out of my house," she growled at him and spat on the floor narrowly missing his shiny boots.

It was a standoff, they glared at each other with hatred, and yet knowing there was nothing else to say or do.

Grunting he turned away, his partner followed.

Chapter 46

The group was silent as they heard Mies Sukkel unfold his tale. They listened carefully to his story of meeting with Sgt. Ger Hults. The more Braam heard the more excited he became. Holding his tongue was hard but he said nothing. His patience was stretched as he waited for the group to process the information. He glanced over at Alida; she too had that gleam in her eye.

He knew she grasped the situation well. Braam suspected that she was already making plans, going over options. He watched her eyes, he knew her mind was working overtime as she plotted and formed teams in her head. Evaluating everyone she would figure out who should be on the team and who worked well as partners for this venture.

Braam focused on what Mies is reporting. "Two trucks are coming this Saturday, two days from now. One truck will have the ammunitions and grenades, the other will have food, blankets and guns. They will cross the river at Nijmegen, and then go north to Arnhem where they will drop off half the load. The remainder is for the troops in Utrecht, Veenendaal and Ede."

"How did you discover this? Is this reliable info?"

"Dik, you know better than to ask those kinds of questions. Except this time it is no problem to tell you because the man is long gone. There was a sergeant stationed at Van Bemmel's who gave up his fight with Holland and is returning home. He traded a lot of information for our help to get him safely on his way home."

"How do you know it is true? What if he is setting us up?" asked another.

"Fair question, but I doubt it very much. He really wanted help with food and directions. I did not give him any of our safe places to stop at. Like you, I did not want to endanger another group. However, I did give him a map with a route that would keep him fairly safe from discovery. Also he was given enough food to last five or six days and he was very sincere in his distaste for what the new breed of Nazis is doing. Besides that Nieske vouched for him.

You know she has a nose for smelling deceit and has watched him supervise his men. She has seen his distaste with the new troops. She thinks he has truly deserted and gone home."

"Some of you have been hoping for this opportunity," he continued. "We can use everything they will have, plus some dynamite. If they have no dynamite we can make our own explosives from the grenades."

"Do you really plan to hijack these trucks? You must be crazy, out of your damn mind! Spouted Dik. "This smells like a trap to ferret out Resistance corps."

The group became silent. It was increasingly fearful that the Gestapo's effort for attaining information was working. Several Onderduikers had been arrested and executed. The push for finding Jews had resulted in mass deportations. Trust was scarce. The Nazis use of food or the need for food bought information. Their intimidation and threats increased the fear causing the weak to yield and become informers.

Braam stood up. "Guys, let's look at how we can do this and figure out how to avoid the pitfalls. When we think it is impossible it will be impossible. We need that ammo and those guns; whatever we prevent them from having they cannot use against us. There must be a way to accomplish this. Let's figure out a successful plan for doing it."

A lengthy discussion ensued. They agreed that they did not have the means to transport two truckloads; however if the shipment was captured after the trucks left Arnhem it would be safer as it was in their own area.

"The amount on the trucks will then be small enough for our trucks. It will take less time to unload and load and still provide what we need." Argued Mies

There are two barns about half way between Arnhem and Ede where the arms could be hidden until the other groups can pick up their share. The group in Nijmegen has access to a phone; they will call the bakery when the trucks came over the bridge. From there Alida can bring the notice in plenty of time to get set up for when

154

they leave Arnhem.

They agreed to capture the trucks after they leave Arnhem. The guards will be relaxed, thinking the small amount left is not crucial to anyone other than their own troops. Stealing the trucks from a beer or tea stop would be wonderful and faster.

"If we can separate the troops from the trucks we can unload them and then dispose of them in a fire," suggested Sam.

"That will never work; how will we know where they will stop for a break, or even if they will be stopping."

"Too much risk of other soldiers being there or a witness who could give us up when questioned," added Alida

"All the soldiers and witnesses have to be eliminated; we cannot take any chances of being recognized or found through interrogations by the Gestapo." ordered Mies.

All conversation stopped as the reality of what they needed to do sank in. Killing German soldiers was one thing but they were hesitant to go farther than that. Collateral killing of fellow Dutchmen was not what they wanted, even if the witness was a Nazi sympathizer. Some even backed away from the direct killing of the Nazi regime, hoping others would do the actual deed while they just played a supporting role.

"What we are planning carries a death sentence. Killing a Nazi soldier will not increase the penalty. Killing the soldiers is a must for our safety. Just look at it as a bonus to our cause. So stop worrying, let's get to work and make it happen." Mies looked each one in the eye as he went around the group waiting for a response.

Slowly each conspirator nodded. *"Ja, we can do it."*

They formed two teams. Each team was composed of two on the ground and one truck driver; six men, two trucks and Mies. The team leader was Henk; he chose Braam, Jap and Gerrit. The rest of the group prayed with them and left, leaving Mies with the team. Only these five would know the details of when, where and how. The fewer that knew the operation the better.

Now the serious planning began. They agreed to stop the trucks in the, *Edese Bos*, (Ede Forest). They would escape from there going southwest through the *Hoekelumse Bos*. There the arms would be hidden or shared with the group from Utrecht and the one from De Hague. The remainder goes to Veenendaal.

"Í know a farmer who is feeding his sheep in the Ede Forest," ventured Gerrit. "We can herd his sheep onto the roadway. They will block the entire *Arnhemseweg*. The trucks will never get around those sheep. When they are yelling at the sheep or trying to chase them off the roadway we come out of the bushes, jump them and take them out."

"Are those sheep near where *Kruislaan* crosses *Arnhemseweg*? If so, we can hide our trucks around the corner," suggested Jap.

Jap knew the area very well. He was from nearby Barneveld where the van Kampen family lived on a farm. Jap had fled when the Gestapo had come to take him to the work camp. He hated all things Nazi because of what the soldiers did when raiding his father's farm.

He remembered well the day the Nazi soldiers arrived, knocked on the door and demanded food. They wanted canned goods, and especially preserved bacon and sausages. When his father had refused to give them food the sergeant had taken the entire family out of the house. He lined them up, from youngest to oldest, in front of the barn.

A machine gun was set up on a tripod. When it was ready, the sergeant walked up to Herr van Kampen and calmly said, "We will start with the little ones, how many do you want to see die before doing as told?"

Watching the soldiers carry off the food and two geese, Jap vowed to get even. Today was one of Jap's opportunities to pay the Nazi's back.

Chapter 47

Alida answered the bakery phone for the tenth time, it was for her. "Yes, sure I can bring the order to you at one thirty today, two loaves and five tarts? How about making it an even six?"

At one thirty the trucks leave Arnhem, headed west. Gerrit has the sheep ready just east of *Kruislaan*. When he hears the trucks coming he herded the sheep onto the road. He has one hundred thirty bleating wooly critters that are some of the stupidest creatures in creation. They are grazing the grass on the roadway shoulders, walking back and forth doing a nice job of blocking traffic. He whistled to alert his truck drivers, they are on *Kruislaan*, the plan is ready.

Arnhemseweg is dark and shady from the huge beech and oak trees lining the sides. The lead truck does not see the sheep until he was a mere two hundred feet away. Hitting his brakes he lays on his horn to frighten the sheep. The sheep ignore the horn; they are used to cars, trucks and wagons. They continue to calmly graze and wander slowly on the road heading to the next patch of grass.

Gerrit yells at the sheep from one side of the road while Jap yells at them from the other side. Completely confused the sheep huddle in the midst of the roadway.

The truck stops, the driver leans out the window yelling and cursing at the stupid sheep and made some vulgar references to the shepherds.

Gerrit takes offense at these words. He walks up to the truck. Everything is going according to plan. Looking at the driver with feigned rage he walked up to the truck. He reaches to the small of his back to make sure his knife is ready.

Jap is on the passenger side of the truck, he runs to the rear; under his coat he is holding his Sten gun. As he nears the rear of the first truck he sees that Braam is coming out of the woods at the rear of the second truck and Henk is approaching that truck's driver.

A soft rain is falling so the canvas is pulled closed. Jap pulls the canvass back on his truck at the same time Braam is doing the same on the rear truck. Both trucks have two guards. The second truck's guards are playing cards. The front truck guards are up front kneeling and looking under the side of the tarp to see what is causing the stop and who the driver is yelling at. The rear is unguarded.

Gerrit shouts at the driver to calm down or he would come up there to shut him up. The driver is now furious and yells back that he is not afraid of some hick farmer, especially not a stinking shepherd. Those were his last words as his head was nearly severed from his neck.

At the same time Jap easily dispatched the two guards. He shot both of them before they could turn. Jap hoped that Henk was taking care of the second driver, fearing the thought of being shot while his back was exposed.

No need to fear, one shot and the second driver slumped over his steering wheel and two more shots made the card players fall onto the cards they had just dealt. Slowly blood drained onto the cards, turning the ace of spades red.

The rain and trees muffle the sound of the shots. The compatriot drivers barely hear the gunfire so are a little slow in bringing their trucks. When they rounded the corner they sped up and quickly each one backs up to a munitions truck.

With utmost speed the two Nazi trucks are emptied of all the arms. They found several hundred grenades, thousands of rounds of ammunition, twenty rifles and ten pistols. The only things they left were the fifty caliber machine gun ammo. They did take the larger anti- aircraft ammo to take apart for the powder.

A little bit west, about half a mile back toward Arnhem a woman jumps off her bike and drags branches and logs onto the roadway making sure no one will drive up on the men unloading the trucks. When satisfied Alida rides east, away from where the men are working.

The raided trucks are driven onto a dirt road leading to a campsite where they are not visible from the road and abandoned there. Braam wants to burn the trucks but knows that might bring attention. This way they were far enough away. Instead he rips out the sparkplug wires.

Running back to the road, fleeing the area, Braam heard a single gunshot. He heard a grunt of pain and saw Jap fall down.

"Go, run, I have been shot!" screamed Jap.

Braam instead fell to the ground, rolled over into the ferns and undergrowth. He crawled back to Jap. He looked at the truck they had just abandoned. He saw that one of the guards had crawled to the back of the truck.

The guard collapsed falling face down dropping his pistol. It lands on the dirt as he sags over the edge, his helmet falling to the earth next to the pistol. "Damn," thought Braam," I thought we took all the guns. These guys were supposed to be dead."

Jap was on his knees and holding his back, blood oozing out from in-between his fingers. He was shot just above the kidney. It did not look good.

Braam tore off Jap's shirt. Tearing it into pieces he made a compress and long strips to hold the compress in place; he stopped the flow of the blood. Pulled Jap up onto his feet he half carried half dragged him back to the truck headed to Utrecht.

Making a detour to Veenendaal, they dropped off Braam, his bike and Jap. Jap could not go to the clinic or doctor office but needed immediate attention for his wound. It was extremely risky to go to Sukkel's bike shop, but it was done in spite of Jap's wishes. Jap did not want to bring attention to the shop.

"Bring me home, let me die there, you will be safe, he ordered.

Ignoring his wishes they carried him into kitchen and laid him on the table. Mies' family doctor came, cleaned the wound and gave him pain medicine.

Winching in pain Jap looked up at the doctor, "I am going to die aren't I?"

Grimly the doctor nodded, "Best call your pastor and family. I am sorry; there is nothing to be done. I did what I can. Brave men should not die like this" and he wiped tears from his eyes.

Within twenty minutes the pastor was there. Jap's mother and sister had arrived a little earlier. His father had been captured months ago and sent away on the train to work in a factory in Dresden.

Jap's mother cried and held his hand as she watched her son die. His sister sat on the other side also holding a hand, crying softly her tear drops falling onto the handkerchief in their hands.

The pastor read from Psalm 23. *"The Lord is my shepherd, I shall not want."* He stopped there then asked "Are you going to heaven, Jap?"

"Of course I am! The Lord is my Shepherd; he has seen me through many dark times and promised me eternal glory."

"Are you sure?"

"Yes, I am sure; I am not worried about death. I am anxious to see Jesus."

"How do you know this is true for you?"

Jap looks at the pastor with a bewildered look. "Are you the preacher who tells us to seek God, live right and be saved by Jesus'? My Bible says to believe in Jesus Christ and you will be saved. I believe Jesus paid for my sin and I have made him my God, so yes, I do know I am saved and am going to heaven."

Jap's mother smiled when hearing the reassuring words. Her son's statement confirmed his faith and her confidence in his relationship with God. With furrowed brow she looks at the pastor, "Do you believe that, pastor?"

"I think so but am not sure; I have always waited to have God call me. I do not know, for sure, if he has elected me."

"You are too Calvinistic for your own good and are making God to blame for your lack of faith. Look at Jap. He knows that God wants people to come to Him and accept him. Just say yes to Jesus, pastor. When you say yes to accept Jesus' payment for your sin, then you too will realize that God elected you. God does not make you say yes, but he does invite you to say yes.

That is why Jesus said, 'come unto me all you who are weary and I will give you rest' you must voice your choice. Saying yes is proof of being elected."

Mother van Kampen was on a roll, she had her theology down pat, and she knew the Scriptures. Now she was giving her pastor a much needed guide to knowing God. "Hyper Calvinism is convoluting Bible truths. You guys twist the reality of election and predestination to make yourself look humble and pretend you are focused on how to recognize the sovereignty of God. Let me tell you something, Dominee. You preach that God is sovereign, but you do not grasp his grace. This sovereign God is offering you his grace; he wants you to accept His gift. Stop trying to be worthy of salvation, you cannot earn it. John Calvin would be disgusted with you!"

Chapter 48

Jon turned off the kerosene lamp and went up stairs to bed. For light he is carrying a candle which he places in a stand next to his bed.

He steps into his pajamas.

He hears a truck turn into his drive. It is after ten. Shouts and orders are heard from the troops, who are on the drive.

"Something is up," he mutters to Nieske. "They are bringing in new stuff or getting ready to move something from here."

Jon goes to the window to see what he can see. Snow is softly falling, not covering the ground, yet. This is the first snow of the season, a bit early but not unusual. It looks nasty out; the snow is drifting in large wet flakes. There is no wind. The snow is covering the earth in a wet blanket. He cannot see what the troops are doing. He is afraid to go down yet curious about the commotion. He sits on the edge of the bed to put on his socks.

Jon jumps when someone bangs his bedroom door. The door bursts open, "Come we need your help, hurry!" shouts the soldier.

Jon dresses quickly and warmly and runs downstairs. He follows the soldier outside.

The new sergeant met Jon as he came out. His name tag said, R. Gunn. "We need your horse, we are moving out."

"You are not taking my last horse, how am I going to farm? Jon shouted.

"Don't get yourself into an uproar. We just need your horse to remove the guns from the pasture. The ground is too wet for the trucks. You can keep your damn horse! Just get him harnessed and follow me."

The snow is coming faster and wetter. With no wind the snow was piling up and making life miserable. The ground was not yet frozen so the soil was turning into slush and mud.

Jon led his horse into the darkness of the pasture, following Sgt. Gunn. The flashlight Gunn carries casts an eerie glow on the falling snow. The small group of men and the horse are surrounded

163

by a halo of light reflecting off the white blanket.

Jon backs the horse to the first antiaircraft gun. The soldier hooks a chain from the gun's carriage to the draw bar of the harness. *"Ik hebben hulp nodig"* I need help, grunted Jon as his horse lunged into the harness only to see the hooves sink into the mud.

Six soldiers line up behind the gun as the horse pulls. Grunting in effort the gun slowly comes out of the hole and slides across the pasture. Jon kept the horse going until the gun arrived at the barnyard. There the soil is packed hard enough to hold the truck.

Two more trips to the pasture. More help was needed. Sgt. Gunn even helped push the guns through the increasing mud. Finally all three guns were in the barn yard. The pasture is now a muddy mess, with ruts six inches deep where the guns tore up the grass and the horse and soldiers stomped the summer clover into muddy holes.

The snow is coming faster and the temperature is at zero degrees centigrade. It is a miserable night to be out thought Jon. But it is a blessed night if it means the Germans are going away. Tomorrow would be great day. The sun may be out or not but freedom was coming at last.

"Am I done?" Jon asked Sgt. Gunn? Are you coming back or is this occupation coming to an end?"

Gunn glared at Jon. "Just because these guns are needed elsewhere does not mean the occupation is over or that the Third Reich is not winning."

"I can see who is winning. Give *Herr* Hitler my regards when you see him. May I put my horse back in the stall?"

Sgt. Gunn glared at Jon but did not respond. Turning away he shouted orders, hurrying his men to load the truck. He turns to watch the hoist lifting the guns onto the truck and the trailer.

Jon took his horse into the barn, wipes him dry and gives him a carrot. While the horse is crunching the carrot Jon gathers a hand full of Timothy hay, placing it in the manger.

The sound of truck engines starting brought Jon to the door. The truck with the trailer is moving out. The remaining soldiers are climbing aboard the munitions truck. Smiling broadly Jon waved goodbye as they turn up *Danmakerweg*.

Standing there in the cold Jon thought about how wonderful life was, with gratitude filling his heart he said a prayer of thanksgiving. When he realized how cold he was he shook his head at his foolishness for standing there in misery when he had a warm bed and a great wife waiting for him. He went in the house and returned to his bed.

"They are gone, honey. I think for good." Then they snuggled in relief as tension began its retreat.

Chapter 49

September 17, 1944

Herve' woke up early, it was dawn before sunrise. He heard the sound of airplanes, not one but many. The sky was filled with loud buzzing, like a huge swarm of bees but much louder. He leaped out of bed, not sure if he should be afraid or follow his curiosity. He runs downstairs. His mother is looking out the kitchen window. Her hands covered with flour and the bread dough is in the pan.

Should he panic or stay calm? Hoping all is well he runs to his mother. His mother is mesmerized; her mouth is open in awe. She leans forward to see better, her nose pressed against the window.

Herve' knew that whatever it was it was not creating fear in his mother. He saw hope in his mother's face. He knew something good was coming. He is too short to look out this window, Herve' rushed outside to see.

Too much in a hurry and overly excited he forgets to put on his klompen. There he stood in his night socks and pajamas staring into the sky.

The sky was filled with airplanes, hundreds of them. They are coming from the west, and they did not have swastikas. He knows they must be American. These are not bombers, but they were dropping things. He had never seen such a sight. He was not sure just what was coming out of these planes. As he watched the items drop out of the plane it soon had a line behind them that blossomed out into a huge mushroom. Parachutes! That is what they are, soldiers jumping out of airplanes with parachutes.

They are only a few kilometers away, right over Ede. Now the sky is filling up with parachutes, thousands of them.

Silently, he watched in awe as the men fell into the sky, a few seconds later the parachute would billow into a mushroom and drift down. He was speechless. Then gliders came, dropping more soldiers and crates. Two jeeps were next; there they were hanging under this huge canopy, drifting down disappearing behind the trees.

Herve' did not notice when his mother, father and Arie come out. The family stood there in a row on the driveway gawking. They did not know that they are witnessing the largest airdrop of troops and equipment of the war. It was happening right here, in Ede, right in front of them.

The planes kept coming. They had a white circle with something like a plus sign in it. No swastikas. "The Americans have come," whispered Jon, in awe and wonderment. "The war will soon be over." Happy tears formed and slowly ran down his cheeks.

But he was wrong. These were Allied troops alright but not American soldiers. They were part of the Allied Forces; these men were Polish, New Zealanders, Canadians, Scots, Irish and the British 1st Airborne. The Americans were coming from the south with armor, tanks and ground troops.

Three days ago on September 14 the Americans had freed Maastricht and much of the southern part of the Netherlands.

The sky seemed full of sky blue chutes, orange chutes and gray chutes. The first wave passed, it was followed by the second wave a short time later, with more troops and crates of supplies.

Jon and Nieske hugged right there in front of the kids. This was a special moment. They were careful to never show affection in front of the kids. Oh, the kids knew they loved each other because they were always kind and nice together. They might yell at the boys but they never yelled at each other. Now they too were hugging and jumping for joy.

Then they each grabbed the two boys hugging them in excitement. Evert liked to sleep, and he was not the curious type so he was not there. Now the four of them were jumping and cavorting in happiness and hope. Hope of freedom.

"Did Gerben know this was coming? Is that why he left?" mused Jon.

"I wonder what info he gave Mies? I bet he knew that his platoon was going to battle somewhere and he did not want to fight with such green recruits who hated to listen to older men's wisdom." replied Nieske.

"*Ja*, those Brown Shirts are indoctrinated to mistrust everyone over thirty. Hitler made them believe that the youth would save Germany and make it superior to the entire world."

"That should have made them distrust him too. He and his henchmen are older than thirty, but he is a master manipulator. The youth think they have power, but actually Hitler is using them to fulfill his agenda, not theirs."

"Good thing they are gone or they would be out there shooting those guys hanging in the air."

"They wouldn't do that! That is not allowed by the rules of war."

Jon scoffed, "Those young soldiers are only old Brown Shirts, and they have no conscience and care nothing for rules of war. They are losing now and will do anything they can to help their cause. They lack any conscience or moral value."

"Come boys get dressed quickly, we are going to where those troops landed," shouted Nieske.

Waving her arms as a hen chasing her brood she herded the boys upstairs. She finds Evert still in bed. Shouting at him to wake up and get up, *"komen naar beneden."*

"Come, hurry downstairs" she admonished. Those parachutes are made of silk and we should get one for us to use. Just leave the chamber pots till we get back."

Normally that was Herve's morning chore, to take the chamber pots to the toilet, empty them and take a pitcher of water to rinse them.

When the three boys were downstairs she had a slab of bread waiting for them. It was the usual fast breakfast, but also quickly becoming Herve's favorite; homemade white or light wheat bread with a nice thick layer of warm hog fat or smeared with lard. Yum; it was better than bread with jam or cheese.

His mother would say. "This will warm you up; it sticks to your ribs."

Off they rode on two bikes. Jon has Evert behind him and Herve' in front on the seat, while Nieske has Evert on the seat behind her. They ride side by side until they came to the paved road, *Apledoornseweg*, leading to Ede.

They were not the only bikes on the road. Everyone they meet or pass waved and with huge smiles and bright eyes make comments about the arrival of the Americans. Excited that the end of the war is in sight.

Just outside the city of Ede is a forest; inside this forest is a huge sandy area with no trees. The wind blows through here creating sand dunes. These dunes are covered with heather and other scrub weeds and grasses, but no trees of any size. It is a perfect place to parachute into.

The air drop is before the sheep that graze the heather are released from the cote where the sheep are kept during the night.

Spread out over the heather are scattered the remnants of the landing. There are parachutes, ropes, wood from the crates and the bindings strewn everywhere.

There are lots of people at the heather picking up what they want. They have come to salvage what they can get. They will use it, sell it or save as memorabilia.

The men are looking for ropes and hardware items, maybe a knife, food or other useful items that may have been dropped.

The women gathered around the parachutes. Soon it became standard for six or eight women to be at each chute, knowing it was best to share. Carefully they worked undoing the stitches in the seams, not wanting to destroy or cut the fabric of these triangular pieces. When the sections are separated each woman took one section.

Herve's mom proudly carries her piece of sky blue silk to her bike. The boys and Jon are waiting with their trophies. Jon proudly holds up two lengths of rope he scavenged.

"Look" she said proudly, holding up the huge blue silk. "I can make shirts for the boys and one for you too Jon."

She was thrilled with the silk as they needed clothes for the boys. They kept growing and even though they handed down what they outgrew she needed to keep finding new clothes as Arie outgrew his meager supply.

Herve' was excited. "Do I get a new shirt? One just for me that is not old and worn out by Evert?"

When he received his new shirt he was very unhappy. Instead of wearing hand me down clothes he now looked like his brothers. "*Bah,*" So he wore his old clothes rather than be dressed like his brothers.

The parents look at each other; they realize that for the first time in Herve's life he has hope. It was great to see. Maybe now that the war was ending Herve' would stop being afraid and asking each time a plane came over if he was going to die.

"What kind of hell have we brought these kids into," thought Jon as he gathered Herve' into his arms hugging him before lifting him unto his seat.

Chapter 50

Mies Sukkel was upset. He grumbled as he paced the floor. The cadre of *onderduikers* was gathered in his shop to discuss what was happening in Arnhem. The battle at Arnhem was not going well.

"I told them!" He shouted. "Did they listen? Hell No! This was the wrong time to attack Arnhem. If they had waited a few days they could have walked over that damned bridge!" He groused. His fists were clenched, knuckles white. His brow furrowed as he told the cadre the intelligence information he had given the Allies.

"No, they had to be in a hurry. They ignored what several of us told them. The group in Arnhem gave us photos. They had visual evidence proving what I told them was correct. Hell, it was plain as day, there were twenty Panzers sitting there under the trees. I knew about those tanks because the soldier who deserted from van Bemmel's place told me they were there. This was corroborated by the photos from our friends in Arnhem"

"Twenty tanks! It only takes five to defend that bridge and make it impossible for jeeps or soldiers to cross. Those soldiers walked into a trap. This is bound to fail; we told them to wait until the tanks were gone."

"Montgomery doesn't listen to anyone; he even argues with Eisenhower and Churchill, Why do you think he would listen to a Dutch citizen?" commented Dik.

"How much did Sgt. Hults know or tell you?" asked Alida?

"Oh man, he spilled his gut, telling me everything he knew and then what he surmised to be the plan. He had been in the western front for four years and for the last ten months was assigned here. He had contacts everywhere."

"If he was so knowledgeable and connected why did he desert and inform us?" quizzed Braam. Braam, too, was pacing, he could not sit with all the tension in the room. Everyone had great fears of losing this battle for the bridge. They knew that losing the bridge would bring retribution and suffering along with extending the war through another winter.

Everyone turned to Mies to hear his response on what truly motivated Sgt. Ger Hults.

"He had been disillusioned for some time with the propaganda and harshness of the SS and Gestapo. The proverbial straw that broke the camel's back was the letter he received from home. Somehow it had not been censored, so he read the entire message.

The message was that the order had been issued, to hasten the destruction of all Jews. Every Jew was to be rounded up, except those working in the war equipment industry. Trains had been set aside to haul these people like cattle to camps in Poland for extermination. This was taking precedence over moving wounded soldiers from the Russian and western fronts to hospitals or home for recovery.

"Sgt. Ger Hults told me, 'When killing Jews is more important than saving soldiers who believe in Germany and are willing to die for Hitler's cause, then leaving them to suffer and die in the field. That is too much, I quit!' That is why I believed him."

The group realized the impact this battle was having on the war. But for them the greater concern was the liberation of The Netherlands. Once this bridge was in Allied control the Ruhr industrial region of Germany was accessible to Allied ground troops and the road to Berlin was virtually unobstructed. The Ruhr area was producing a lot of the war equipment. Capturing it would break down the German defense on the France, Italy and Russian fronts.

The idea for capturing the five bridges was a great plan; a stroke of genius if it was successful. While the main armies were engaged to the south the plan was to use the Airborne to launch attacks to secure bridges at rivers and canals, thus opening up a sweep from the North West into Germany's back door. This part of Holland and into Germany normally had only Occupation troops to control the local citizens. Sweeping through this area should be easy as the artillery, tanks and main army were at the front lines.

Mies stopped pacing, facing the group he explained the plan and what was going wrong. "The Allies knew that entering

Germany was going to be difficult, the closest way to divert from the western front would be to cross the Albert Canal. Having anticipated this Hitler had called *Generalfieldmarshall* Gerd von Rundstedt out of retirement and he had installed Panzer divisions and troops along Albert Canal."

Continuing, he reported, "That made it possible for *Fieldmarshall* Walter Model to focus on reorganizing the other fragmented divisions and units. To do this he moved the 9th and 10th Panzer divisions to the Eindhoven-Arnhem areas for rest and reorganization before going back to the front lines. Model had created a new and improved Division."

"That reorganization plan, my friends, is how there happened to be six to seven thousand troops with tanks sitting right here near the Arnhem bridge." He fumed.

"Hell, we knew they were there, we saw them. Our informant told us that Model had set up headquarters in Oosterbeek, just 3 kilometers from the bridge. His headquarters was on our side of the bridge! He has tanks sitting on the bridge, how are we going to capture a bridge that has a row of tanks sitting on it and artillery lining both sides of the river?" he fumed. His face was vivid; the veins in his neck were throbbing. "That arrogant chump does not listen to anyone; they should fire Montgomery and put that American general Patton in charge. Patton listens; he knows how to make plans. Patton makes things happen!"

"Montgomery does a good job posing for pictures." Piet spat with disgust, "Patton kicks ass."

One of the others stood up. "My brother says that artillery is knocking down the building one floor or one room at a time. The Poles occupied the building right next to the Rhine so their snipers are picking off German machine gunners and artillery. Now that five story building is three stories with piles of rubble on top."

Alida began to sob. Everyone looked at her, "What's up Lida?"

"'That building is where those bastards imprisoned people going to the camps. That is where they kept my mom and dad before shipping them off. It has been two years now, I suppose they are dead, at least I hope so. That is their only relief from the hell of the camps" She bent over to put her head on her knees, weeping.

Weeping for what she could not control or do anything about. "Damn them to the hottest part of hell", she cursed!

Braam walked up to Alida, placed his arm around her shoulders. "*Ja*, this is not going to turn out well, there goes the hope of liberation by Christmas; too bad Field Marshall Montgomery is not here to witness his mistake."

"*Ja, 'de klootzak'*, should be here and get his butt shot up instead of sacrificing Urquhart and his troops."

"The church in Oosterbeek is full of wounded as are several houses near it. Kate Ter Horst has turned her house into a first aid station and hospital. Those guys are stuck, even if help dropped in today, it will be too late. I suspect they are evacuating right now and some of them will need our help to avoid capture."

"Let's go rescue and do what we can; we will regroup next week to see how we did." Mies led them out to their bikes.

Weeping in anger, sorrow and fear he, too, rode off.

The German army buried most of the slain Allied soldiers and took their own back to the German side of the river. Some mass graves with thirty or more, some single graves under trees burying them wherever the soldier had fallen. They buried more than twenty in Kate Ter Horst's garden.

A dark, sad day for the central part of Holland; not only did it rain hard with gusty winds but freedom had escaped them. The weather was miserable and life was dismal.

The surviving soldiers retreated, running, hoping to find safe harbor. They did not speak Dutch, but the Dutch would help these men who sacrificed in the attempt to bring freedom.

Chapter 51

October 1944

General Brian Horrocks did a masterful job liberating the southern section of The Netherlands. Fighting with limited supplies they managed to secure enough bridges to free the towns south of Nijmegen. Stories drifted north about the bravery and dedication of the troops, the Dutch were amazed and gratified that these men left their wives and families to come to Holland to bring freedom to a people they did not know nor owed anything.

Alida brought three survivors of the battle at Arnhem to the meeting at Marinus Sukkel's. Alida discovered them hiding in the woods, or maybe they found her. She followed footprints going off trail into the undergrowth then spotted the heel of a shoe. Softly she called out, first in Dutch and then used the English Braam had taught her. Holding her hands open so they could see she was unarmed, she coaxed them out.

She brought them to a safe house. There they bathed and had their first warm meal since the battle began; they ate potato soup. Not great soup but warm and filling; made of potatoes, water and a little cheese. That was as good as it gets.

They are trapped behind the German lines, inside Nazi occupied territory, unable to rejoin the Allied troops just thirty kilometers away.

They were British so Braam became the interpreter for these three paratroopers. They agreed to help the *Onderduikers* as much as possible for as long as it took to find a way through the lines to reconnect with an Allies command center, they had guns, but not much ammo. That had been a major problem, not getting supplies during the battle. They saved their last clip of ammo for protection during the retreat.

~~~

A new wave of German soldiers swarmed the countryside.

They built pillboxes for defense and brought tanks to patrol major roadways across Gelderland. They created a line across Holland from Germany to the sea to keep the Allies from penetrating north.

Connecting these three Brits with the Allies was nearly impossible, but Braam had a plan.

Chapter 52

Braam took these paratroopers west, to get away from Arnhem then used the underground route used to move Jews to move these men south. They hoped to have Jon van Bemmel transport them under a load of hay or other products to Otterloo where the next secure" safe house" was. Mies nixed that plan as too dangerous. "The *"moofen"* are back, Jon cannot help now." he grumbled.

It was near midnight when Braam crept to the edge of the woods. What he saw sent shivers up his back. Grateful for his caution he slithered back to his group. They noticed how pale he was.

"What did you see?" one whispered.

Placing his finger over his lips, he moved backwards deeper into the woods and away from the trail. Two minutes later he stopped, they had not gone far but moving slowly and silently they could talk.

"The Germans are back at Jon's place, but now there are more than ever. Two groups of three are walking the path along the fence; they stopped for a smoke not fifteen feet from where I was."

"Damn, now what do we do?" asked Richard. He was a corporal giving him rank on the other two.

"The hard part is getting across the road; it is a few hundred feet away. After that we will follow the tree line along Bykerk's farm to the next woods. If the moon stays behind the clouds we can stay out of sight pretty well until we get to Otterloo."

"How far is that?"

"With any luck we will get there well before daylight. If not we dig a hole under the pine needles and brush and wait till tomorrow night. Do not worry, we will get there. Wilco will wait for you. He will get you to the American sector."

Four thirty in the morning they arrived at the auto repair shop. Braam did a surveillance tour around the perimeter, and then checked the buildings and houses in the area for any signs of Nazi presence. It could be Gestapo or soldiers bivouacked at some one's place. He found that things had not changed since last seeing Wilco.

The four of them hunkered down next to a cluster of wagons. Braam left the soldiers there; he approached the side door to the shop. It was unlocked. Slowly he opened the door, pulling it toward himself while keeping his body out of view.

A candle was burning in the corner. Sitting at his work bench was Wilco, sound asleep. Braam slid in and closed the door softly. "Wilco, it is Braam" then moving closer he again whispered, "Hey, Wilco, it is Braam, wake up."

This time Wilco stirred, and saw Braam in the shadows of the flickering light. His hand was holding a wrench, a big wrench.

"It is me, Braam!"

Instantly awake and alert he looked to see if Braam was alone. "Are we alone?"

"Yes, just sleepy; are the men with you?"

"They are hiding outside. I will get them."

Thirty minutes later Wilco drove his 36 Dodge truck he bought to haul parts and equipment, out the front door. He stops, gets out and closes the door, then drives away. Two men stashed under the false floor in the bed and the other sitting up front with his new Dutch hat and coat.

"Here, take this and put a big chew in your mouth in case we are stopped." He tosses a pack of chewing tobacco to Richard. "Don't say anything, just spit a big gob and let me do the talking. Hopefully nothing will happen."

Braam, climbed to the loft with a blanket. Soon he was curled up on some hay, wrapped in the blanket sound asleep. He was at peace, confident that the men would soon be safe.

Chapter 53

Herve' was crying. His shoulders shaking as sobs racked his body. He knew today his life would end. Terrified he looked up at his mother. He looked into her eyes and saw fear and dread there too. He wrapped his arms around her legs as he waited. He waited for the gunshot that would take his life and his mother's life. He knew that she too realized this was the end.

The new sergeant and two soldiers were in the kitchen; one had his pistol in his hand. All of them young; Sgt. Frans Dietz was barely twenty and the soldiers could pass for sixteen. They had not even started growing good facial hair, just kids being tough. Sergeant Dietz was pointing his finger and yelling at Nieske. Herve' and his mother were all alone on the farm. Jon was at the mill and Arie and Evert were in school.

"You butchered a pig; you know that is against the rules," he shouted.

"I did not" she replied, "and if I did it would only be so we could stay alive!" Trying to stand tall while defying this man in the uniform she hated.

She was only as tall as his ribbons, but that did not stop her from looking into his face with defiance. She knew cowardice would kill her sooner than bravery; as long as it was bravery and not insolence.

A smile creased his lips, "*Ja*, you religious people do not lie, you just do not tell the truth. It was your husband or his friends who butchered it, right?"

"We have the count of how many there were before we left and now there is one less. Where is it? You cannot have eaten it all."

Turning to his men, he pointed to the fireplace chimney, "Start looking there for the smoked meats and sausages. The rest is canned so find those jars, and we will have a fine dinner tonight."

Nieske sat down, dejected and angry, she brought Herve' to her side. He was not sure if she needed to feel the warmth of a body or was trying to protect or comfort him. He snuggled real close hoping she could protect him from this enemy.

She knew they would find most of the meat; they had slaughtered a small pig, just over one hundred pounds. They had enjoyed two meals of fresh pork and the remainder had been canned or smoked as sausage or slabs of bacon and ham. The smoking was normally done in the smokehouse, attached to the barn. This time they secreted the bacon and sausage by hanging them inside the chimney. She watched as the soldier pulled two racks down from inside the chimney, both loaded with meat. The sausage was her own recipe; she had tweaked her mother's recipe to make it better with less salt and more sage and nutmeg. The sausage was known as *"Boer worstje"* farmer sausage.

If only they had stayed away another week this meat would all have been cured and stashed where they would never find it.

Just then the other soldier walked in carrying six jars of canned pork, setting them on the table. "There are more, maybe seven or eight."

"You should be shot!" He stormed, "You and the kid!"

Herve' began to cry quietly, wiping his tears on his mother's apron. Then sobbed uncontrollably, the end was coming. He knew it was inevitable, today he was going to die.

Nieske jumped up, "Who would provide your food then?" She almost added, 'you dumb shit', but held her tongue.

"Jon will be more careful to obey and do as he is told if he comes in the house and sees you dead. That would teach him and the neighbors a good lesson."

This time she did not hold back, "You are an idiot; do you think for a minute that Jon would not strangle you with his bare hands? You are nothing. Compared to him you are a jackass." She spat on the floor of her own kitchen. A kitchen she kept spotless and orderly.

"He would be shot before he had a chance."

"That would be fine with him; he would never harvest another potato or sheaf of grain for you to get your hands on. Then you would be without food; you need us, we do not need you! She shouted. "Now get out of my kitchen!"

Herve' hid behind his mother; never had he seen such a display of anger or bravery.

Nieske collapsed into a chair relieved that she had survived this confrontation and amazed at her bravery or was it stupidity? Her anger and frustration had removed her fear, now she wondered how much more she could take. She began to shake and then trembled in fear for what might have been.

She began to weep; her emotions draining her strength, she fell to her knees. Herve' hugged his mother comforting her as he wept tears of relief.

When Jon came home for lunch she told him about the confrontation and the meat being found and confiscated.

"It is October, Jon, we do not have enough food to feed us and twenty hungry soldiers. What are we going to do?"

"We still have the stash, they have not found that."

"It is going to be a real trick to sneak that out as we need it. We have to keep this a secret from the boys too. If they find that stash they will shoot us for sure. They will take us to the Centrum and make an example out of us."

"When the choice is to use that stash or die from starvation, the decision will become easier."

Chapter 54

Evert Bultan rode onto the farm. Leaning his bike against the house he knocked on the side door. Side doors are for family, friends and workers. People who do not know you use the front door.

Jon saw him turn into the drive; he checked his watch to see if it was coffee time. They had no coffee but continued the ritual of a ten o'clock break each morning. Nieske had a small stash of coffee somewhere but she made a drink with crushed acorns and tree bark. It was strong and bitter. He seldom drank it preferring hot water with a little molasses or if available tea.

Occasionally, like a dutiful husband, he drank that bitter stuff. When he did drink it he added lots of milk. He preferred a tablespoon of sugar with it, a teaspoon would not be enough to sweeten it but sugar and molasses were in short supply.

Using cream was the only luxury left. Four years of occupation brought living standards to survival mode. He was afraid things were soon going to be worse. The extra soldiers ate a lot of food.

Imports were decreasing since Japan captured the islands of Indonesia. He wondered how his brother was doing there. The last he heard of him was two years ago. That was before Batavia was captured and the Dutch Army imprisoned. Was Bernard dead? Was he a POW? The silence was ominous.

Less food and fewer spices were coming from there. The Americans were sending less food as they were working hard at feeding their own troops. All of that probably did not matter much as the German navy had U boats enforcing the embargo of all goods coming to the Netherlands. The worst part or at least the part that angered Jon most was that these soldiers wasted food caring little for what the Dutch had left. He spit in anger.

"Goedmorgen vader" (Good morning father) he said as he walked into the kitchen. "Come for coffee? He chuckled."

Evert looked around. Jon realized he was looking to see if they were alone, so he scooted his chair closer. We are alone in the house right now."

"Good, I have an assignment for you."

Nieske approached the table with a plate; on it were thin slices of heavy rye bread. She made good pumpernickel whenever she had molasses; today's bread was dry and not sweet. To make up for this she spread a nice layer of butter, churned yesterday and topped it with a thin slice of homemade Edam cheese.

"Eat first, then business, Papa."

"How are the boys doing? I wish we could see you more often."

"Two are at school. Herve' is playing with the cats on the hay. He just lives to be with animals or trying to take things apart, so playing with cats is good. It keeps him out of my hair.

Arie and Evert are doing well in school?"

"*Ja*, they both have excellent grades and like to study. Only problem is they came home with head lice and now we all need to be treated with poison powders."

"Thanks to the *moofen*. Hopefully the Allies will end this war soon. Then we can settle down to a normal life."

"Normal life?" she scoffed. I do not remember what normal is. Just ask Herve' what he thinks normal is? Poor boy, everyday he thinks it may be his last. He has not known life without soldiers, guns and rockets, death and fear. Every day we go to bed hungry. So what is normal?" Tears welled up in her eyes.

Picking up the last crumbs off the plate Evert leaned over to Jon. "I have a man who needs your help."

"A Jew?"

"*Ja*, and his life is far worse than ours. This has some danger to it. He has lost his mother and father and last month they arrested him and his wife. He escaped but his wife was shipped to a camp."

"Escaped, how did he do that?"

"They were arrested in Utrecht, taken to Arnhem to wait for the next train. While locked up in the old hotel the local Commandant asked for help in cleaning up the rubble from the battle for the bridge. Ben, that is his name, seized the opportunity to

186

be outside and look for a way to escape and he did."

"How did he manage that? They have armed guards watching them, right?"

"The way he tells the story makes it look like God had his hand in this. Apparently there were two guards, one on each corner of the building they were working on. When he saw the guard nearest him light up a cigarette he hit him just under the helmet on the side of his head with a brick. Before the guard was on the ground Ben ran down the *"Steeg"* alley and got away. The other guard shot at him but could not chase him or all the workers would flee. Ben was hit in the arm, but will be all right.

That is part of what makes this risky. If he is found they will know or suspect he is the escapee who killed the guard."

"All he has left are two children. They were shipped to France two years ago and he has not heard of them for over a year. Now that the French are mostly free, he wants to go find his children."

"What do you need from me?" asked Jon.

Nieske interrupted, "No, you cannot consider doing this. You are a dead man if they catch you."

Jon looked at his wife, and then turned back to her father. "Where from and where to?

"He will be at my house tomorrow, I can keep him for a few days but the longer he is there the greater chance he has of being caught. Then he needs to go to Otterloo."

"Wilco's place?"

"You know Wilco?"

"Yes, I do and I will take care of it."

"No, you won't! I will not let you. You guys sit there and plan how to help somebody we do not know. Well, think about somebody you do know; me! They will shoot you and leave me with three boys." She began to cry.

Jon got up; he pulled her with him onto his chair, holding her on his lap. "Sweet heart, you know I love you, but if I do not do this, this man will die. I cannot let that happen. I understand the danger, but a man has to do what a man has to do. It is in God's hands and he will protect me."

Herve' stood there next to the table listening to his father. They had been too engrossed to hear or see him come in. He felt the anxiety of his mother, yet was proud of his father; a brave and righteous man.

Nieske scowled at her father when he left, neither one saying anything. She thinking that her father was exercising his Calvinistic belief in God and trusting God while putting her husband into great danger. He liked to quote the Bible to give confidence about God keeping all of them safe. He was a strong believer in providence; for him nothing was by chance or luck. He firmly believed that when you were faithful in doing God's will that God will honor that with blessings.

The Jews were chosen by God so who was Evert to go against that? Besides this man would be killed if he did not have help. God placed Ben in his care and he was going to trust God to see it through.

She sighed, knowing this was true. She had seen it often. Now it was her turn to trust God and place the welfare of her man and this Jew in God's hands.

Chapter 55

"Why are you questioning me? I have done nothing!" Nieske was defiant in her response to questioning by another new sergeant replacing Sgt. Dietz. Her confidence had grown since the last episode, so she stood her ground.

Walter held had three stripes, not great rank for fifty a year old. Nieske realized that he had been demoted or passed over for promotion which explained his salty attitude.

He had seen Jon leave with his horse and wagon, carrying only two pitchforks. The Dutch pitchforks have two tines on a handmade replacement handle carved from a beech tree.

"Where is he going? Does he have permission to travel?" growled Sgt. Held.

"What permission? He is not going anywhere different. How far can he go with one horse and no feed? If you must know he is going to my father's to haul some hay for him."

"Was he the man visiting yesterday? Why does he need help, he looks young and strong enough to handle it alone."

"What do you know? He is older than you think. He will be seventy next birthday."

Sgt. Held paused, this questioning was not going anywhere useful, yet he had this gnawing suspicion that something was going on. "Hauling hay, you said? Why?"

"It is extra hay; my father sold it to a farmer on the other side of Otterloo."

"Extra hay? How did he get to have extra hay, we need hay for our horses"

Nieske backed up from her aggressive stance of the sergeant. "No," she thought, "I cannot show fear or he will think Jon is up to something wrong."

"Yes, extra hay. Your troops killed or stole half of his cows, took his horses so he cannot haul it himself. Now he has some hay to sell and he is not going to sell it to you. You would just steal it!" She stamped her feet in anger and frustration.

Sgt. Held did not like her attitude. He took a step toward her, now standing within arm's reach he said, "If we take your cattle why does this farmer need to buy hay?"

"Because some of your stupid troops smoked while lying on the hay stack; you guys screw up everything you touch. These youngsters are still wet behind the ears, no training in common sense, just ignorant and stupid!" she screamed at him. She hoped she had not over done this but she wanted to be sure Jon was safe and stayed safe.

"He will be back this afternoon before milking time, you can ask him and see if I am telling you the truth." She stomped her feet and turned to go.

"You better be telling the truth or there will be hell to pay!" he shouted, his face red with anger and frustration.

"When the Americans come you will have hell to pay" she shouted after him then turned and entered her house.

She paused just inside the door. She began to shake and shiver, not sure if it was due to fear or the anger and hatred she had for anything Nazi.

~~~

Jon loaded the wagon with hay, nearly five feet high on the wagon. In front of the wagon just behind the seat was a man sized box with some tools. The plan was to make any inspector look in the box and ignore what might be under the hay.

Jon knew the man's name was Ben, that's all. The less he knew the better. In fact, Ben may well not be his real name.

A few boards had been placed in the center of the wagon starting two feet from the front and going back to three feet from the rear. They created a breathing tube so Ben could be in the center of the load without suffocating. The boards also provided protection when the Gestapo or inspection troop's jabbed pitchforks into the hay from the sides searching for bodies under the hay. The boards prevented those pitchforks from puncturing a body. Jon knew the Germans figured out that hay was used to hide things but they were mostly too lazy to unload the entire load of hay.

Evert Bultan hugged Ben and helped cover him up. Then he clapped his son-in-law on the back. He opened the barn doors to send them on the way. "Go with God; see you next Sunday at church; then you can tell me about today."

Jon kept his Belgian/Morgan cross mare at a slow but steady walk. This was more than an hour's drive and he did not want to tire her out, nor did he want to look like he was in a hurry. He conserved her energy so he could use her to pull the plow tomorrow. Thinking about home he wondered how Nieske was doing and he wondered what explanation he would need to make if questioned upon his return.

An hour and a half later he arrived at Wilco's shop, he drove right past the shop to the barn. Wilco's wife opened the barn doors. Safely inside they quickly opened the front of the load, freeing Ben. She took him to the harness room then came back and helped unhitch the horse and took him outside for water and some feed.

Meanwhile Jon unloaded the hay. He thought about taking it back with him. Just then Wilco came in, "I do not need all that hay, Jon."

"It is yours, buddy. If I take it back it will be very risky for me as several soldiers saw me going west and if they see me going back with it? He left that question hanging. He and Wilco both knew the answer to that.

It was lunch time so they went to the house for some bread and cheese, with a glass of water. Water, something they rarely drank, but now with the shortage of everything else water took the place of coffee, beer or tea.

"Food is getting scarcer Jon; it will not last the winter or certainly not till the next crop comes in," ventured Wilco.

"*Ja*, we need to conserve, I suspect we will all be sharing what little we have with lots more people soon enough."

Hitching the horse up to the wagon he headed out of the barn. He heard a door squeak open and a voice behind him. "*Dank u wel*" Thank you so much.

Then Jon was off, going home. All was well; at least this far.

Chapter 56

Evert Bultan was enjoying a cup of tea and sharing an apple strudel with his wife Martha at the *Tie Kamer(Tea Room)* at the corner of *Achterdoelen* and *Doelenplein* in the Ede Centrum. They are sitting at the table in the front corner by the window. Martha's pastime is people watching.

Evert is sipping his tea and listening to her chatter on and on about the bike traffic, the ladies hair styles and whatever action is going on outside. Evert is paying scant attention until she mentions the small group of SS standing at the corner leaning against a black truck. Letting her words go in one ear and out the other Evert is more interested in his tea and watching the people inside enjoying what little of life there is to enjoy.

Evert noticed that one of them is keeping his eye on the *Tie Kamer*. Are they waiting for someone to come out? Evert is uncomfortable. Are they watching him? Or is something else happening?

Evert scans the dining room to see what other possibilities there might be. Across the room he sees a familiar face. Two men are conversing over tea; one is dressed in a pricey grey suit. They both appear to be business men discussing something. Evert studies them to determine what is going on and recall who that familiar face belongs to.

The tea room is not large, maybe thirty feet wide and forty deep. Tables are set for four along the window, six in the center and along the rear wall the tables are for two; this is where these men are. They each have tea and a pastry.

Evert nudges Martha with his foot to get her attention. When she stops talking he leans into her and asks her to be discreet and see if she recognizes the blond man. "Who is he and where do I know him from?"

"The man in the gray suit is obviously German; I have seen him at the city hall talking to troops. He is a commander or civil authority. The other guy I have no idea, he looks like he could be

German too."

"Ah ha, I got it. He is the guy that Herr Sukkel meets with sometimes; his name is David Slager. He has been of assistance to Mies. Why is he with a German official?"

David Slager finished his tea, wiped off the last crumbs of his pastry and walks over to two women who are sitting across the room with a small boy. He smiles at them and says something. They look up at him in surprise but say nothing.

As he turns to leave he gives a small nod to his companion, then walks out the door. When David is out of sight the German official goes to the door and waits. The SS officers meet him at the door. There is a brief exchange of words and the official steps outside and walks away. He goes in the opposite direction of David.

Three officers walk up to the two women and the boy. Each officer takes one of them by the arm and march them out to the truck.

Evert and Martha turn pale at what they just witnessed. The officer at the door looks around the room. He makes sure everyone is busy with their food or tea or at least faking it to stay uninvolved.

"I think we just witnessed a 'catcher' at work.

"What do you mean "catcher?" asks Martha.

"That is a street term for people who assist the Gestapo in finding Jews. They work for the Search Service and are paid by sharing assets that belong to those they inform on. The catchers are really good at figuring out the disguises and uncovering Jews for the Gestapo. The rich Jews who can get false Identification Cards and have the means to disguise themselves are the targets."

"I do not understand, what do you mean the catcher targets wealthy Jews?"

"Those are the ones with jewels, art and cash. The catcher goes for them first so he can attain wealth and power. "Catchers" have a good life, plenty of food, freedom to move around the country and they hoard jewelry, gold and arts owned by those they rat on. Real low lifes, they are *verraders* (traitors); Traitors to the Netherlands and to their own race." He spat into his napkin with disgust.

"Those poor ladies will never be seen or heard from again. Unless someone here knows them and tells the family, it will seem they just disappeared."

"*Ja*. Just like the other thousands that have been lost to the camps."

"I wonder if Herr Sukkel knows Herr Jager is doing this. His group could be compromised too."

Chapter 57

Alida hands Mies Sukkel a letter. It has no writing on the envelope to indicate who sent it or to who is to read it. Mies opens the envelope takes the letter and begins reading. His hands start shaking and his eyes narrow. He looks at Alida. With a quiver of angst and terse anger in his voice he tells her the contents.

"We have a *verrader* in our ranks. It seems that so far he has only betrayed Jews, but who knows what he has said or what his plans are. He is capable of putting us in extreme danger."

"Who is it? I knew something big was happening when Herr Bultan came to the shop today. He was clearly upset. He made sure I knew the urgency of getting you this letter as soon as possible. I left early to get here before dark."

"It is close to curfew, you must spend the night here. We can discuss what to do. It seems that our friend and I mean that sincerely, as he has done lots of good for and with us, like setting up and operating the printer. Now it seems that David Slager has a side career or something happened that caused him to become a catcher."

"From this letter is looks like he is working with the Gestapo. He helps them find Jews! Evert witnessed an arrest yesterday which appeared to have been set up by David. *Verdoeming!* Damn it, I really liked him too."

Alida was shocked, she had never heard him swear or use bad language.

Together they reviewed the possible implications this has for the team, the printing press, the plans of actions they have in place, etc. They tried to figure out if David was knowledgeable of the pipeline for transporting Jews or knew details of the operation. Did he know drop off sites and pass words and codes? Did he know or suspect their involvement of the heist of weapons outside Arnhem, in the *Edse Bos*?

"Saturday, that is day after tomorrow, I have a meeting scheduled with him. We are to meet at the café at the university in

Wageningen. I will find out the truth."

"You better have someone with you; this could blow up on you. I know he is always cool and has great self control, but what if he flips out and attacks you and sets things in motion to destroy our cadre?"

"Right, you are absolutely right. I think it will be good to have Piet and Dik there. David does not know them so they can be nearby in case we need to protect me or to take David out."

Tears sprung into Mies's eyes as he said this. "I really trusted him; he has been so sincere in his hatred of the Nazis and has willingly helped. He has never asked questions or tried to get information from me. If it becomes necessary to take him out it is going to kill me!"

Chapter 58

Saturday, just before noon, Mies Sukkel walked in the café. David was already seated at corner table near the window.

Dik and Piet were seated by the back wall. They each had a beer and were talking about raising chickens and how it was difficult to find feed that would produce eggs with strong shells. They bantered back and forth with suggestions for improving the feed. One idea was to mix some rye grass into the feed, it helps build calcium. They wanted to sound like farmers when David walked by them.

"This place has some real coffee, would you like a cup?" asked David.

They each ordered coffee and a ham with cheese sandwich. Ham was available to this restaurant but the slices were becoming thinner each month. Looking at his sandwich Mies commented, "If they slice this ham any thinner we will be able to read *De Trouw*, the local newspaper, through it."

David asked how the bicycle shop was doing. Mies told of the troubles of finding parts and learning how to make do with homemade remedies for holding bikes together.

Then David asked how the "other enterprise" was doing. "Printer still working okay?"

David noticed a change in the facial expression and the hesitancy in the response. "What is wrong? You do not seem yourself. Are you angry about something or angry at me?"

Leaning forward with his elbows on the table Mies looked directly into David's eyes. "Not angry with or at you, just worried. Worried about you."

David leaned back and away from Mies, his eyes dropping down, avoiding direct contact. "What? Worried about me, why? I am okay."

"Look at me! You were seen pointing out Jews to the SS troops. Tell me that this is not true. No, do not look away, look straight in my eyes and tell me that what I heard is wrong."

David looked up, shook his head with sadness. "Can we go for a walk? I will explain everything to you."

David dropped enough guilders on the table to pay the bill and they walked out.

They walked into the University's gardens, strolling slowly like great friends in deep discussion.

"Remember when I was out of touch about two months ago? I told you I had not felt well while visiting a friend. Well, that was to cover up for being arrested."

"Arrested? What were you arrested for?" Then the light grew bright in Mies' mind. "You were picked up for being a Jew?"

"Yes, I was to meet my friend, the man who is in charge of my store. Instead the Gestapo was waiting for me. The man I made wealthy turned me in. I guess making good money and skimming profits is not enough. He wanted the whole store."

They sat down on a bench, facing each other.

"The Gestapo took me to the interrogation chambers. There they set me down to watch while another man was brought in. This man was tied to the chair, his hands tied behind the chair and his feet to the chair legs.

They proceeded to beat this man, first with blows to the stomach until he vomited. Then they began on his face and shoulders. He eyes were swollen shut; blood was coming from his nose and his ears. He fainted away.

A few minutes later they aroused him with water in the face, untied his hands and proceeded to break his fingers, one at a time.

Then they took me out of the room and asked if I wanted that prior to being sent to Auschwitz-Birkenau. If I cooperated with them by being a catcher I would avoid this pain.

They knew I had connections in the world of arts and jewels. Turning me would give them access to my clients and those wealthy enough to get false identities and who hid their valuables. They love wealth as much as they hate Jews. They cajoled me and threatened me.

I turned them down. They took me back into the room.

The screams and groans became unbearable. The man was now hanging from rings in the ceiling. His feet were just touching the floor. They beat his back and his kidneys until the poor man vomited blood, all his fingers broken, his face broken; he passed out and so did I."

"That is what it took to turn you into a *verrader*?"

"Yes, I knew I should be strong and die like a man, but it was too much. I could not stand that kind of pain, my store was gone, and I had nothing to live for except self preservation. They promised me a share of the jewelry, money and arts that would be confiscated. I gave in.

Looking into Mies' face he said, "I am so sorry."

With a combination of horror and disgust Mies asked, "What about my shop, the cadre, have you informed them of us too?"

"No! No I have not and would never do that. You guys are the only active thing going that hurts this evil system. I watch to see if I am followed. But they leave me alone to do as I please as long as I find Jews for them. I know my days are numbered. When I no longer produce or they are tired of me they will execute me too, right after they torture me to tell them where my share of the jewelry is hidden. I need to be one step ahead of them. Soon I will disappear where they will not be able to find me."

Mies stood up to leave. "If you sincerely want to escape see me tomorrow and we will arrange it. If you do not show up we will relocate the cadre and they will hunt you down like a rat."

Chapter 59

November 1944

The rain is coming down as if the bottoms of the clouds are broken open. Like a bucket turned upside down, water is gushing, and pounding the farm. It is raining so hard it sounds like hail on the tile roof. Huge drops hammer the roof like a butcher tenderizing meat. Water is pouring off the roof, the flower beds are full, and the fields look like a huge lake. The buildings and the cows are all that is showing above the water. The ditch has overflowed and turned the road into rocky mush.

The soldiers stay inside the barn looking out the double doors. They stay dry while keeping an eye on the guns in the pasture. The guns and ammo are covered with tarps. The crates of ammo are stacked on blocks keeping them out of the water.

The guard keeps a close eye on the guns. These are the latest model of anti-aircraft weaponry. These are *2cmFlak 38 Flugabwehrkanone* (airplane canons) that fired 220 rounds per minute. That is a lot of 20 millimeter bullets flying through the air.

Wet days are common in a Dutch fall, except this year it seems worse. The dark clouds and rain add to the gloom covering the land. Despondency permeates every house, farm, mind and soul. The grim weather and a glum outlook on the war combine to bring an oppressed people into despair bordering on depression. The gloom and doom is obvious in the house and the barn at the van Bemmel's. These are desperate times. Despair has settled in as the war lingers on. Food is minimal; a balanced meal has not been seen in almost a year. Hatred for the Nazis and the occupation is intense and at the danger point of exploding.

The lines of commitment are defined; families and neighbors are divided. They are divided about how to proceed into the future. Many feel that the war is lost. France and Italy may be free but Holland and Poland will never be free.

An increasing number feel the need to support Germany, just

to get the food they need. These are hopeless, desperate times. So many just want to give up; the will of the Dutch is nearly broken.

The Germans have strengthened their hold on the northern part of Holland. They are intent on starving the Dutch into submission. The embargo on shipping food to Holland is stringently enforced. No food is coming into the occupied area. France, Belgium and South Holland may be free, but the Allies are bogged down and settled in for a long winter. Twenty percent of the people want to concede to Germany and get on with life. Another twenty percent want to expand the resistance into sabotage, assassinations and general riots.

The majority just hates the Nazi occupation and despises the SS and the Gestapo but feel helpless, discouraged and hopeless. They just want to get along. Food and security are foremost in their minds.

Therefore, this day was gloomy long before the weather darkened the sky and the rain turned the earth into mud.

Chapter 60

Sloshing through this water and mud is a family; a father, mother and two preteens, a boy and a girl. They are bundled up and carrying umbrellas. The rain running off the umbrellas filled their (*Klompen*) wooden shoes; their leather shoes are in their packs protected from the water and mud.

They turn into the drive; hesitant but hopeful they approach the house.

The guard soldiers see them walk up the drive. They pick up their rifles or place a hand on their side arms. Wary and vigilant that this may be resistance fighters taking advantage of the weather they are on alert.

Jon hears the soldier's voices. He, too, looks out the window and sees this small family.

"Refugees coming," he says to Nieske. "The big cities are empty as people spread over the countryside looking for food. The markets are empty; farmers are their only hope. The embargo has cut down the amount to a few bites a day."

"*Binnen komen*, Come in," was Jon's invitation as he opens the door into the kitchen. The four of them come in. Water is dripping off their heads, down the arms, making a big puddle on the floor.

"Go get towels" ordered Nieske, she shoved Herve' off his chair. He ran to the cupboard and came back with an armful of towels. Jon took the umbrellas and the hats and coats to the barn area. There he hung them on pegs to drip dry. The *klompen* were placed by the stove to dry.

"Bring those coats here; put them by the stove." She lined up four chairs with the back toward the stove. Jon came back with the coats; he hung them on the backs of chairs near the heat. Nieske gave each visitor a towel.

Herve' saw that the oldest was a girl and the smaller was a boy about his own age; almost four he thought proudly.

Drying themselves they huddled near the stove. It was a cast iron stove where they could cook and heat the room. It burned coal whenever it was available, or else wood or bricks of peat, all of which are getting scarce.

Standing by the stove, getting warm they introduced themselves. "I am Gerard Stephanus and my wife Marijan, my daughter Rika and son Joseph. We live in Rotterdam. We are without food. The coupons allow us five hundred calories a day. That is if there is food available."

"You are welcome here. As you can see we have occupation forces staying here, so our food supply is low too but we make do." She was careful to use correct words so not to insult the troops. Nieske had been very circumspect and gracious around Sgt. Held since the day she had tangled with him.

"Would you like some soup? I was making some for our dinner; tonight for supper we will have sandwiches.

It is potato soup. I am sorry but there is no meat. Not much potato either but the peelings are surprisingly good. Lowering her voice she glanced toward the barn, "the *moofen* take all the meat and most of the potatoes. There are some turnips in it though; we rotate them with carrots or rutabaga. The Nazi do not like rutabagas very much so we grew extra of those to provide something for ourselves."

During the meal Bernard and Marijan told their sad tale. A story of their city, that was in the throes of hardships, starvation and death. Herr Stephanus told them that people were eating anything they could get their hands on, flower bulbs, tree bark, just about anything to quiet the rumble in the stomach.

"It all changed when Hitler began the embargo. All food shipments stopped, only ships with German cargo are allowed in port. Sweden's airdrop of bread ended too. Their planes were shot down for delivering bread. Hitler is intent on breaking our will. May God send him to hell!"

Those who work the docks or fishing boats stayed in the city, they manage to hide some fish they catch. This along with what is handed out in food lines helps them survive. Many others beg or steal what they can find. Coupons are hard to get, and nearly worthless as there is very little food on the shelves.

People stand in line to get food. Mostly it is porridge or soups. "I think they mix in sawdust to extend it. Everyone brings a pot or bowl along with proof of how many are in the family or house."

Marijan broke in with, "My sister, Emmy, is an *Onderduiker*; when she is out doing her work the family divides their food into four bowls, one for her father, mother and sister and one for Emmy. When she is late returning home they wait twenty minutes past curfew; if she is not home by then they assume she is captured or dead. Then they eagerly divide her portion up one teaspoonful at a time."

"*Ja*, the family is emotionally torn up. The feelings range from hoping she is safe and will return and yet happy she is not there so they can have the extra food." Tears roll down her face as she thinks about death for a family member being weighed against having a few more spoonfuls of broth.

Gerard, too, had tears in his eyes as he related the hardships. "I am an honorable man. I have always worked and earned my way, now I am reduced to being a beggar," he lowered his head and wiped his eyes.

Joseph came and leaned against his father; a four year old who did not know how or when to hug, but sensing his father's sorrow. Gerard picked him up onto his lap, Joseph snuggles close.

"What are your plans?" Asks Jon.

"We have no plans. We just try to survive by roaming the countryside to find goodhearted people with some food to eat and get through this winter. Maybe next year the war will be over; one way or another."

"You must stay here for a while, at least till the weather clears."

"Thank you, thank you, we do not want to be a problem. We can sleep on the floor."

"You will all share a room in the attic; the chimney goes through it so it is not too cold to sleep on the floor there."

That night Jon took out the shuffle board for the adults to play and dominos for the kids. Four days later the weather cleared.

Refugees are again wandering the country roads. Two more families stop at Van Bemmel's. The Stephanus family stayed three weeks and moved on.

The parade of refugees continued through winter and into spring. The farm was never without guests. Sometimes there were three or four, many times six or more. Meals became simple; warm cereal grains with milk or water for breakfast. Dinner was a carrot or half of a turnip. Supper was soup. Soup that was made of whatever the soldiers did not eat; potato peeling soup seasoned with turnips, rutabagas or beets was as good as it got.

The citizens of Amsterdam and those northern cities went into Friesland and Groningen and those in Utrecht, Rotterdam went south and east for food.

In January, the Stephanus family returned. They had the same clothes except for a different scarf for Marijan and Gerard had a different coat. Jon and Nieske welcomed them back.

"I did go to our house once he said, it was still there and doing well, nobody has broken in or stolen things, so I took what clothes we needed. Then I rejoined Marijan at the farm just outside of the village of "De Steeg.""

"Stay awhile; we still share what we have. It is not as good as when you came first, but we still eat."

That day the soup was made of potato peelings and carrot peelings; for vegetables they ate turnip greens. No meat, no eggs, no proteins.

By December the chicken count is down to thirty hens and one rooster. "No more eating the chickens," ordered Sgt. Held. "We need to save these so we can have eggs."

Now there were no eggs for the family, but at least the nights were quieter as the soldiers stopped their pistol practice on the chickens sitting on roosts.

Many a night Herve' and Evert jumped out of bed, shocked and frightened by the gun fire. Sometimes they hid under pillows or go to their parent's room for comfort and security.

The main meal of the day varied little; it is potatoes or potato peelings, carrot peelings, kale or cabbage, the rutabagas or whatever vegetable is available. It was all cooked together in one pot then mashed and mixed. The excess water is saved for soup broth.

Nieske places the pot on the table and doles out a dollop of the mixed food for each person. There was always some for everybody but never enough to fill the stomach.

Plates are wiped clean with bread to make sure nothing is wasted. When there is no bread the plates are licked clean. "*Ja*," moaned Nieske, "what have we come to? We lick our plates and our fingers just as if we are barbarians."

Heer Stephanus reminded them that they had it better then city dwellers. Those staying in the city only get a small bowlful of soup or cereal per day. "In the city, they get enough food to not die, but not enough to live!"

Herve' was a little bolder or less mature then his brothers, or maybe not as wise; he complained about being hungry. But there was no more. They were all thin, not gaunt but the ribs could be seen and counted without touching them.

"Mommy, will I ever get to eat as much as I want?"

Chapter 61

April 1945

Germany was losing its grip on Holland. The winter of hunger was nearly over. Refugees were returning to their homes. Sweden restarted air drops of bread and ships were freed from the threat of U-boats. Fishing improved when the U-boats went north to protect the German and Polish harbors. Germany was hanging on but in its last breath of surviving the Allied bombing and ground attacks.

Life in the big cities continued to be horrible; death is everywhere. It is far too late for the weak to recover. The hearse carts patrol the streets picking up the dead. People die while scavenging for bits of food, eating grass, paper or whatever might be digestible. It is no longer about nutrition; it is about quenching the pain in the belly.

There are bodies along every street and alley. Death saps their last bit of energy. They lie down or drop wherever they are. Bodies curled in fetal positions with bony hands grasping their stomachs. Too weak to get up they die where they fall.

Grandparents give what little food they have to the children and grandchildren so they could survive; knowing the only thing they have left to give is their own life. Death comes quietly for them during the night as they sleep.

Thirty thousand Dutch starve to death during the winter of hunger. The war takes its toll on the battle field and in the homes of citizens. The great socialist effort of the Third Reich does not care; these are just collateral damage. The elderly are dying; the Jews are sent to concentration camps to be experimented with and then exterminated. Yet there is not enough food to save the remnant still alive.

Hitler and Goering realized that the tide of war had turned against them. Their hatred of Jews and Gypsies was greater than their fear of losing the war. The search for and transporting of Jews to extermination camps increased. Goering made a determined push to exterminate Jews before they lost the war. The pressure was on; cooperate or the food embargo would return.

Old men knew that survival of the Dutch required sacrifice. They gave their portions of food to their wives and children. These men were the bodies found dead on the street; fathers using their last ounce of strength searching for food for their children. They would rather die than bend to Hitler.

The will of the Dutch will not be broken!

Because the Dutch kept detailed municipal records the Netherlands had the highest percentage of its Jewish population arrested and killed. Over one hundred twenty thousand Dutch Jews were killed. This is nearly half of the total Dutch citizens lost to the war and occupation. The others died from starvation or were arrested for helping Jews or for refusing to work at Westerbork or in factories in Germany.

The *Onderduikers* raided many city halls to destroy these records. With family trees easily traceable those with Jewish names were tracked and hunted down. Humans were hunted like animals, prey to hatred and the socialism of the fascist.

Neighbors of Jews were interrogated and accused of assisting Jews escape. Most Jews fled in the darkness of night; using the underground to help them escape to England or America. Destroying birth records hindered but did not stop the Gestapo in its search for Jews.

The VII rockets still came overhead; the only difference is that fewer of them crashed in Holland. Now when the kids are outside and hear the rocket coming, they stop, stand still and counted to ten. That is how long it takes to calculate the rocket will not crash nearby, and then go about playing.

Chapter 62

Breakfast is over when Jon heard the plane. It came from England and was flying under the clouds, indicating there was a target nearby. It was an American B17 Flying Fortress.

The Nazi soldiers hear it too. They remove the camouflage covers from the guns and commence firing.

Nieske ran out of the house. Screaming in terror, she calls her boys to come in the house. Like a mother hen harboring her chicks she gathers then under the stairwell.

Hundreds of 20milimeter shells are fired from the pasture. Poor training or too eager youths or God's protection but the bomber was not hit. The sound of the propeller driven motors grows fainter as they disappear into Germany.

Nieske is terrified that the bomber will make a U turn and take out these guns, or call in fighters to strafe the farm. She knows that if the Allies drop bombs on these guns they would take out the munitions truck too. This truck is parked two meters away from the back of the cow barn, which made the truck twenty meters from this stairway.

The only hope was for these planes to not come back and to not radio for others to come and wipe out the guns. Death is imminent.

"Pray," she ordered the boys, "only God can help us now!"

Arie immediately began, "Please God protect us, keep the Americans away, do not let us die!"

Evert copied him as best he could.

Herve' being only four did not know how to pray other than the prayers he had been taught to say before eating and before going to bed.

The guns were now silent. The plane has passed. The family waits for the aftermath. Would bombers or fighter planes come and destroy the guns? Would the house be hit? If the munitions truck was hit the house would become a hole in the ground.

Herve' prayed, he prayed earnestly and loudly. He chose his bedtime prayer as it mentioned death. First he said, "Now I lay me down to sleep, I pray the Lord my soul to keep and if I die before I wake, I pray the Lord my soul to take!"

He stops, "wait, I do not want to die; I do not want my soul going anywhere. I want to live." He starts over, "Lord bless this food for Jesus sake amen."

He prayed that prayer over and over, thinking it made more sense than having God take his soul. They did not have much food to bless but eating is better than dying. Dying is something he is expecting but does not want to do. He hopes God understands.

He is acquainted with the concept of death. He heard the stories of executions, of prisoners not coming back and soldiers dying in battle. For him death meant not breathing, being cold and being put into a hole in the ground. He does not understand death. He just knows he wants to live.

He learned a prayer to say when he awoke every morning too. He was not sure what was worse, the night or the day, because every day he realized that this may be his last day.

He did not want to pray the Morning Prayer yet. He scratched his head trying to remember it. All he recalled was "now that I am awake, thank you that my soul you did not take;" after that he could not put the words together. So he went back to his mealtime prayer.

The bombers did not come back and no other planes came either, not that day or the next day or ever.

Nieske and Jon talked about this at supper that day. "God heard you boys and granted your request."

"Ja, but Herve prayed the "Bless this food prayer," said Arie. "Bet God laughed about that stupid prayer."

"You didn't" moaned his mother, embarrassed with her son.

Herve' ducks his head in shame. Why do my brothers ridicule me and why is my mother so ashamed of me he thought. Seems I cannot do anything right or make them happy. He looked up with a look of sorrow mixed with defiance, "I did my best, I prayed hard just like you said to do, and tried to do what you wanted."

"Wait, wait, hold on a minute. How do we know it was not

214

Herve's prayer God answered?" asked his father. "I think God was very happy with Herve's prayer. Herve's prayer was probably more sincere than those you guys made, so stop pestering him."

"We know that God hears what we say and he knows what we think too, so when Herve' asked for God to bless the food, God realized he was really thinking 'God I do not want to die' and God honored that because it came from Herve's heart. God has a way of answering what is in the heart, not just what is said. That is why so many prayers are not answered because they are selfish prayers and not expressions of reliance on God."

Turning to his little boy, he smiled, "You did real good. God knows what we want to say even when we do not say the exact words" and then patted him on the head.

Chapter 63

Two bikes turn into the van Bemmel's driveway. One is Alida and the other is a tall young man. He is lean and gaunt. His eyes are sunken deep back behind his cheekbones. They reflect extreme pain or hardship. Deprivation, fear and destruction have taken their toll. When he set his bike against the house wall he stayed stooped over a long time before standing erect. His hands are bony, his face emaciated. Slowly he straightens up to reveal his face. There is fire lingering deep behind those sad eyes.

The door opens before Alida knocks. "Come in, what have we here?"

"Nieske, this is Cobus Eldersveld, he is from De Hague. Do you have something for him to eat? Then he can tell his story."

"Come, come, sit, I will get some warm cereal ready and make coffee. It is almost coffee time."

"Cobus' eyes lit up, you have coffee?"

"Well, not really, it is bark and acorns. But it tastes pretty good, would you like tea instead, I have a little left?"

She hustles about the kitchen, getting out a bowl and setting a small pan with a cup of water on the stove. When it begins to boil she put a cupful of crushed oats and barley in it. It was somewhat like oatmeal or cream of wheat; a mixture of coarse grains that satisfy an empty stomach.

Cooking for a few minutes she pours it into the bowl and adds a spoonful of molasses on top to help it go down.

Cobus has his spoon ready. As soon as she set the plate down and stepped back he attacked this food as if he has not eaten in weeks, which was sort of correct. This was more food than he had eaten on any single day for an entire month.

While he was eating Nieske went to call Jon, whom she met in the feed storage area as he headed for the house. "We have a visitor, another refugee. Alida brought him; I think he is in trouble."

"I saw them arrive."

"Come, let's hear his story, he has been starving, so he is eating something now."

As Jon and Nieske came in Cobus leaned back in his chair with the cup of bitter make believe coffee.

After introductions they sit leaning back in the kitchen chairs. Herve' comes out too and sits on his father's lap.

"Thank you. That was the most kind of you. I really needed that."

All eyes are looking at him so he begins his story.

"I live in Scheveningen, or at least I did until the occupation. My father's house is near the sluice gates of the dike; you do not have them here as you are above sea level. For us those locks or gates are critical in keeping the sea water out when the tide is up.

The Germans took over all the houses near the locks, water gates and the harbor, so my family was displaced.

The Nazi's plan was to control the water. They could flood the area with salt water if they wanted to punish us for resistance efforts. They care nothing for the crops, the people or the city.

"My family moved to The Hague. We have an uncle there who took us in. There I found others who had been abused and lived on the streets. Most of this group helped in the resistance so I, too, joined the resistance and became an *Onderduiker.'*

"How old where you then?"

"I turned nineteen six months before the occupation, I am now twenty three."

"For these past four years I have lived with various people, families and places, always staying on the move.

Looking at Alida, he continued. "I met Alida when she and Braam were planning the raid for the food coupons. Our groups have worked together a lot. The Gestapo and SS officers in Scheveningen and The Hague are extra tough and strict; they see the seamen as enemies who are too independent to control. They enforce the curfew and check papers of people riding on the streets. You know how they reacted when we killed their general. They grabbed the first fifty people they saw and executed them on the streets. I hate those bastards," His eyes shone with intensity.

218

Last November when our food supply was cut off we spread out into the country for food.

That did not guarantee food either as some of the farmers decided to sell food to the starving. Many houses are now empty of furnishings and some barns are full of household items from trading for food. It is a shame that those farmers have no pity for fellow countrymen. They strip them of what little they have, trading what they own just to stay alive while these farmers gain wealth. When this war is over lots of city folks will be destitute."

"We knew it was bad in the cities, the refugees tell us the horror stories about searching and scrapping for food, some even eating flower bulbs." Nieske was weeping.

Herve' did not understand this but he felt the angst, anger and fear in the room. He snuggled tighter, looking for comfort.

"The entire city is like a concentration camp. We are not gassed to death, although that would be more humane. Hitler is trying to break the people's resolve. He wants us to accept the Third Reich; turn in Jews, Gypsies and *Onderduikers*. Death was everywhere. The mortuary truck drives down the streets and stops whenever someone waves them down or they see a body of another victim."

Outside it began to rain, big drops that could be heard falling on the tile roof. Then it began to pour. It was a typical spring rain, good for the crops but not fit for man or beast to be in.

Cobus was done with his story; except for why he was here now and why Alida brought him to their home? Before Jon could ask, Alida picked up the story.

"You do not want or need to know very much more, just be sure that this man is a patriot who has sacrificed much for his family and our country. The Gestapo is looking for him, and he has no idea where to go. They were doing a door to door search for him, but he was in a new hideout. That is where I ran into him."

"Everybody cleared out of this hideout. We removed all trace of us having been there. We fled to different places and cities. Cobus and I managed to get on the train to Ede, stole two bikes and here we are."

"Today is not a good day to travel anyway," started Jon. Then looking at Nieske with questioning eyes he continued. "You must stay for a while; you will sleep on the floor in the boy's room tonight. Some refugees are leaving today. It is best they not know who you are so stay away from them. We will bring food to you and feed you until you are stronger and ready to travel."

Looking at Nieske, Cobus said, "Oh, and I have news about your brother, Geert."

Chapter 64

Cobus began. "It started early last week."

"What started last week? Come on, how is Geert, what happened?"

"He is on a farm near Leiden, the family is okay but everything they had is gone. It is a tough story. They were moving from place to place seeking refuge. He is devastated with the loss and the kids are scared to death. The kids duck and tremble when they hear airplanes and loud noises."

Jon and Nieske leaned forward anxious to hear what happened to her brother's family. They knew he peddled milk, eggs and whatever dairy products he could find. As the occupation dragged on the Nazi raided farms for dairy products and grains, which depleted Geert's supplies. Geert used his bike to pick up and make deliveries. He made a large square crate on the front of his bike to hold the milk and made a saddle over the rear wheel to carry eggs and produce. His route was spread across town, unlike his brother Kees, whose clients were all in his *"wyk"* section of town.

Kees operated a store attached to his house in Doorn. He had walk-in customers plus his milk route. He delivered milk by wagon pulled by his Newfoundland dog. The wagon carried two milk cans from which he ladled a liter into the housewife's container. The butter and cheese were sold by the gram and weighed on the balance scale.

But this story was not about Kees. It was about Geert who was suffering. She turned back to listen to what Cobus was saying.

"De Hague became a hub for German attacks on England. With the two local airfields in their control they were near to England and flew short missions to bomb London. The V1 rockets were replaced with the V2 missiles. They brought these new V2 rockets to De Hague. The new rockets also had new mobile launchers that were hidden in the forest. They take them out to use and then hide them under the trees.

Their attacks are now very efficient and effective, England is taking a beating. Along with the launchers they also brought in a huge stockpile of missiles and an arsenal of bombs for the planes."

The V2 launchers were hidden in the *Haagse Bos* (Haagse Forest). On March 3 they began the assault on London and High Wycombe, firing hundreds of V2 rockets in two days."

"Ah, so that is why we have not heard any rockets for the past months," observed Jon, "they moved the launchers from across the Rhine to De Hague."

"It was a disaster and extreme mess," continued Cobus. "Seventy rockets malfunctioned and fell on the city and surrounding area; others fell into the ocean."

"How many hit London?"

"The best guess right now is that about six hundred hit London or the surrounding area. That is why England retaliated. They needed to take out those V2 launchers."

"I got this story straight from Geert. On the day the disaster occurred he left home at daylight, to find milk for his clients. When he was a few blocks away he saw two Nazi soldiers working with a team of Gestapo. They were stopping people. Geert patted his pocket to check on his ID and travel documents, they were not there so he hurried home to get them.

When he entered his house the first bomb hit, taking out the back wall and blowing out the window glass on the rear side of the house. The noise was deafening. The sky filled with planes and explosions of the bombs. The house next door was also hit, taking a piece of the roof and the chimney."

Astrid, the eight year old, began screaming in terror, grabbed her little brother and hid in the bathroom. She said 'she chose that room because it had no windows, so the flying glass would not hit them.' Geert had to break down the door to get them out.

When she came out she said that she had prayed to Jesus to save her and her brother. I told her Jesus knew she was going to need help that day and that is why her father forgot his ID and travel documents.

They tied their valises on the bikes, loaded the children in the milk crate and left. There were people lying on the streets dying or holding their wounds crying for help as blood oozed out between their fingers. People were in a panic, running out of their houses. Some just sat on their front steps too dazed to know where to go or what to do. Bikes and runners were everywhere, going in all directions, hoping to avoid the next bomb. It was bedlam.

More planes came, the forests lit up with fire, trees were falling down and debris filled the air. Almost every house on the street had holes in the walls or roofs, chimneys were falling down, roofs sagged causing the tiles to rain down on the street. The house nearest the forest was on fire with flames coming out the hole in the roof.

Geert stopped a few blocks away, turned for his last look at the home they had lived in for eight years. He saw his house hit with two bombs, one took out the front wall and the other one removed the remaining portion of the roof. Everything they owned was now gone. All they had was the clothes on their back, one change of clothing each, a box of family heirlooms and a few photos and memories of better times. "

Nieske began sobbing, she sank off her chair. Hunched over she wailed for her brother's loss and miraculous escape. Her mind's eye saw the pile of rubble with smoke and dust rising from what used to be a happy home.

Looking at Jon, she apologized. "I was feeling bad living with the Nazis but we still have a house, the farm and all our things, I will never complain again."

"What are they going to do, Cobus?"

"They plan to stay out in the country; there is more food there, as you know, so they will stay with family, mostly the ones in Drenthe and Gronigen. They have enough cousins and uncles to stay with a few weeks at a time to not be a burden to any one family. It is the kids we should worry about, they are petrified with terror and grief.

At least her family will share what they have, just like you are doing. Only you share with complete strangers. At one stop the farmer told them to get lost. He had nothing to share. He said he was taking care of his family and no one else."

Chapter 65

May 2, 1945

Jon and Nieske are outside surveying the farm. Their arms around each other they are at peace. They are content and calm. The family and the remaining refugees have finished supper. It was special; it was the first time in weeks or was it months, that they ate meat. Peace invades their lives.

Two days ago the Nazi soldiers packed up and loaded the anti-aircraft guns onto a trailer. No words were spoken, no explanation, no thank you, no apology, nothing. They finished after dark. Jon heard the trucks drive out and by morning they were gone.

The war was going extremely bad for Germany. Most of the occupation troops moved to the heartland of Germany. They needed to stop the advance of the Allied Armies coming in from two fronts, France and Italy. The Rhone Valley was liberated. Berlin was next.

This morning Jon opened the cache of canned meats. Jon took two jars. He did it by himself, not wanting his children or anyone else to see where they came from. The two jars would be enough for two or three day's meals.

Tonight's meal had been like dinner instead of supper. The pot was on the table, per usual; it had potatoes and the greens of beets and turnips mixed in. Eyes got big and stomachs rumbled when they spied the meat. Canned pork never looked so good.

Prayers were full of thanks for the food as well as the great hope that the war would officially be over soon.

Jon looked out over the fields with pleasure. He smiled to himself, looking up he sent a quick thanks upward. All the grains are planted; Pete, Case and Gerrit and the refugees were a big help the past week while the rain was gone.

"Jon looked down at Nieske, "They are grateful for having a place to stay and food to eat, so they were happy to help out. Even Gerard helped, he carried the seed out to the planter filled it after each row was planted. He helped sow the grain seeds, which are cast by hand and not with a planter. His soft office hands and back could not do the tilling and harrowing to prepare the soil. He had tried pushing the planter but soon had blisters on his palms; but he did what he could.

Bless him. Jon was happy with his new friend. War created bonds with people he would never have met or known.

"It won't be long and we will be back to just the five of us. When the war ends in a few weeks and food shipments start coming in everyone will be going home. It will be strange to have the house to ourselves again and not play shuffleboard, checkers and monopoly almost every night."

Nieske stepped back a little so she could see Jon's face. "It will not be just the five of us, it will soon be six." She smiled when she saw the reaction on his face.

Slowly the realization dawned on Jon. A grin crossed his face. "Are we going to have a baby?" he stammered.

"Yes, sometime in November or early December. I hope it is a girl. I will name her after my mother, Cornelia."

"Are you happy with this? It has been four years when you said no more babies and you have not been happy with the last one."

"I have new hope, the war is almost over, spring is here, and the crops are in. Yes, I am happy. She will be the delight of my life."

"I wish Herve' was just a little bit more of a delight for you; he really is a good boy."

"Times were horrible then, Survival was all I could do, there was not enough food for one more child. I try to love him, but it is difficult. I don't know if it is just me or is it that he is rambunctious. He is always into something."

Looking up at Jon, she added, "It is mostly me; life was too complicated, terror filled me and I was desperate to take on more duties. I am sorry for him and for me. He has inherited your view of life and your kindness; he will do well in life."

"He is rambunctious, as to the other stuff, we will see" laughed

Jon. He may be the one who accomplishes more than you expect. He is a good boy, at four years old he has a serious relationship with God."

Looking deeply into Nieske's eyes he shared what he thought. "It is not that he is difficult; the problems you faced and the times were difficult. The Nazi's created fear and made it difficult to open your heart to another baby, no matter who that baby was."

"You may be right and sure he loves Jesus. But then everybody in Holland loves Jesus now. Living under the cloud of death makes people call on God. The question is, will that devotion to God last beyond this war?"

Jon laughed with joy, "look at Herve', he is not a fair weather friend or a foxhole believer. His heart is pure, he really gets it. He grasps the reality of a God who is committed to his life."

"I hope you are right."

Turning to go, Jon looked back.

"Now that the grain is planted and the guns are gone we can fill the holes in the pasture and turn the cows into that pasture to eat that nice clover. At least that is one good thing that came from having those guns there and not having cows grazing. The clover has come on real strong and healthy. Maybe this year I will make it into hay."

Those holes get filled tomorrow!

Chapter 66

May 5, 1945

"Wish this war would end" muttered Jon, "It's been five years already."

"Cheer up Jon, it is almost over The Americans are in Germany, things are looking up." She was feeling cheerful. Being pregnant was good for her. Now that the soldiers were gone she had renewed hope, the future looked bright. She was going to have a girl, she was sure of it.

"Look, we even have an egg for breakfast and I made some white bread. I had enough yeast to make one loaf and enough yeast left to raise more bread in a few days. Celebrate with me, be happy."

"I am happy."

"Your face doesn't say so. Would you prefer some pumpernickel to go along with your dark face? Come on, wash your hands. You smell like cows."

"Of course I smell like cows. I do every day, I just milked them. Hope they each have a heifer calf this year, we need heifers to grow the herd."

"Here come the boys, hungry as usual."

"Herve', did you empty the chamber pots? You forgot again, didn't you?"

"Aw, mom, why do I have to do all of them? Why can't Arie and Evert help or at least carry their own?"

"You are old enough and it is time you do some chores too; everybody in the family works."

"Sure we do, but why do I get the yucky work carrying pee pots? Besides, when you aren't looking Arie makes me do his chores too."

Arie jumps up, anger all over his face, but before an argument could start they heard a bicycle ride onto the gravel drive.

"Jon, Nieske!" they heard grandpa shouting before he was off the bike.

Arie ran to the door to let his grandpa in.

Evert Bultan almost ran into the house. "The war is over," he shouted! Then he repeated it as if he could not believe his own words. "The war is over! The peace treaty was signed this morning, or maybe it was yesterday. I heard it on the news this morning. All the church bells rang for an hour yesterday. It was awesome to hear bells from all over town ringing the good news of liberty and freedom." He paused as a chill ran up his back recalling the sound of freedom. "It is wonderful!"

"It was on the news again this morning. The report stated who signed the treaty and gave some ideas of how Germany will be divided up. Germany will never again be big enough to create another war.

"Hitler committed suicide and his top leaders have all disappeared."

"News! Do you have a radio?"

"Yes, I had a radio the whole time, just could not let anyone know."

"Sure, like that was more dangerous than taking care of the Jewish couple and shuffling the others along the underground."

"When helping Jews it is possible to cover up or maybe explain it away. When you need a secret to stay a secret, no one can be trusted to keep it secret. You know that. Never ever share a secret. Anyway, the war is officially done."

Herve' began jumping up and down, waving his arms, "We are free!" he yelled at the top of his voice.

"Yes we are free, we have been liberated. The Canadian army took control of most of this section of Holland. The German troops are in custody. We are free! Free at last, I just cannot believe it."

"We had meat yesterday, Grandpa. Dad had some in a hiding place" reported Herve'. We are celebrating every day!"

"Meat, aha, you do know how to keep a secret," he smiled at Nieske.

No one worked that day. Everybody celebrated. The refugees

and the van Bemmel family stood and talked, the men were clapping each other on the back. They would have hugged but Dutchmen do not do that. They are far too stoic for such displays. But the smile on the face and the shine in their eyes showed their excitement.

Two refugee families announced that they would go home tomorrow. "Enough food will soon be there and we have been blessed to be here. Thank you so much for your kindness!"

Jon gathered the entire group in the kitchen. The room was full, everyone was standing close, and some were holding hands, especially the ladies. They are all looking at Jon, expecting him to say something. And he did.

"It has been a long war, a terrible time in life and for humanity. Many of our family members have been killed or died. We have been through terror, cold and hunger together. Now that this hell is over we should say thanks. Thanks for having our prayers answered. Thanks that we have survived; truly God has protected us."

He then led them in a prayer of thanksgiving, recalling the mercies of God against the onslaught of evil. Grateful that God had brought victory over Nazism and spared everyone standing here.

When he finished there was not a dry eye in the room. It was a happy but somber group that went to their sleeping places and began gathering what belongings they had. In a few days they would be home.

Home or what was left of their dwelling place. All of them concerned about what lay ahead; a new start, cleaning up, picking up and going forward with what was left.

As they left, Nieske gave each a grain sack containing potatoes, vegetables, some wheat and a loaf of pumpernickel bread along with a wedge of cheese.

"You will need this tomorrow." She handed the sack to them as they came to the door.

The women did the triple cheek kiss and cried. Then they headed to the road; stalwartly they walked down *Danmakerweg* to start a new future.

The men shook hands, more firmly than ever before. All would remember that firm hand shake from the farmer who provided life; his hard calloused hands revealed a warm caring heart.

Gerard and Marijan stayed for one more day. Happy to have one more night of playing shuffle board and checkers, one more supper, a night to cherish. A deep friendship had been developed during this harsh Dutch Winter.

Chapter 67

May 6, 1945

"We are going home boys; it has been very nice to get to know you. We will miss you. Now, you boys do what we taught you, okay?"

Marijan had Arie, Evert and Herve' standing in line. She hugged each of them, kissed each one's cheek and gently shook them as she said her farewells. Gerard did the manly thing shaking their hands. Marijan gave Arie a toothbrush and a small cake of tooth polish. In those days it came in a bar like a soap bar.

The entire family walked out the side door with them, excited yet sorrowful to see them go. A bond had developed with many of the refugees but none like the love and respect that blossomed with the Stephanus.

One last hug and best wishes are exchanged. Nieske gasps as she looked over Marijan's shoulder. Gerard and Marijan see the fear in Nieske's eyes. They step sideways to see what scared her.

Jon did not look at her; instead he looked to see what she had seen. On the path alongside the farm are six German soldiers. They are walking single file, rifles at ready across their chests, as if they are on patrol.

Petrified, they just stood there. Don't they know the war is over? Silently they watch the troops as they move along the trail toward their road, *Danmakerweg* .

Arie was the first to react; the war was over so these soldiers have no power over them. At least that is what his mind says. But it looks like these guys may not know the war was officially done, or that the peace treaty had been signed. They walk like they are on patrol, ready for battle.

Arie yells, "You rotten *moofen*, go home!" Quickly a hand is placed over his mouth. The war may be over but if these guys shoot you, you will still be dead.

"Hush your mouth." Nieske takes him inside. "You shoot off

your mouth too much!" she scolds.

Fortunately, the soldiers were too far away. Likely they had not heard Arie or understood what he said.

Jon pushed everyone back inside, "The Canadians are just up the road with tanks, they are camped at *Harskamp*. Better stay inside until these guys pass."

He and Gerard went back outside; they peeked around the corner of the house to see what is going to happen when these Nazi soldiers cross the road in front of a tank.

Jon and Gerard can see the Canadian tank sitting on the road just south of the path, it is facing their way. The six Germans cannot see this tank through the dense trees and brush.

The first two soldiers step onto the road and spot the tank. It is too late to stop or go back. They run across and dive into the ditch; the last four dive into the ditch on their side of the road. The first two begin firing at the Canadians.

"Shit," moans Jon. Gerard who has not learned farmer talk remained silent. "Didn't they hear the bells yesterday? The war is over, guys, it is over, you do not have to do this and die!" Even though he hated the Nazi regime he sees no sense in more killing, even when it was German soldiers who terrorized the country for years."

The tank's turret slowly moved to the right and down. It pointed at the four sprawled in the ditch. Flames spew from the barrel instantly followed by the boom. Dirt, gravel and grass flew everywhere as the grenade blows away the top edge of the culvert. All four soldiers lay still. Are they dead?

The turret moved to the other side of the road and did the exact same thing. "These guys are good shots," muttered Jon.

This time only one soldier laid still, the other one jumped up out of the ditch, without his rifle. As he rose he tore off his shirt and pulled his white undershirt off over his head, waving it in surrender.

Four Canadian soldiers approach the lone survivor. Rifles at the ready they split up with two going to each side of the road. The lone man standing has no gun and the others are not moving. They have their hands outstretched as if reaching for their rifles; empty hands, dead hands, the guns lying where they fell when the shrapnel took their lives.

The five dead were buried there alongside the path. A shallow grave with soil mounded on top. Their rifles are stuck into the ground at the end of each grave. Each rifle was standing erect on its bayonet. The man's bullet riddled helmet set on the butt end of each rifle. Empty helmets, with the straps hanging down. A sad sight.

The survivor is escorted to a jeep parked behind the tank. The last POW taken after armistice is driven away to the barracks at *Harskamp*.

The boys and their father go to the grave site, to view what tanks can do with two shots. They step around the blood soaked ground and stood at the foot of the graves. The blood is now brown, all that is left of life soaking away. Death makes a gruesome scene, one that will stain Herve's memory for life.

"*Ja* boy, it is awful. You should have stayed home like your mother wanted, but no, you came running after us. Now you see death and it will always live with you."

Standing there next to the graves of the enemy they see the holes in the helmets; helmets that offered no protection from tank grenades.

Would death never end?

Arie spat on the grave, but Evert and Herve' just held their father's hand, looking up at him with anxiety. This could have been them; any day of this war could have brought this result to them or their father.

Jon picked both of them up into his arms, glad the war is over and happy that this late event had only harmed the enemy.

Looking at them he said, "Boys, you have seen terrible things and have feared death; remember this day because war is a terrible thing. Hatred brings death and abuse of power is evil."

Are these the last to die in this terrible war? Who knows for sure? They did not have to die, that is the truth. Poor communications has cost five men their lives and made five more widows and five mothers mourning for sons who died in a futile attempt to rule the world.

Chapter 68

The war is over but the hunger continues. Every day refugees come by on their way home. Some just need a meal while others spend a night. All have new hope, happy to be going home. Going home to cities damaged by war, where neighbors are missing or dead. Their house may be looted or destroyed but they are going home.

They are thin and emaciated having spent the winter and now spring wandering the countryside surviving on the goodness of others.

The slow plodding steps as one going to the gallows are replaced. Life has purpose again. Now they walk upright and with determination. The eyes are sunken and rimmed with the darkness of starvation, but there is a new light, hope shines in them. Smiles come readily, laughter is not common, humor and pure joy is still foreign to them. How long has it been since they laughed or experienced pure joy?

Jon reminded them that good times will come when they restart their lives. The common answer was always sad. "Life will never be the same again, too many have died. Look at our children, most of them do not know a day without fear or a day without hunger."

~~~

People are still dying from malnutrition, for some it is just too little too late. That is what the government called it, but those who witnessed these deaths knew it was starvation not malnutrition.

Malnutrition is a serious factor which will affect the younger children for the rest of their lives. Especially those born the last year of the war or were conceived during the Dutch winter. These silent victims were undernourished while in the womb and their bodies did not develop properly. They will have weak optic nerves and softer bones, bones that are just a little thinner and chests that do not fully develop. Children, who have not seen or experienced war, yet would carry the results of war for a life time. Many lives will be cut short; having old worn out bodies when middle aged. A life shortened by optic deficiencies, pulmonary and renal problems or other ailments caused by the Winter of Hunger.

Chapter 69

At nine o'clock Jon saw Braam Koster pedal up his drive. He stopped planting potatoes and went to meet his friend. They embraced; two men that have a huge amount of respect for each other.

Jon recognized the gift Braam gave Holland to help fight Nazism when he could have stayed in America. Braam recognized courage, dedication and generosity when Jon jeopardized his life to aid the resistance and help those in need. Jon helped people he did not know as a response for what God meant in his life. Only men who have defied death understand this embrace; they have no need for cultural decorum or stoicism.

"Come, it is almost coffee time and Nieske will want to greet you, too."

"Not yet, I want to talk to you first."

"What's up, are you leaving us?"

"Yes, I am leaving; I board ship a week from Monday. I wanted you to know. I am not saying my goodbyes now; I will be back with Alida."

"Ah, Alida, you guys did a lot together. She is a good woman, not difficult to look at either." He nudged Braam with his elbow.

Braam grins, "Alida and I have been through a lot together and have decided we want to do a lot more. She is coming to Minnesota, too."

"Wow, that's quick work. Is she going with you?"

"No, she has things to do, her immigration papers will take months to approve. Fortunately she will get preferential treatment for her work during the war. She has only a brother to say goodbye to. You know her mom died in Auschwitz and her dad died somewhere in Germany; there is no record of him dying at any camp."

"Does she need help? We will do what we can for her."

"Thanks, but she just needs to take care of her mother's things and plan what to take to America. The house will be put for sale.

Her brother wants her to keep all the money, but she is going to split it half way. She will leave in a month or six weeks. We will be married in America."

"This is great news and Nieske will be tickled pink, she loves romantic stories. Come; you can tell her over some coffee."

They stopped when they heard the sound of marching feet and rumble of trucks; it has been eight days after liberation.

Shouts and cheers are heard from down the road. Coffee is forgotten. Houses emptied as everyone went to the road to see what the noise and cheering is about.

Soon *Danmakerweg* is lined with hundreds of people. Farmers, family and refugees cheered as the procession passed. In front was an American jeep. Besides the driver there were three more soldiers, two of them with their feet hanging over the rear fenders. One is holding a flag,

"A beautiful flag" thought Herve'.

It was the Stars and Stripes of the United States of America, the people cheer loudly. *"Huzzah"* Then they saw the Nazi flag tied to the rear of the jeep, it was all torn and ragged from dragging on the gravel. They cheered again! Louder than before.

A roar of approval went up when that hated symbol came by in humility. "Hup, hup hooray!" became the chant along the roadway.

Next were trucks carrying soldiers and behind the trucks are more soldiers; hundreds, maybe thousands, all marching, well not marching but walking. Every one smiled and waved to the Dutch who are honoring them. They are grateful for the thanks and praise. It was the same everywhere. Each village or town they pass through there are grateful crowds shouting in gratitude and thanks.

The soldiers, of course, are happy to be alive, happy to be going home, happy to go see family and now excited and happy with the thanks they receive from the Dutch.

Some soldiers toss packs of cigarettes to the people; others hand out or throw candy bars to the kids. It is a parade of pure joy and excitement. The Dutch are grateful to these heroes who came from the other side of the world to bring liberty and freedom.

Arie caught a chocolate candy bar, which said Hershey's on it. No one knew what this was. Herve' caught a pack of Phillip Morris cigarettes and then Evert, too, caught a Hershey bar. It was a glorious day. Even the sun shone, warming the cool spring day after the night's rain. God was good.

Jon took the cigarettes and Nieske took the candy bars. "Aw, come on mom, I caught it, it is mine," complained Arie.

The people linger long after the soldiers are past, waving to them as they turn onto the *Apledornse Weg*.

Slowly the family and Braam go into the house. The coffee was still on the stove, so they ate pumpernickel with cheese and drank coffee.

Nieske took one of the Hershey bars, unwrapped it and broke it along the little rectangle lines. Everybody gets one piece of the chocolate.

Arie and Evert had eaten chocolate before, but this was Herve's first chocolate. "Do all Americans eat this?"

"*Ja*, I am sure most Americans get all the chocolate they want, it is a land of plenty, which is why they share. Right, Braam?

"Can we go live there?

"No, Herve', we have a farm here and grandpa and grandma are here" responded Nieske

But Jon smiled," that might not be such a bad idea," he thought.

One of the refugees gave one of the candy bars she caught to Nieske, "for the boys," he said.

These bars were eaten, one at a time for the next two Sundays. Each person getting one square, but dad got the extra square.

That night Jon smoked his first manufactured cigarette in four years.

"Too bad the Canadians did not get to march through and receive this kind of adulation." He thought. "Seeing the Maple Leaf alongside the Stars and Stripes would have been nice."

Life was good once again. Hope had arrived!

241

Chapter 70

Jon and Nieske went to town. This was the first time to shop and walk without being watched or carry ID to show to the Gestapo. Besides enjoying the freedom Nieske is going to see the doctor and talk about her pregnancy. Freedom never felt so good.

Jon whistled a happy tune as he loaded Arie and Evert on his bike; then holding Nieske's bike when she loaded Herve'. They had a long list of things to do. The primary goal was to obtain a loan for repairing the damage on the farm and maybe, hopefully, buy a cow or two. He heard that American dairymen were donating Holstein cows to help rebuild the dairies in Holland. The price was reasonable as only the government fees and veterinary expenses were being charged.

"Is there no end to the generosity of Americans?" asked Jon. He did not expect an answer, just thinking out loud about life.

The Agriculture Bureau approved Jon for three of the donated cows. The farms that had suffered the most during the occupation were given first rights. Jon was pleased with the system and the opportunity to replace some of the cows lost to Nazism. The milk would increase the income and provide cash for family needs.

Second, was to buy a bicycle for Arie, he was eight now and the news was that the Free States, (the United States) had also shipped bicycles to Belgium and the Netherlands. Plus Nieske wanted to just look around the shops to see what was available. New items were being made and imported from nations eager to help rebuild the economy or improve their own economy. A new dress might be nice. How long has it been since she bought new clothes?

As they neared the Centrum they heard the noise of many voices, some shouting, some screaming and hoots of derisive laughter. Nieske looked at Jon with questions in her eyes.

"What is going on, do we want to go further?"

"Let me lead the way, I am sure it's all just good fun."

"It does not sound like fun to me. Those screams are terrifying

243

and most of the shouting is in anger. Let's be careful, the boys are with us."

They parked their bikes in the stands by dress shop on the corner of *Driehoek and Raadenhuisplein*. When they rounded the corner into the Centrum they saw a crowd gathered in a semi-circle around a truck parked against the brick wall of the grocery mart.

One man stood on a wooden box making announcements. Several other men went into the canvas covered truck bed and brought out a woman.

"This woman betrayed her people, her family, and her nation!" He announced. "She collaborated with the enemy; she sold her body in exchange for favors and money."

The announcer enumerated some of her misdeeds, and then pronounced the punishment for her sins. Two men sheared the woman's head with scissors, till she was nearly bald, just a few short tufts were left by the ears. When her crude hair removal was complete they tore off her clothes. With a smack of a broom handle on her naked back they set her loose.

Nieske quickly covered the eyes of Arie and Evert, Jon was holding Herve' on his shoulders and did not get him down in time to avoid seeing the nude woman. "Have you no shame?" she scolded Jon.

He shrugged; shame was one of her favorite words when she wanted to condemn something. This was brutal justice and not at all erotic, it was best to not make a big deal of it. The shame was on the traitor, she was paying a small price of the pain her actions had brought. After all, she lived well while her countrymen suffered, now was payback time.

While she ran away another woman was brought out. This one had collaborated with the enemy by providing sex and informing on her neighbors. She too was shorn and stripped, and then beat numerous times with the broom handle before turning her loose to run home or to someone who would give her shelter.

The crowd hooted and jeered at these traitors, no one covered them up or helped them. A few added injury to the insult by punching and kicking them as they ran by. The ones who had informed on neighbors and friends received the worst beatings.

Nieske felt sick, she hated to watch the humiliation. Jon was more stoic, "Who knows how many people were arrested, beaten, shot or sent to camps because of what these poor excuses for Dutch women did. They are fortunate to not be executed."

"You are right, it was because of people like them that my cousin was shot and Alida's mother and father were sent to death camps." She spat to show her disdain. "But I do not want to watch this, or have the boys see it either."

Leaving the Centrum they went to see the banker first. Mr. Kamerling saw them come in the door.

Chapter 71

"*Mijnheer en Mevrouw* van Bemmel," he greeted them. "How are you? How can I help? Hope all is well on the farm."

Jon explained his plan and thirty minutes later they had a promise of enough money to do the repairs to the hog and chicken barns, and pay for the three cows. The loan was promised to be paid on warrants when the jobs were completed and the cows delivered. The bank had very little cash on hand but the money was coming.

Cows were coming too; the entire country was short of milk and short of beef cattle. Five years of eating the old cows and new born calves had depleted the country of livestock. Canada, America and Brazil were sending replacement cattle to help reestablish farmers. Milk was a high priority to provide the calcium and vitamins needed to overcome the winter of starvation.

The Centrum was back to normal with people sitting in the outdoor cafes drinking coffee or beer. All had lots to talk about. Some discussed the war and survival but most talk was about their plans for the future. Woven into the talk was the justice meted out in the Centrum; was it enough? Was it fair? Should court trials be held? Scorn for the traitors was not enough, but what does justice look like?

At eleven fifteen Nieske walked into Dr. Voorman's office, she was right on time. Her doctor liked being prompt and expected his patients to be prompt, too.

"So you think you are pregnant? You should know, it has happened four times now?"

"Yes, I am sure; it has been three months since my last monthly," she murmured. She was very uncomfortable discussing personal things even with a doctor.

After the exam Dr. Voorman said. "Yes, you definitely are having a baby. This is not the best time to have a baby."

Nieske raised her eyebrows, "Why?"

"The famine has caused much damage to mothers; the lack of

proper nutrition starves the fetus of nutrients needed to develop healthy babies." Holding up his hand he silenced whatever she was going to say.

"However, I realize that you have not starved but your diet has not been well balanced either. You had vegetables and potatoes but protein was missing. Having said that, it may well be that this baby will be mostly alright."

"You should have practiced birth control a little longer. Now you must make up for what has been missing in nutrients."

"We love each other too much to abstain. You know that during hard and difficult times the need for closeness grows. When fear encompasses the day it is especially needful to feel close and reassure each other that there is love in the world and that you really do matter to someone."

"I understand that. Abstaining is difficult, but my father taught me the next surest method is to 'leave the church before the choir sings'.

"Be sure to eat lots of protein, you are eating for two and take a large table spoon of cod-liver oil every morning and every evening during this pregnancy. Fortunately you have six months left, with good food and enough milk I expect minimal damage to the baby. Eat eggs and meat every day; it is not a cure all but the cod liver oil will help."

"Yes, doctor, will you need to be at the birth, or will your mid-wife be okay?"

"The mid-wife will be fine, the birth will be just fine and if you eat right the baby will grow up healthy as well."

Sitting at a café table she shared coffee and this news with Jon while the boys were busy eating and watching others. They overheard others talking about the morning's events. The events began with the beating of traitorous men. These men were crudely shorn and stripped of clothing before setting them loose. These men had not fared as well as the women; they had also been beaten with fists or tree switches and doused with kerosene and tar before they were released and ran away.

Arie was proud of his new bike; he peddled it faster than the others, staying in the lead. His mother cautioned him and scolded him all the way home.

The next day Jon began the repairs, sawing the wood, nailing roosts in place and making the hog pens strong so the sows could not break out or turn around to kill their babies. It is common for sows to kill or eat the piglets, so Jon made sure the pen was too narrow for the sow to turn around. It was confining for the sow but necessary for the piglets. He could afford no further loses and it was only until the piglets could run around.

He was down to two sows and no boar; the rest had all been eaten by the Nazis. Fortunately both sows had been bred by the neighbor's boar and would have piglets soon.

The pasture looked good. The holes were filled and new clover and rye was growing. The barbwire fences were repaired. By July the farm was back to normal; normal as in looking good, but not normal in replacement of lost livestock.

Jon bought three young cows, one was having her first calf soon and the other two were four months pregnant. He was pleased to have them. The rest of the herd were getting older and soon beyond the age of having calves. At this point it was more important to have them produce calves then to produce a lot of milk.

Farming was going to be tough for years, but at least they were free.

Chapter 72

The docks are crowded. Passengers are standing with suitcases in hand waiting to board. Well wishers and family fill the space. The Queen Mary looms in the background, standing high above the dock, her three masts point strongly into the sky. She was a troop ship but now most of the passengers are emigrants. She dwarfs the other liners with her size and grandeur.

The crowd is anxious; many passengers are hesitant to get on board. They want to take just one more minute to shake hands, one more hug or, for the men, to slap each other on the back before saying goodbye.

Everyone knows that this is the last time to see family and friends. Emigrants seldom return and those staying need money to reconstruct war damages. The voyage across the Atlantic will take a week, longer if there are storms. The ride on trains will take several more days to get to the final destination. America is a big country, those staying in tiny Holland have no perception of the size or why it takes days for a train to cross the country. In Nederland a train will go from one end to the other in three or four hours.

Braam Koster is there. He has two suitcases standing next to him. His sea chest and a small crate, containing family heirlooms and household items, were loaded yesterday. The crate held items from his mother and things Alida was sending with him. Braam is willing and joyfully taking these items; they are for the new home she will share with him.

A big group gathered around Braam and Alida. He is in love; he adores this brave woman. She sees the bravery of many of the men gathered here. Yet she has a tender heart that expresses kindness to everything not Nazi.

Marinus Sukkel is there along with seven others from their group. Jon van Bemmel also came to say farewell to his friend. Nieske was home with the boys because she was having pregnancy problems. She insisted Jon go; Braam had been a vital part of keeping their hopes alive. They would miss this brave man and would hold his memory dear in the years to come.

At last the group broke up giving Braam and Alida the last few minutes together.

The ship's horn blew its loud and mournful toot, giving final notice. The engines are started; ready to sail. Just one stop before America; they headed to England to complete the passenger list.

Jon and Braam shook hands for the last time. "Write us about your journey and give my greetings to Klaas and his family," said Jon.

He had never met his cousin and did not know the family, but family is family, so greetings are sent along. "And thank them for sending you, Braam. Holland is blessed to have you here."

At last the ship drifted away, slowly heading west. The ship's railing is crowded as final waves of goodbye are made to those standing on the dock mourning. Many tears roll down cheeks of the women while men quickly wipe wet eyes hoping no one sees them. They felt alone, left behind by those going west to new adventures and opportunity.

A war has taken many and now America is taking more family. Hearts ache for missing these loved ones, yet happy for them.

Chapter 73

Seven days later the Queen Mary slides into its dock in the New York harbor. There is no one waiting for Braam. The reunion with his family and friends will take two more days.

It is early morning; when Braam disembarks. He is carrying two bags. The crate will be shipped on a truck and will arrive in Pease in five or six days. He has three hours before his train leaves but he hustles to the cab stand. He is anxious to be home. He opens the cab's back door, and throws in his bag. He gets into the front seat.

The driver motioned for him to get in the back.

"I speak English," he tells the driver, "I don't sit in back seats."

The driver expecting that his fares were mostly foreigners and spoke little or no English, especially this one dressed in frumpy Old Dutch clothing.

"Train Station, please," ordered Braam. It was great to speak English again. Even if it was not his mother tongue, America was his home.

"Where are you headed from here?"

"Minnesota, I have been gone over four years and I am going home!"

"Home? You sound like a Dutchman or German. You are not German, are you?"

"No, I am from the Netherlands, I hate Germans." He bit his tongue to stop the expletive that formed in his brain. "No," he said to himself, "the war is over, it is time to move on".

"Me too. If you were German I was going to tell you to get another ride. Those bastards killed a lot of my people."

"Ah, you are Jewish," stated Braam.

All the way to the station Braam told him about the war and his escapades while in the Resistance. When they arrived the driver hustled out to get the bag from the back seat.

"This ride is free; it is my way of thanking a real *'mensch '*, thanks for helping my people!" Then he quickly hugged Braam. He had just met and blessed a real man, a hero.

"A real *mensch?*" Braam thought about what that meant. To be a real man, a man strong enough to live by his moral obligations and principals.

"Yes" he said to himself he had met many real *mensch*. He thought about Herr Sukkel, Herr Bultan, Jon van Bemmel, Sjoerd, and the other guys in the cadre. And of course Alida, she was not a man but towered in her *"menschness."* If that is a word," he mused.

Darkness crossed his mind and his brow furrowed as he thought about those who failed at being upright and lost their honor. David Cohen aka Slager came to mind. Sadness and sorrow filled his heart and his thoughts.

How does a man stand up to the pressure David faced and not collapse? But a real *mensch* would not collapse and sell his soul to become a "catcher" betraying his own race. Yet, David had done much to assist the cadre and the cadre had been blessed because David had not turned them in to the Gestapo.

David had not fared so well. Mies was there the day David died. They were to meet in the theater in Veenendaal. Mies went up to the balcony where they had met before.

When Mies walked up the stairs he saw only one person there. That was expected as it was two in the afternoon on Wednesday. Sitting next to David he noticed how pale he looked. Then Mies saw David was gripping his side. Blood oozed through his fingers.

David began, "Just listen; I do not know how long I have. I have been stabbed. The brother of some people I turned in found me out. He followed me on the train today and when I was walking here he came up behind me, shoved me in an alley and stabbed me. I made it here to see you."

With that he reached into his coat pocket. He gave an envelope to Mies. "Here take this; it has the information for where I have secreted the money, jewels and art objects. You are to take them and use the money and diamonds for the cadre. Maybe the art can be returned to families if they return home. There may be a few, else give it their children or heirs."

"No, I will not take that. I will bring you to the hospital and take care of you."

"It is too late," he wheezed. "I have only a short time. Tell the group I am sorry for failing to be the man I should have been. I am proud to have known them."

Mies stayed till David died. Grieving about another life lost, Mies closed David's eyes and slipped away, leaving David to be found by the usher or cleanup crew.

Braam awoke from his revere, looked out the window at the country flashing by.

Chapter 74

The train ride is uneventful. Between naps he stared out the window admiring the expanse of the country. He dreamt about getting home, finding a house and preparing it for Alida.

The Minneapolis train station was crowded with people waiting for the train from New York. Seven of them are from Pease, anxious to greet their friend. He was brash and gutsy before he left; what was he like now? What happens to a man in war, a man that volunteers to risk his life? They are anxious to hear his story.

The welcome in Pease is even greater. Friends, neighbors and interested people fill the Christian Reformed Church's reception hall. They came from miles around. Dutchmen from Princeton, a cousin from Prinsburg and another from Pipestone are there to welcome him home, anxious to hear first hand news of the war and family.

He loved this country. It was so open compared to The Netherlands where the landscape is broken up with ditches, canals or rows of trees. Towns or villages are only a few miles apart. Here there is corn as far as one could see on the softly undulating land. The nearest town is ten miles and the nearest city is twenty or more miles. The green is only broken up by the occasional house and barn or the scattered towns or villages. He loves Pease for its quiet peacefulness and he loves his church.

Driving down Main Street he sees the nice brick building that replaced the white wood sided church built in the 1890s. He recalled the cornerstone the settlers had placed there in 1907. The words inscribed on it are *"Eben-Haezer,"* an ancient Hebrew phrase meaning "Thus far the Lord has helped me."

Those were appropriate words when this land was settled and it is appropriate now for him as he returned home safe, sound and in love. Surely this is the same God who brought him back.

He is looking forward to seeing everyone although he disliked the attention. They would want him to speak or as the preacher liked to say, "Just say a few words."

Braam Koster was embarrassed, he was not a public speaker and hated all this attention, yet he was pleased that so many people cared. He much preferred the work he did in Holland, where he was behind the scenes and with one or two partners. He liked the "very little" talking and loved the trusting and a lot of doing.

Before Braam left for Holland he attended church because it was expected that every Dutchman went to a Christian Reformed Church or a Reformed Church. Now he wanted to go to church; he had a new relationship with God. He fully realized that it was God who sent the Guardian angels who had protected him. He recalled those evening times where Marinus Sukkel had led the group in Bible studies where he presented Jesus as a real person who cares about your life and your soul.

Long prayers he could do without. Every Sunday the pastor has what became known as "the long prayer." These prayers were used to remind God of what God already knew.

They contained flowery phrases and preached a message to the people listening. Those prayers did not make an impression on Braam. He figured God was not impressed either. Braam thought prayers should be addressed to God and God only. Prayer should never be used as a tool or hammer to convince the audience of the preacher's knowledge, his vocabulary or his point of view.

During those years as an *onderduiker* he was a regular visitor with God. Braam's conversations with God are straight from the heart, no bull, just a lot of thanks to a God he trusts. His new attitude toward God or relationship with God was not based so much on staying alive but on what he saw in Christians. He was amazed that it was the Christians who protected the Jews, often at their own peril. It was the Christians who endangered their own lives to assist others. Only a relationship with Jesus motivates that much good will. Good will that results in sharing, harboring and caring for people who are not immediate family, sacrificing for absolute strangers.

After the food was served, it was time for him to tell his stories. He related a few incidents, mostly what others had done. He told the story of Jon van Bemmel transporting Jews in his load of hay, of Wilco providing a way station in the underground and of Evert Bultan harboring and shuttling Jews. He paused a moment, uncertain what else he should say.

Suddenly he could not stop talking as he told his friends about this amazing woman he met. She was a patriot, who challenged danger, risked her life and worked tirelessly in helping those in need.

Embarrassed with his ardor he stopped, and gave his thank you speech and expressed his gratitude for their support, love and prayers.

"Who is she? What is her name? Are you going back to her?" were questions popping up from the audience.

Blushing a deep red he rose to his feet one more time. "Her name is Alida Mollengraff; yes, we are in love. No, I am not going back, this is my home; I love Minnesota, I love America."

A groan rose from the ladies in the crowd, they thought they had a love story to share; now that dream was shattered.

Braam's face split into a huge grin. "I may not be going back, but she is coming here, we will be married soon."

"How soon, Braam?"

"Maybe six weeks, she has her immigration papers and small pox shots. She is selling a few things, giving a few things away, packing and saying goodbye. If all goes well she will board the Queen Mary in four weeks."

"Oh, and do not feel sorry for me that I have to wait; feel sorry for those staying in Holland. The country is a mess and it is going to take years to rebuild and get back to normal. Pray for Jon. His place was nearly destroyed and yet they gave food, assistance to everyone who came to the farm."

Chapter 75

It is a peaceful morning in Ede. After a night of rain the sun peeks out from behind the billowing white clouds. The clang of the church bells in Ede carries out to the farm under the amphitheater of clouds. Jon cocks his head in wonder; after all it is nine on Wednesday. What is happening?

Is this another big event? Freedom keeps these wonderful days coming. Jon wrapped up his chores, hurries to the house to find Nieske. They load the boys and ride into Ede. He does not want to miss out. The bells rang a long time, so it must be great news.

He liked being free. New horizons and hope filled his soul, he could go whenever and wherever they want. No papers, go guards, no soldiers and best of all, no fear.

The streets are again filled with people. Everyone is happy, smiling and laughing in joy. Orange flags are everywhere. "The Queen is back, the Queen is back!" Others are shouting, "We are truly free, the Queen is home! Hurrah"

The church doors are open for those who want to say a prayer of thanks. Gratitude creates an exuberant crowd. The Calvinists are not accustomed to this display of joy.

The *dominee* mentioned this on Sunday. "That is how much joy and exuberance there will be when you arrive in heaven he admonished. He, too, felt guilty for showing his exuberance during the celebration.

"This is a happy day, come let's get a cup of coffee and a tart to celebrate." Suggested Nieske

It is a great day in the Centrum. The crowd was lively and fun. Two impromptu bands, with horns, drums, a flute a saxophone and a homemade drum or a pot with a wooden spoon are strutting in front of the shops playing loudly and sometimes off key. Nobody cared; it was a joyous occasion with lots of shouting, whistling and clapping. The cafes were flooded with families drinking tea and eating pastries. Men lifted glasses of beer, yelling *"Proest"* at the top of their lungs.

261

Good news met them when they arrived home. The postman was there with a package. "You have a package from America. Do you have family there?"

"Yes, an uncle and some cousins we have not met."

"Well, this is a good family; they have sent you a large package."

He took a letter out of his bag. "This is your day for mail from faraway places. This letter is from Indonesia."

Jon, Nieske and Herve' gather around the package on the kitchen table. "It's from Uncle Klaas, in Minnesota. Wow, the last time we heard from him was just before we married."

"Open it, don't stand there staring at it."

Inside neatly packed and folded were three shirts, one for each boy, enough fabric to make two dresses along with an envelope of the latest style of dress patterns, and two shirts for Jon and socks for everybody. In the middle of the package was a bag with two round objects that felt like balls.

Nieske picked up the package, "Why send balls or toys?" She wondered.

They were not two balls. They were oranges, bright, shiny oranges. She peeled off the wrapping and the aroma of fresh citrus filled the kitchen.

Herve' wondered what made mom and dad so excited. He knew this was the royal family's color but what are oranges?

"How nice, we will eat one Sunday and put the other one away for Arie's birthday."

That evening they tried on their new shirts and socks, the first new clothes in three years, except for the blue parachute silk shirts.

Jon grabs one orange. "We should enjoy this tonight, not wait till Sunday."

The entire family watched him peel this fruit. Forgotten is the letter from Indonesia. Nieske's excitement made everyone eager to taste this exotic fruit. When the peeling was off Jon squeezed the peeling to make it spray a fine mist of scented moisture. The boys tried to capture the mist, taking deep breaths, inhaling this wonderful aroma.

Jon separated the slices, giving a slice to each in turn. When there were two slices left Jon and Nieske each had the extra slice.

"We must thank uncle Klaas for this." So they all sat down to write a note of thanks to go with Jon's letter. Evert helped Herve' write "*Dank u om Klass.*"

Six weeks later another care package came from uncle Klaas. This one was larger; it contained more clothes, more socks and two pair of nylon hose. A letter accompanied the package explaining that Braam had told stories about the family in Holland and how devastating the war had been. Things are good in America so they wanted to help.

That started a new relationship, between family members who did not know each other but the bond of being family did matter and it grew.

Herve' was a happy boy. He learned how to smile, fears faded away. Now he remembered the good things, chocolate and oranges provided by Americans. New clothes, not hand-me downs but clothes no one had worn before. Life was better. He is home alone with his mom when his brothers are in school. He liked that because he loved his mom and hoped she enjoyed being with him.

Soon he would have a new brother or sister. His mom wanted a girl. Would having a sister change how his mother spent time with him, or lessen his chances of having his mother love him?

For the first time in months he felt uncertain and lonely; that night he cried himself to sleep.

Chapter 76

"Jon, Jon! We forgot to read the letter from Indonesia. It is from your brother Bernard!"

Jon was finished with chores, the cows are milked and livestock fed and ready for breakfast. Forgetting his hunger he opens the letter, anxious to know what his brother has to say. The last letter was four years ago.

That letter was written the week before Japan invaded Indonesia. Jon presumed that Bernard and his family were dead. Bernard was stationed on the island Samboe, protecting British Petroleum facilities. This letter is postmarked Batavia, Indonesia.

Dear Jon,

I am happy to say that I and the whole family are safe and doing well. We are recovering from the trauma of war. Probably like you are. Please give this letter to the rest of the family as soon as you see them.

We will be returning to Holland in a few months. We are waiting for permits and other matters to be finalized. We intend to emigrate to America or Australia when the possibility comes, but first we will return to Holland, see family and finalize the applications.

Just briefly, I will tell more when we arrive. I was captured and taken to a prisoner of war camp. My wife Tina and the two boys, Theo and Tun, were also captured and imprisoned in a camp with Tina. We did not know the other was alive although the camps were on the same island.

We are grateful to be together again and look forward to visiting with you and Nieske in the near future.

Love, B&T

Jon leaned back. "They have been through a hell of their own, haven't they?"

He gets up and hugs Nieske, "At least we always had each other."

Chapter 77

Six weeks later Jon and Nieske waited in their driveway for the taxi. Bernard's telegram said he and his family would arrive at eleven, just in time for dinner.

Nieske had prepared a special dinner for Bernard. She made mashed red potatoes; breaded pork chops with mushroom gravy, red cabbage and sour kraut, chunky homemade apple sauce, a loaf of wheat and a loaf of white bread with lots of freshly churned butter.

The boys loved to have visitors because mom always made extra food and it was really good too!

Hugs, kisses and tears streamed down their faces, the family was overjoyed that those who were thought dead and buried in the jungle are alive and well. Nieske hugs Tina one more time when they were in the house, just thankful for life.

Dinner was ready, so they sat down to eat. As soon as the prayer was finished and everyone said "Amen" the boys dug in but the adults talked.

In his prayer Jon thanked God for the miracle of life and that the entire family had survived the war.

"We better eat" encouraged Jon or these boys will have it all gone.

Silence invaded the home as the lost and returned family smiled and munched on their first home cooked Dutch meal in four years.

When dinner was done the family settled in for the long tale of Indonesian adventures or in reality trials and troubles.

Bernard started. "The men's camp was in the jungle ten miles from Batavia and the women's camp on the opposite edge of the city. The men tended gardens to feed themselves and the Japanese captors.

Tina dug holes for fence posts to enclose their camp. Their camp was a section of confiscated houses. Both camps had lots of armed guards, who spoke no Dutch or Indonesian."

"The work was hard and food was scant until the fence was completed and the gardens began to produce.

The hard part was the not knowing if your wife or husband was dead. You felt all alone, that loneliness and uncertainty of life ate our hearts and tormented our dreams. Dreams that the man or woman you loved was dumped in the jungle to feed wild beasts."

Theo joined in, "The best part was when the Red Cross trucks came to our front gate. The Japanese soldiers left the day before and we had no idea what was happening. The Red Cross brought white bread and jam with peanut butter."

"Yes, the end was strange" continued Bernard. "The war over but the camps did not know it. The Japs just disappeared into the jungle, leaving the prisoners to fend for ourselves. It was a surprise; we had no idea we were free. We had no place to go, had no idea if the Americans or Australians were coming or what.

"What happened next was a parade came our way!" added Tun. The parade was all men, many American soldiers carrying their flag. The others were men freed from the men's camp."

"That is when I spotted my dad, Theo chimed. "He was walking on our side of the group. Mom and I ran to him. We hugged we cried we hugged some more."

"What are your plans?" prodded Jon.

Bernard looked at Tina, "We have not agreed yet. Tina likes the idea of going to Australia but we also like the United States; either California or Washington. The military is giving back pay for the years in prison, so we have a bit of cash to start a business. America looks pretty good to us."

Chapter 78

July, 1946

School is out and crops are growing. The rye and barley are already six inches tall and the wheat is doing well. Jon loves this time of year. Seeing the first sprig of green protruding from the soil always exhilarates his heart. It is similar to having a new baby, the pure joy of seeing new life where seed is planted. Hope is renewed bringing peace and contentment.

Hope for the future, seeing the grains and vegetables grow to maturity providing food for the coming winter and through spring and summer until the next crop.

He was at peace. Today was easy, he only had to milk the cows and feed the livestock. The heavy rain last night precluded any work in the fields for at least two days. "Perfect," he thought, "we can go to Oosterbeek's war cemetery today and church tomorrow free from field work." He would tell the family his plans at breakfast.

Breakfast was ready when he came in. The aroma filled the kitchen and the boys woke up to the smell of frying bacon.

Today is Saturday so breakfast is not the normal fare. Saturday and Sunday there is time for a special breakfast. On Sunday they eat boiled eggs on homemade white bread. Soft and sweet with no preservatives, buttered with homemade butter and covered with slices of boiled eggs; the second slice of bread was pumpernickel with butter and cheese. Then, just as if it was dessert, the third slice was also buttered white bread sprinkled with chocolate sprinkles called *hagel* (hail).

Not today, today was Saturday. The bread is not the fresh loaf. Saturday is the day the old dry bread gets used up. Nothing is wasted or thrown away; even the heels are eaten along with the entire crust.

None of that matters. Everyone is eager; mouths are salivating for what is coming off the stove. The bacon is on the table and the stale bread is frying in the bacon grease. The sizzle of frying is accompanied by the aroma. Clutching their forks they wait.

"Come on pray, Dad," begged Arie, "before the food gets cold."

Jon looked at Nieske, who nods her approval. She stays at the stove flipping slices of bread that will soon be smothered in dark brown corn syrup. Then they disappear down these hungry mouths along with a well done fried egg and a glass of cool buttermilk. Nothing like homemade buttermilk chilled in the cellar.

Food is no longer scarce, not that it is plentiful, but there is enough. They have all the vegetables and bread they want and eat meat three days a week. It is a small amount but a bite or two of pork or beef or the occasional chicken is great!

There is no wasting of food. They eat well but whatever can be sold is sold to generate income to fund restocking the farm with cows, pigs, chickens and implements that had been broken or stolen.

As the boys ate Nieske warmed a bottle of milk for her new baby girl. Cornelia is lying in her crib watching the family eat. She is a good baby, now nearly seven months old. She smiles a lot and loves it when the boys play with her and tickle her under the chin.

It has taken awhile for the boys to adjust. They went from wonder at seeing a baby to resentment when this little bundle took mother's attention away from them. They soon learned that when they are nice to Cornelia that mom is also nice to them.

"Say, let's go to Oosterbeek today. We should visit the new cemetery and pay our respects to the men who died in the battle for the bridge in Arnhem."

"What does that mean, to pay respect? What is at Oosterbeek?" chimed Evert and Arie.

Jon leaned forward putting his forearms on the table. "Remember the day we saw the parachutes coming down at Ede?"

Evert continued licking his plate but Arie and Herve' both looked up, their eyes big as they recalled that day when the sky was full of airplanes and parachutes. "Yes, dad, that is when we got the silk shirts."

"Those soldiers came from England, Australia, New Zealand and Poland." He listed these faraway places, knowing the boys had no idea where these countries were except that they flew in airplanes.

"Those men came to bring freedom and liberty to Holland. They did not know you or anyone in this country, yet they came to fight for us. Sadly they lost the battle for the bridge. Those men and boys who were killed in the battle for the bridge are buried in Oosterbeek."

"Boys? Did boys, like me, die in the battle?"

"Not boys like you but older boys, like young men. Many of them were teenagers, not old enough to marry but old and brave enough to fight wars."

"All the soldiers they found buried at the battle sites have been moved from the temporary graves in the woods, in the gardens and along the bank of the river to a new place. The people of Oosterbeek have provided a place of honor where they will have head stones and a memorial with their name."

Nieske agreed, "We should go. It is a nice sunny day, Cornelia will be fine. I will pack a lunch so we can picnic on the way home. It is the honorable thing to do; we must show our gratitude for what they did."

Chapter 79

An hour later the little family was on the way. Jon took Evert and Herve' and Nieske had baby Cornelia, while Arie rode his own bike.

In Oosterbeek they rode up *Johnnaboeveweg*. The tree covered road created an impressive canopy open at both ends with bright sunlight. Coming out of this tunnel they entered pasture lands where brown and white cows grazed peacefully next to the fence around the cemetery.

Inside this fence were majestic, old beech trees. They parked their bikes near the entrance.

The family walked into the arched entry. They pause to look at the names of the fallen inscribed on the wall in alphabetical order listed by their nationality and their rank. The graves are laid out in perfect order in this expanse of beautifully manicured grass. A white headstone marks each grave. It has either a cross or a Star of David engraved on it. At the far side of the cemetery, across from the entry, is a memorial obelisk. The monument's base is covered with wreaths, flowers and hand written notes of thanks.

It is a solemn moment.

With awe and respect they walk down the grass in the center toward the obelisk. Three men are laying a wreath of red carnations with an Easter lily in its midst.

Their voices are muted in respect, not wanting to disturb the peace of this place of rest. It is an awesome sight to see seventeen hundred fifty white headstones. When other graves are discovered the bodies will be transferred to this revered resting place.

The family stops, Jon closed his eyes to stop the moisture gathering there. Nieske too blinks her eyes as tears roll down her cheeks. The three boys gaze at them, not understanding the cause of this display of emotion. Watching mom and dad they too realize the intensity of what these graves mean.

"The words are all in English, Jon," mentions Nieske.

"Well, these all spoke English except for the Poles, Nieske."

Jon sinks to his knees in front of his sons. "We must never forget what these men did; they came and died for a people they did not know. These men are true heroes and we honor them for their sacrifice. We must pray that God will bless the families. Families that are now missing a son, a husband or a father.

"Is this like what Jesus did, dying for people he did not know?" asked Herve'.

"Yes, something like that, dying so that others may live. Only Jesus died to give eternal life; these men died so you will live in peace on earth."

"Can we pray for them, dad?"

"Sure." The family got into a small cluster holding onto each other while Jon prayed. He thanked God for these brave men and the sacrifice they made. He prayed for those who loved them that God would comfort them and heal their pain. Then he asked God that all who came here would cherish freedom and be grateful for those who paid the price for liberty.

They walked the entire cemetery, stopping to read the names and rank, but not comprehending the words written below them. Jon began counting the stones with the Star of David; Jon understood why these Jewish men had come to fight Nazism. It is an honor to die saving your people. Some graves had no name. For these the inscription read, "Known only by God."

"Ja," said Nieske, "what is better than to be known by God?"

When finished they walked somberly back to the entrance, where they met several Dutch soldiers coming in. These soldiers stood at attention and saluted the cemetery before entering.

The boys stopped and turned back to the cemetery watching these soldiers. Jon smiled when he saw Herve' and Arie stand straight as if they were standing at attention and give a salute to the graves before turning and following the family.

Chapter 80

Klaas van Bemmel stopped sending care packages when Dutch stores reopened, but he continued writing letters.

Nieske started knitting dresses again. New patterns and post war designs changed the fashion to go along with the new wool colors and other yarns, now plentiful in the market place. Nieske sold these custom designed and fitted dresses at the upscale women's shop in Ede and Utrecht. Her favorite sales were private orders from the wealthy ladies in town.

Klass' next letter was not like the previous letters. They used to be full of events in Pease and what the family was doing since Alida's arrival. She lived in Klaas van Bemmel's home for two months before she and Braam married.

They admire Alida. Klaas loved the story she and Braam told about when they raided the German camp at Utrecht. Sneaking in late at night, just before three in the morning they stole guns and grenades. The moon had gone down so it was very dark when they caught a guard snoozing.

Sjoerd had dispatched him with a quick thrust of his knife to the heart and left him there propped up against the tree where he was napping.

The armory was the brick storage building behind City Hall. There the three of them overpowered the guard when he heard them open the door but was too slow to raise an alarm. They chose the hour just before dawn when sleep or drowsiness overcomes every man.

They worked fast, taking as much as they could carry before anyone else awoke. They filled four fifty kilo grain sacks with pistols and grenades then hustled out. They kept in the shadow of the buildings until they came to the back alley where they got on their bikes onto *Kettlestraat*

The sad thing was that a few weeks later Sjoerd was killed at the raid at Jon Van Bemmel's place.

Klaas was impressed that Alida could strip, clean and

reassemble any weapon and fire it with complete calm. She was a good match for Braam.

Wow, now we hear about more escapades then we knew of; those two got into a lot of action," noted Nieske.

"They thrived on the adrenaline rush of being an *onderduiker*. I sure hope they can handle the peace and calmness or boredom of operating a store," responded Jon.

This letter was not about Braam and Alida. This letter informed Jon that Klaas is moving. They had an offer from the neighbor to buy the farm. They accepted the offer and decided to relocate to California. The plan is to live in the Bellflower-Artesia area as there was a sizable Dutch settlement there.

With Dutch farmers settling there the influx of other Dutch migrants grew, especially with immigrants and those moving from the mid-west states of Minnesota, Iowa, Illinois, South Dakota and Michigan. It was a great community with three Christian Reformed Churches and a Christian School. Klaas is going there too.

The letter closed with the suggestion that Jon consider immigrating to America. Klaas would keep him informed on what California was like and what the opportunities were.

Jon and Nieske looked at each other. Both were thinking about what she had just finished reading out loud to Jon.

"Have you thought about leaving Holland?"

"Yes, but not seriously. My thoughts are about what our boys will do; farm land is scarce and this farm will not support more than one family. So, yes the idea of moving has been on my mind."

"To America? Leave my dad and family?" moaned Nieske. "Cornelia will never get to know her grandpa."

"I do not know; my thinking has not been specific. I have thought about the Ukraine; there is lots of good farm land there and the weather is similar to here. Then South Africa sounds pretty good too now that the Boer war is over and the country is prospering again. There is good farm land there too. In California the weather is nice, they grow oranges there."

"I don't care where oranges are grown. I do not want to go

276

anywhere; I want to stay near my family. Won't you miss your brothers and sister?"

"Hey, there is no plan to go anywhere. This would not have come up if Klaas had not mentioned it. We have a lot of years to decide what to do for the boys."

"What do you mean, boys? We have a daughter, too, you know?"

"Of course, I know that; but I do not need to provide a farm or career for her. Hopefully she will marry a good farmer."

Just then Evert came in. "Oranges, did you say we have oranges?"

"No, we do not have an orange, Uncle Klaas is moving to California. They grow oranges there."

"Oh, good. Can we go too?"

"No, we are not going," snapped Nieske.

But the seed had been planted.

Chapter 81

Six months later the offer came.

"We love California, the opportunities are endless. Come and we will help you," wrote Klaas.

It is Saturday and everyone in the family has taken their weekly bath.

The galvanized tub was put away. Arie and Evert brought it to the kitchen where mom put pots of water on the stove to heat. A pile of towels are on the table along with a bar of homemade soap. This soap will remove dirt and your skin if you scrub too long. This soap is like sand paper, no dirt can withstand its onslaught.

Jon is fond of saying, "this stuff will keep you clean for a whole week; dirt is scared to death to come in contact with it."

Nieske made it from rendered beef fat and lye, she adds lavender petals to give it a hint of pleasantness; the lye eats away all grime, sweat and skin.

The kids play in the living room when mom and dad bathe. Mom bathes first and dad bathes next. Not every house has this order but Nieske told Jon he would still become clean if he bathed second. She would come out of the water dirtier if she followed him. Wisely he agrees and consents to second place.

The tub is emptied and new water put in for the kids. The oldest goes first, then Evert and lastly Herve'. Mother stays to help and to be sure they wash behind the ears, wash the hair and to add hot water when the tub cools. She rinses their hair with clean water.

Arie complains about his mother tending his bath. "I am old enough to wash myself, mom."

He is embarrassed to have his mother see him naked. He wants to be a grownup. Nieske tells him that he is too young to handle the pots with hot water. She did agree to leave when he stood up to dry himself.

After the bath they dutifully kiss their mom and dad goodnight.

"Remember your prayers and get up when I call. We do not

want to be late to church," she scolds.

Sunday might mean a special breakfast but there is no sleeping in. The chores still need to be done and church was farther away than school so it takes longer to ride into Ede than to school in Bennekom.

Finally it is quiet. Nieske pours two cups of black pekoe tea and sets a plate with four windmill shaped ginger cookies on the table. They agreed that tonight they would discuss the future and what to do with the invitation to go to America.

Jon is trying to hide the eager expression on his face while Nieske is worried and apprehensive.

Jon starts the dialogue. "That is a big gift to offer sponsorship to us; he is taking a risk on people he has not met and does not know."

"Braam must have said some nice things about us."

"It is a big deal. Getting a sponsor is difficult, lots of people are looking for sponsors and we get an offer without even asking. That makes me think it might be a God thing. If God is making this happen we need to check it out; if not I want to stay here."

"My mother was pretty wise. She said when you have decisions to make; clarity comes when you process it objectively and spiritually. We did this when we bought this farm and now we should do it again so we can see if we should sell the farm, or stay," began Jon.

For the next hour they made a list of why to emigrate and set up in a new country; writing down what the benefits would be. This included the opportunity for the boys to someday have a farm, the economy is better in California, there is a group of other immigrants, there is a Christian Reformed Church, a Christian School, the weather is always nice, the sunshine will be good for Cornelia to catch up on vitamin D and many more pluses.

The negative list included: leaving family, learning a new language and culture, would the sale bring enough money to pay the passage and get started in California. This is a concern because the Dutch government limits the amount of money taken out of the

Netherlands.

They discussed Cornelia's health issues for some time. How will going to California benefit or affect her health. She is battling the effects of Rickets, whooping cough and scarlet fever. Dr. Voorman explained the cause of Rickets being a lack of calcium, vitamin D and phosphate.

Since the diagnoses they had supplemented the breast milk with cow milk, added cod liver oil and taken her outside as much as possible for exposure to sunlight, even rainy cloudy days is better than staying indoors.

All of them, especially Herve' and Cornelia are suffering from the lack of a proper diet during the winter of hunger. Arie, Evert and Herve' have been sick off and on for months, first coming down with mumps, then measles, which were followed up with chicken pox and finally the whooping cough.

"*Rats!*" thought Jon. "That war killed thirty thousand by starvation, several hundred thousand in the extermination camps and it is not over yet."

"I think it best we go to America."

"My dad does not like the idea of us moving to America. He thinks it is a land of depravity and especially Hollywood where those provocative movies are made. He thinks it is a heathen land, especially California. He was okay with California until he discovered that Hollywood is in California," sighed Nieske.

"Heathen, evil, what is Evert Bultan talking about? These are the people who liberated us. If it was not for them we would be living under Nazism. That is evil! Sometimes I think your dad is stuck in prejudice and ignorance."

"Please, don't talk about my dad like that, he is a great man. He took great risks saving people of other faiths and cultures. To him people are souls, when they are in need he helps. It is not every one who gets honored by Israel for helping. I am proud of him and my stepmother too, although I still do not like her. It is just that he has puritan morals so he thinks all movies are satanic."

Jon knows he just stepped into a sensitive area and he needs to back up and prevent this from becoming a fight that will disrupt his happy home. He adores his wife and tries to please her as best and often as he can. He just wishes she would worry less and trust him in making plans for their future. Saying anything more about her dad is not helpful. So he changed the topic.

"I saw the certificate Israel sent. It is a real honor to be recognized and to have a grove of trees planted honoring him and others who sheltered Jews. When he dies it will be nice if you can inherit that certificate."

Nieske cooled down and agreed they should pursue immigration and to petition the Dutch government for emigration papers and apply for immigration to the United States of America. "At least we can check it out. If God has that for our future, I do not want to be in the way."

Chapter 82

Life changed rapidly at the Van Bemmel's. Letters went back and forth every two weeks. As soon as a letter is received the next one is sent with more questions.

What is the economy like? What does housing cost? What is the income to be expected from farm work, from construction? Can Nieske sell her dresses?"

"Yes, business is very easy to start, yes, the weather is always nice; no snow, no ice. Klaas mentions that if they miss snow they can go see it on the mountains.

"Mountains," thought Jon, what are mountains?"

Jon contacted the United States Justice Department's Citizenship and Immigration Service for entry. He also applied for exit visas at the State House in Den Hague. They filed form I-485 applications for immigration and legal residence with work permits for the United States.

Meanwhile Herve' started school. He is excited to learn, he already knew how to read simple phrases, He was jealous of his brothers who could read and took turns reading the Bible during supper for the family devotions.

Herve' hated to miss school and was perturbed when he had to skip a day of class to travel to Amsterdam. His first train ride was great; it was a true Kodak moment to see three boys with their noses pressed against the window, watching the countryside rolling by.

Amsterdam was awesome; they gawk at the tall buildings, the thousands of bicycles and the electric trams. Trams in the middle of the street, people running across the street between cars and the trams, it was crazy. In Ede they have only four story buildings, a windmill and high church steeples and no trams. They had seen five story buildings in Arnhem but here whole city blocks have buildings as tall as the Arnhem tower.

The next day at school the kids and the teacher asked questions about the big city and what they saw there. Herve' told about the

Small Pox vaccination.

"It is important to stop Small Pox as thirty percent of the people who get the pox die and the rest have scars and other problems the rest of their lives," he grumbled. "You will need those shots; America will not let you in without them."

This bothered Herve' as he had just become used to the idea that he would live and now this Pox thing might kill him?

At lunch break he took his lunch outside. He wanted to sit by himself and think about what he heard about Small Pox and why the vaccinations are vital to the world's health and his own well being.

He took out his sandwich of two thick slices of white bread with a thick slice of pork fat in-between. He finished that and then took out the half sandwich with berry jam. He is still hungry.

His eye looked at the apple tree on the other side of the fence. This tree is in the school master's garden right next to the fence, some branches hang over the fence. On the ground are lots of apples.

His hunger spurred him to think about those apples lying there going to waste. He knows those fallen apples probably have worms, but so what? Eat around them. He hated being hungry, his family ate everything and never wasted food; they ate wormy apples at home. You just had to be careful where you bite and do not chew until you look at the part left in your hand. Spitting out a bad piece was better than going hungry or wasting food.

He jumped over the fence.

A group of kids gather at the fence. They reach out for an apple, soon there are twenty hands reaching for an apple. Herve' put an apple into each hand. He knew to not pick from the tree but those on the ground are different. These apples are going to waste, if the School Master wanted them he would have picked them up. He picks up more apples and gave them to the stretched out hands.

Then he noticed his brother, Arie, running to the school's office. Herve' felt a creepy feeling go up his back, something is wrong. I bet he is going to tattle on me, just like he does at home.

Herve' jumped back over the fence and waited for the inevitable.

Sure enough the School Master came out of his office. Everyone ran, leaving Herve' alone. The School Master face was twisted into a scowl and anger in his eyes.

He grabbed Herve' by the arm and towed him to the office. Herve' could hardly keep up. When he was too slow the school master jerked his arm and pulled harder. Herve' stumbled and nearly fell.

He pushed Herve' into a chair, then scolded him for leaving the school grounds and stealing apples.

Herve' saw the wooden paddle on the wall; he knew what was coming next. "Grab your ankles" was the order. Herve' got up slowly, looked at the door contemplating escape. He knew better, if he did his punishment at home would be terrifying.

Three hard swats across the rump and he is outside again.

On the walk home Arie berated Herve'. "I am going to tell mom what you did. Wait till mom hears you took those apples, she is going to pull your ears and have dad beat your butt" chortled Arie.

Arie ran home and blabbed to his mother telling about the apple event and the paddling Herve' received for leaving the school grounds.

"What were you thinking? Have you no shame? You have embarrassed the whole family, again. How can I hold my head up among the parents!" she shouts. "Just wait till your father is done with the milking; he will teach you a lesson."

"But mom, they were just lying there going to waste, there was a hundred or more. I was hungry and so was everyone else. I am the only one getting beat it is not fair," he grumbled.

"You are an embarrassment. How can I go to church or face the parents or teachers, I am so ashamed of you! I am too embarrassed to go out in public and face those people."

Herve' decided he better get away from here fast as his mother was building up a head of steam in her anger at him. He ran to the barn, best tell dad before Arie or mother does.

He blurted out his confession. He explained that the apples were lying there going to waste and how hungry everyone was.

With sadness in his eyes Jon hugged his son, sorry that hunger is such a painful memory. He is also sorry that these apples were wasted by the School Master. No spanking that night, in spite of his mother's anger. His dad understood. His father was the only person to ask if he picked any of the good fruit off the tree.

Chapter 83

It is Saturday and Herve's turn to go with his father. Herve' loves to listen in when men talk man stuff like world events and religion.

The Dutch are a headstrong people and love a good debate. Voices become loud and intense as the debate rages. For most of them it is an opportunity to express their thoughts without their wives interfering and without creating divisions.

When the time for discussion is over they will still be friends. Religion may be the exception, especially with hard core Calvinists, who at times are less tolerant.

These discussions occur at the mill where Jon brings his grains. Sometimes they drift over to coffee shops or beer gardens. The mill is the safe place as no self respecting Calvinist goes to a beer garden. The miller joins his clients to keep the conversation under control.

When bored Herve' will go watch the workers. He is fascinated with how they move the grain sacks up to the grinding floor. The pulley system and the huge grinding stones intrigue his young mind. He is fascinated by how the grain kernels are turned into dust. All are powered by the wind, which Holland has plenty of.

Herve' loves watching the men's muscles flex and bulge as they lift the fifty kilo sacks of grain off the wagon or onto to the stones. After milling, they lower the flour down on a pully system to storage or onto wagons.

Sometimes Hans, one of the laborers, will take him out on the outside platform to watch him adjust the sails on the vanes. One day, when there was only a slight breeze, Hans showed Herve' how to climb the vane and untie the sail cloth so they would have more power. From that height he viewed all of Ede, the train depot, the houses and the woods. Beyond those trees he saw the field where the paratroopers landed for the battle at Arnhem.

These conversations are different from the group discussion that takes place in the living room. There the men smoke cigars or pipes and sit to one side of the room while the women sit on the other side. The men talk religion, war and work, while the ladies talk about children, dresses and recipes. Although they always keep an ear tuned to what the other group is saying, they only interrupt and comment when they wanted to clarify something. It is mostly the women who interrupted the men's conversation as the men do not give a fig about dresses or recipes.

Chapter 84

Four men are sitting on piles of grain sacks or stools. Nobody smokes inside the mill because the grain dust is highly combustible. Only snuff and chewing tobacco are allowed inside the mill.

Today's topics began with the visiting preacher, Reverend A. J. Wiersink. He is filling in while the church is looking for a full time pastor. Their pastor retired after being in Ede twenty three years.

"That guy is the most long-winded preacher I ever heard," moaned Jon

"He is a tough old coot, alright. He loves to hear himself talk," said Peiter, who is interrupted by Henk.

"He repeats himself all the time; he could easily cut his two hour sermons in half if he just said it once."

"Yeah, and his long prayer is really long and boring. He doesn't know anyone in this church and still finds enough things to talk about to make most of us fall asleep."

"Does your wife pinch you when you fall asleep, like mine does?" asked Jon.

They all laughed knowing that this was what wives do. It was the wife's spiritual duty to keep husbands and kids awake and not embarrass the family.

Herve' loved hearing this grown up talk and knows to never interrupt or they will change topics or how they phrase things. Long sermons and long prayers are why mothers carry a roll of peppermints to church. King Peppermints were the most common as they were cheaper than Wilhelmina's; both were hard candies that dissolve slowly, hopefully to last till the next boring period. Mothers hand out one peppermint to each family member for every point of the sermon and often one prior to the long prayer.

Reverend Wiersink's prayer is a master piece of poetry and prose. He started with quotes from the Bible praising God, and then moved to the greatness of the Sabbath, then going on about the beauty of the day. From there he mentions every ache and pain or death that could possibly be tormenting those sitting in the pews.

(By now Herve's rear was tormented.) Then like catching a second breath for a runner Wiersink launches into teaching some pet peeves. He uses the piety of prayer to convince the audience to comply with how he wants them to live. He thinks farmers and workers have as much time to read and pray as a pastor has. He expects them to start the day with a whole hour of prayer.

"I never did get what his point was; he said he had three parts but he lost me somewhere when he described what happened to Jonah."

"I do love how descriptive he was but it did go on and on. He had some interesting words about what it could be like to be inside a great fish or a whale and what Jonah looked like when the fish coughed him up onto the shore, with seaweed hanging on his shoulders and dead fish hanging out of his pockets."

Henk picked it up from there, laughing, "What would you do when you see a guy walk into town covered with kelp and other things from the fish's belly telling you to repent? That would freak me out. I would repent of everything I ever did, or said, and whatever else I could think of."

"Never to sin again," adds Henk.

"Sure, but his message was good, about not running away from God. That it is best to do what God says when he says it. God has a way of changing lives and hearts for their own good" adds Jon.

"You are right, Jon. If he would condense the message we all would have gotten it. The way it was he went on and when he got to the end he did not know how to stop. So he halts and says, 'What more can I say?' I wanted to shout, 'Just say amen, Dominee."

"That is what he finally did say, Amen."

"Talk about Friesians all you like, but those guys have guts and did a lot for the Resistance during the war," reminded Jon.

Herve' is proud of his dad; he always seemed to stay level headed during these discussions.

"Talk about war, have you noticed that church attendance is down since the war is over?" asked Pieter.

"You talking about me?" asked the miller. "Why should I go to church? Everything is going well, business is good, we are safe, things are pretty much back to normal, I do not need God anymore. I can handle it from here."

"So you expect God to be there for you whenever you need him? What about maintaining the relationship out of gratitude? Asks Jon.

"He saw us through the war, kept me from starving during the 'Dutch Winter' and kept me and my family safe. Now what I am I supposed to do, kiss up to him forever?"

"No, nothing like that; let me explain what it means to me. Sure God protected me during the war, but a relationship with him is bigger than that. It is waking up every morning knowing that God Almighty cares about me; he is with me everywhere I go. He provides for me daily and best of all he has paid for everything I ever did that was wrong or will do wrong in the future. That means he has guaranteed me a future in heaven. When he comes back he will remove all evil. He will throw Satan into hell and purify the earth. Now that is a God whom I can respect, love and walk with every day."

The place is silent as they think about what Jon said. The miller thought for a moment and responded first. "That's only true if one believes there is such a place as heaven and a place called hell."

"Of course, you are correct on that. Just remember that believing or not believing there is a heaven and a hell does not change the reality."

"Think about this. Why would Jesus leave heaven, come to earth, teach about heaven and hell and then die to atone for sin if there is no heaven or hell?"

Chapter 85

"We have a buyer for the farm, Nieske!" exclaimed Jon happily. "Boer Lambertus, who sold us the farm, wants to buy it for his son who is graduating from the agricultural school in *Wagenigen* in May."

Two weeks before Christmas the deal is consummated. Herr Lambertus came with his wife, his son and the son's fiancé to wrap up the details. Jaap Lambertus wants the horses, wagons and implements; the plow, harrow and cultivator.

"I will buy half your cows, all the sows and the chickens, if the price is right," said Jaap.

The bartering begins. The women are not part of this; they go into the house for tea while the men lit cigars or pipes and commenced dickering.

"You need to buy all the cows or none of them."

"I do not need all of them. I just want the top six milk producers."

"That means I will need to sell the remainder at auction and everyone will know the best cows are gone, the bids will be very low, it is better for me to sell all at auction."

They agreed that Jon would sell Jaap the two cows of his choice and he could bid at auction for the others he wants. They struck a deal on the pigs, chickens and horses.

"Come, let's join the ladies for tea and a shot of *Jenever* (Dutch gin) to seal the deal. I have a new bottle of Bokma."

The Saturday after New Year's is auction day. Farmers and onlookers came to the festive event. Everyone is in a good mood. The five days of Christmas and two days of New Year celebration left everyone happy and over fed.

Chapter 86

The next day was a peaceful day on the farm. Jon and Nieske relaxed with their morning coffee. Jon noticed a head pass by the window.

He waited a moment before going to see who is there. Standing there with his knuckles up ready to knock is a man. The man looks familiar but Jon cannot place him or remember the name.

Offering a hand for a shake the man smiled and introduced himself, "Remember me? I am Ben, Ben Driesen. You transported me to safety."

"*Ja, ja*, I see it now. What brings you here? Come in we are having coffee," Jon swings the door open inviting him in.

Nieske poured Ben a cup of coffee and offered him a slice of pound cake. She was not excited about meeting this man who endangered her husband.

Ben took a big swallow and began his story. "I made it safely to France, then England and from there to Tel Aviv, Palestine. I have lived there for the past year and am now on my way to America."

"Are you going by yourself, or is family traveling with you?"

"Let me get to that part later. I came back to Holland on my way to New York to find the people who helped me. I came to personally thank each one for their bravery and compassion in saving me."

Looking directly at Nieske, he continued, "A special thanks to you, *Juffrouw* Van Bemmell, for your sacrifice and courage in letting *Heer* Van Bemmel transport me. I know those hours of him being gone were anxious hours. So thank you."

"We are both happy to have been part of helping you and are so very pleased that you are doing well and took time to find us. God protected us and you too. Is your wife or family traveling with you?"

Ben looked them in the eye and bowed his head as tears formed in his eyes. "No, I am all alone. Part of my reason to come back was to find family. All of my family is gone; my father, mother, uncles, aunts, cousins and my wife and daughter all perished. My mother died on the train ride, the others died at various camps. I only have one aunt left, she lives in New York. She sponsored me to go to America, but she too died, just last week."

"As for God, you may believe in him if you need, but not me. I am done with religion. I think God is a figment of man's creation to find something bigger than ourselves to look to for help. There is no such thing as God who created or loves the world. "

"You do not really accept the idea that there is no God, do you?"

"Hell yes, I do. Oops, sorry for cussing. If there is a god, why would I trust him or love him when he brought Hitler, Stalin and others like them into power. Look at all the evil and suffering in the world, look at me, I am all alone. Does God exist? Bah!

Jon was stunned at these words and feelings. "Ben, it was not God who did this. It is Satan; in his hatred for God, Satan blames God for the evil and suffering he (Satan) brings. That is the core reason Jesus came, to undo the evil hold Satan has on the earth."

Nieske rose from her chair, went to Ben and hugged him, crying with him over his loss and his pain. Alone, all alone in the world, she gave him their address in California. "Stay in touch," she ordered.

Chapter 87

The bidding started. The auctioneer called a price for each item as it comes up for sale. He explains the reason for his starting price, extolling the value. From the stated price he slowly descends the amount until someone shouts "*yup.*"

In three hours everything was sold. The buyers wished the Van Bemmels traveling mercies and blessings on their venture.

After everyone left the auctioneer and Mr. Kammerling, the banker, reconciled the proceeds with the expenses. The bank loans are paid off and Jon received a deposit receipt for the balance.

It is a sad day for the boys as they played on the hay for the last time. They climbed every tree just to remember the good times. Tomorrow they will go stay with Grandpa Bultan, for a week, untill it is time to board ship.

That evening Nieske used her sewing machine for the last time. With great care she cut the stitches in the inside of Jon's winter coat. It is the one he will wear onboard ship. Under the lining she inserted a packet of Guilders and sewed them in place.

The government prohibits taking Dutch currency to other countries. The extra eight hundred guilders she sewed into the coat will help them get started in California.

January 30 is coming soon; the tension is thick enough to cut with a knife. There are so many goodbyes to say. Every day is spent riding to see relatives, people Herve' has only heard of.

By the end of the week Herve' imagined that they have been to every village and town in Gelderland. He is glad to be done with all the kisses and tears.

Nieske was sad and wept but Jon was exhilarated and eager to go.

"We will never see them again," wept Nieske.

"We will make new friends, people we chose to be with, not people we are stuck with just because they are family."

"You never did like my family, did you?"

"Of course I like your family; it is you who doesn't like your step mother."

That was the closest they had ever come to a fight. It was the start of an anxious night. It was not the first disagreement between them but Herve' was worried because this time his mother cried a long time. When she stops talking he knows she is really upset or angry. When he broke a vase that was a wedding gift she did not talk to him for three days.

"When we get settled and make some money we will take the family back to see Holland," Jon offered.

"Sure, when will that be, twenty years?" She snorted, forgetting she had determined to not talk to him.

"If it takes too long then at least you can go see your father and family. I promise. We can use the cash we are leaving in Holland."

The next day the postman delivered the expected letter. It is from Uncle Klaas. Actually there were two letters as one envelope could not hold all the information he sent.

The envelopes contained pages with notes to use on the journey. One side of each note was written in English and the other in Dutch. Nieske put them in her purse.

The notes said things like. "I need to go to the train station, I need tickets to Fullerton, California, where is the bathroom, how much does that cost? Notes covering most of the situations they might encounter or need after arriving in America.

Jon smiled with confidence, reassured that he can manage the journey to their new home.

"California here we come!" he beamed.

Chapter 88

The family checked into their first ever hotel. It was their last night in Holland. The hotel in *Voorburg* had beds with mattresses and springs instead of ticks. The boys found that you could bounce on these beds; they jumped and laughed until Nieske scolded them to knock it off. Boarding time was ten o'clock the next morning, plenty of time to have breakfast and still clear customs.

That evening Jon and Nieske's brothers and sisters came to bid bon voyage. The group tarried in the dining room following the Dutch custom of having the restaurant's table for the evening. They ate fish and ham along with an array of carrots, peas and two types of potatoes. This was another first as the boys had never eaten French fries, *frietjes*. Jon's brother ate and left. He did not pay, leave a tip or say thanks; just snuck out the side door.

Jon served several bottles of wine and a box of chocolates to enjoy while they talked of old times, of survival and hopes, of joys while playing as children when life was innocent. Behind each smiling face was the reality that this was the last time they would be together and likely the last time they would visit in person.

Promises were made to write letters faithfully. Yes, we will send photographs of America; yes we will send photos of our new house and of an orange tree. This was a blessing they were all proud of; none had ever seen oranges growing on trees. Wow! That must be like living in paradise.

By ten o'clock they all left for home; no one wept because showing that much emotion was not acceptable. However there was not a dry eye among them. Quick wipes with a handkerchief wiped away the sorrow. After a kiss on each cheek they left the dining room. They waved good bye as they pedaled away.

Jon and Nieske went upstairs to their room; it was the last night in Holland. The chocolates were gone but they had a glass of wine to finish after reading the Bible and saying their evening prayers.

Nieske wanted to read Psalm 86, so Jon started with verse one.

"*Incline your ear, O Lord and answer me; do preserve my soul, for I am a godly man; O my God save me for I trust in you, be gracious to me for I cry all day long.*"

Jon stopped there; this was a sad and sorrowful psalm. He wanted to read a psalm of hope and assurance. So he turned to Psalm 23. "*The Lord is my Sheppard, I shall not want.*" *And it ended with,* "*Surely goodness and loving-kindness will follow me all the days of my life and I will dwell in the house of the Lord forever.*"

Nieske smiled, "That is good. I really needed that. I am really happy it is California and not the Transvaal of South Africa."

Too tired to finish the wine they got into bed and slept, dreaming of mountains and orange trees, which they had never seen. Three hundred feet above sea level is as high as they had ever been.

Chapter 89

January 1947

By nine o'clock the family was standing before the Customs inspector.

"Where are you going in America?"

"We are going to California, on the other side of America. My cousin is there."

"What are you going to do there? Are there other immigrants there?"

"I will work for a dairyman until we can buy our own farm."

"Going to work a long time unless you are smuggling money with you," he glared at Jon.

Fear gripped Nieske as she wondered what the agent knew or was he fishing. She bent down to pick up Cornelia to hide the in her eyes. Would Jon be arrested if they found the money? Or would they just take it?

Then she heard Jon say, "My cousin will help us. We will be partners for a few years."

"Ah, that is good. Please take off your coat."

"Sure", replied Jon as he nonchalantly shrugged off the coat.

The agent then stepped up and frisked Jon's waist and his legs, making a slow check of his ankles to see if anything was anything inside the socks. "Just checking for a money belt or hidden cash," he explained.

He looked up, nodded his head in the direction of the doorway, "You are clear to go, safe journey."

If he had listened closely he would have heard the loud thumping of Jon's heart.

Heer and *Juffrouw* Stephanus and *Juffrouw* Schneisthorst were waiting for them when they exited. They lived in Rotterdam and came to say goodbye and once more express gratitude for aiding them during the Winter of Hunger. Mrs. Stephanus brought a bouquet of tulips.

"Your last gift from Holland should remind you of the beauty and is a token of the good you did for us," and she wept.

Lots of hugs, kisses and well wishes along with the promise to write. This promise Mrs. Stephanus kept for thirty five years, sending her last letter two weeks before she died at age eighty three.

When the ship's horn sounded they broke off and hurried on board. Passports and papers were checked once more as they stepped on board.

No turning back; going to America!

Chapter 90

Everyone is on board. Lunch is being served on each deck. The first class tourists and wealthier immigrants are on the upper deck. The lower decks are for immigrants in steerage or low cost cabins. Each deck has a dining hall. Immigrant families do not mingle with tourist and travelers in first class. During the meals announcements are made for activities of the day, events on ship and news of Holland and the United States. The first announcement was that departure was delayed due to malfunction of a propeller.

The people out on deck wished they could get off and spend time just a few more minutes with the friends who have stayed on the dock to watch the ship sail away. Hundreds of well-wishers have braved the damp chilly breeze to wave goodbye one last time.

The people on the rails went to their cabins or the lounge. A band began to play, attempting to bring some cheer to a group of melancholy passengers.

The bar opened, providing cheer juice; be it beer, schnapps, wine or *Jenever*. The passengers mingled and got to know each other. The drinks accomplished what the Captain wanted. The bar filled with laughter and the buzz of conversation. The band struck up a polka that brought several couples onto the dance floor.

Nieske grabbed Jon and the kids. "Come, we do not need this ungodly stuff," she muttered. "Besides, it is near bed time."

Several families leave the lounge. This group gathered in the hallway and introduced themselves. They discovered that they are members of the Protestant Reformed or Christian Reformed Church.

"We are not liberal or permissive as some of those people in there who claim to be Christian but act like this ungodly dancing is permissible," states one dour old man.

~~~

Herve' woke up when the ship began moving. He poked his brothers and gets them up on deck.

They put on their clothes, added a sweater and snuck out the door, careful to not waken Cornelia or their mother. They share a cabin while their dad sleeps in the cabin next door with a man who is traveling alone.

They ran up to the deck arriving panting and out of breath. Two tug boats are pushing the Veendam from the dock. In awe they watched the ship glide out to the open sea. Leaving the city lights behind as they sailed into the Atlantic, it was one-thirty in the morning. The boys were alone at the railing. Three boys filled with awe and adventure.

The ship shuddered when the engines powered up and the propellers engaged. They are on the way.

After breakfast the steward gave safety instructions. He demonstrated how to put on a life vest and gave directions on using life boats.

The final word shocked them. "As we sail between here and England there is a possibility of encountering a mine. Germany laid thousands of mines during the embargo and not all of these mines have been recovered. It has been months since the last one so we think we are safe."

There were gasps and expressions of great fear at every table. "It has been three years and now we may become a casualty of war?" moaned Nieske.

The steward assured them all would be fine. But then he ruined his calming speech with the instruction, "should you hear a loud boom, do not panic, just calmly come on deck. If there is serious damage the life boats will be deployed in plenty of time and the captain will send out the call for help."

One lady began to cry. Children looked for assurance from their mom or dad. They thought death was behind them, would a mine sink them at sea?

A man strode to the podium. He is short with dark receding hair and walks with purpose in his steps. He reached for the microphone, which the steward handed over.

"I am Reverend Vander Zwaag, I am, like you, going to America for a future. I am confident that since God has sent us He will not allow disaster to overcome us on this journey. I rest on his promises; please join me in trusting His goodness."

All eyes turned to him and a hush falls on the room.

"We will pray together for safety and confidence in Almighty God. Before that I will read you God's word to you as found in Psalm 91."

He began reading, *"He who dwells in the shelter of the Most High will abide in the shadow of the Almighty. I will say to the Lord, 'my refuge and my fortress, my God in whom I trust.' For it is he who delivers you, he will cover you with his pinions and under his wings you may seek refuge; his faithfulness is a shield and a bulwark. You will not be afraid of the terror by night or of the arrow that flies by day."*

Then he led them in a prayer asking for safety and telling God they trusted in Him.

In mid afternoon they anchored off shore near Hampton, England. The Van Bemmels stand at the railing watching as a boat comes out to them. It closed in so the sailors lashed the two ships together with thick ropes.

A rope ladder is draped over the side of the Veendam and people climb up and boarded. Eighty six new passengers came on board. Now the ship has four hundred seventy six passengers, plus the crew. That is a lot of souls, bobbing on the sea.

They set off on the beautiful blue green waters to their new home. The clouds cleared away to create nice warm sun, a rare day in January on the north Atlantic.

Chapter 91

A soft wind from the north-east made the next day feel like a pleasure cruise. A great day to stroll on the decks, grab a lounge chair to read, relax or visit with a fellow traveler.

The pleasantness of the day was the calm before the storm. The breeze became a light wind; the sun disappeared behind a wall of clouds. The sky darkened long before the sun set and the wind became strong. Those who needed to be on deck leaned into the wind; the sea became choppy with white caps. By nighttime Jon and Herve' were bent over the railing feeding fish. The waves became bigger, the sea became very rough. The sky was totally dark, hiding the setting sun. Most of the passengers became sea sick. Going to bed lying flat on your backs was the only hope for preventing dry heaves.

Those who went to the dining hall heard the announcement about the monster storm they were headed into.

"Going to encounter?" grunted Jon, "What then is this raging wind called?

"We are going to redirect our route. The eye of the storm is heading in the exact direction we are going. Therefore, we will tack north-west to skirt the worst of it. Unfortunately this will add a day or two to our journey."

Jon reported this turn of events to his brood. Nieske was very unhappy. "I hate this ship, I hate being cramped in this small space, I hate having my room full of people all the time and I hate feeling like a cork on the sea!" She almost uttered an expletive but bit her tongue.

It got worse. The next day she was sick and vomited like the rest of the family. The crew was busy mopping up the rooms and halls. The waves crashed over the decks. No one was allowed on deck for fear of being washed overboard. Most passengers stayed in their cabins, prone on their beds, fervently praying. Groans and moans accompanied the groans and creaks of the ship.

The winds became a fierce gale blowing the rain and

sometimes hail against the ship as the ship plowed through the waves. The ship's progress diminished to fifty miles a day and even less on the fourth day of this monster storm.

The van Bemmels stayed in their cabin, lying on the bunks listening to the noise the storm created as ropes, chains and life rings bang against the walls.

The crew lashed everything to the walls. All the tables, chairs, game sets, anything that could move was tied down. Netting was strung along the railings to keep the crew from being washed overboard. By the eighth day of the seven day voyage they were not half way. The sleet is driven horizontal by the fierce wind. No one is on deck. Everyone is too sick to walk or afraid of being washed overboard. The relentless winds howl through the night, no one slept. Even the crew is afraid.

One more day and the sea began to calm. The netting was taken down. The dining room is opened, but few come to eat. The storm moved on, leaving the sea with huge swales and deep troughs. No crashing, cresting waves but swells that lift the boat high and then drop down into the trough only to rise up the other side. Ice hung from the rails and covered the decks. Only crew members ventured out.

Finally the sun broke through. The ice melted. The swells still lifted the ship onto the peaks and dropped it into deep troughs; the kids love it. Evert and Herve' are feeling better.They race from the stern to the bow trying to reach the bow before it rises, then turn around to race to the stern getting there before rising on the next swale. They ran until they gasped for breath, happy to be outside. Panting they leaned on the railing, they looked west, hoping to see land. But America is still hundreds of miles away.

Those standing at the bow gasped in fright. The next sound was the ship's engines shut down. The silence is deafening. For a moment the ship bobbed up and down before the engines reversed and turned to the left.

Two swales ahead, maybe two hundred feet, was a huge iceberg. The blue white ice glistened in the sun. The pilot spotted it at the same time as those on deck. Fear gripped everyone as they stared into the same fate that sank the Titanic in 1912.

The ship veered leeward and slowly moved away from the ice berg. Fear became relief.

Skirting the eye of the storm brought the Veendam into treacherous seas. Many passengers stay at the railing looking for icebergs until it is too dark to see. The ship turned south/west to safer and warmer water.

Good news was announced at dinner, one more day before they will see land. Cape Race will be visible when they sail past Newfoundland. A warning is attached to the good news; another storm, although smaller will bring wind and snow as they pass Cape Race.

After a calm night the Van Bemmel family wakes at six a.m. refreshed and healthy. The sun is bright, the air is cold. It is thirty eight degrees and predicted to drop below freezing. The sky to the west was dark and ominous; they will soon be sailing into a storm. When the flash of lightening broke the darkness Jon took his family down to the dining hall.

The breakfast menu has changed. The boiled eggs, deli meats, chocolate, yogurt and cheese have been replaced with American foods. The bread is the same, except for the raisin rolls but the eggs are scrambled, the bacon is fried and there is cold cereal; Cheerios and Corn Flakes.

Nieske grumbled about the food but the boys are happy with the change and eat some of everything. Herve' loved the Cheerios with half and half milk and all the sugar he wants. America is going to be good.

Chapter 92

Light snow fell but the sea was calm. Cape Race was history, New York was next!

It will be their last Saturday at sea. Sixteen Jews gathered for worship in the dining hall. Several have tattooed numbers on their wrist or forearms; living proof of socialist's depravity. The others survived by hiding with sympathizers; now they will reunite with what is left of their family. This remnant has left or hopes to leave the horrors and memories of Europe. They have traded horror for hope and fear for freedom.

Their bodies have recovered from the camps but the effects of terror and pain was etched into their eyes and souls forever. Wary and fearful they stayed close together, they want to never be separated again. All have lost spouses, uncles, aunts or children, killed in this holocaust.

America has offered hope. They leave behind the ghosts of fear and memories of being hunted as prey. The pain in their eyes and hearts will dissipate. They will bury the awful memories but they can never be forgotten.

They invited Reverend Vander Zwaag to the first part of the service. He prayed that the God of Peace will bring them restoration and peace in a new land and that their future will be prosperous. The Rabbi, Isaac Gouldwasser, thanked him for representing those who had saved them from destruction. Saying, "We worship the same God and it was the Christians who stood up and stepped up to be saviors for the Jews. We thank you."

That evening the dining hall served an American supper of creamed corn, peas, carrots with mashed potatoes and beef roast with gravy.

"That food is almost like Dutch food," says Nieske. "But why they serve lettuce before the meal. Why do they even eat rabbit food? Raw too, who eats raw greens? And what is with eating maize? Is this what Americans eat, rabbit and pig food?"

"They do not cook as well as you dear," replied Jon. "I wonder if all Americans eat what we use as animal feeds. I will plant a garden with kale, beets and turnips, Brussels sprouts and rutabagas for you."

"The kids do not seem to care; it is best that we get used to the new ways. We are not just going to America; we are going to become American."

"Yes, we are, aren't we," and she smiled up at Jon. She is proud of this man who has the foresight to seek a better place for her and her brood.

This voyage may have been rough but that will soon be over. Tomorrow is Sunday and the next day they should be in the New York harbor.

Chapter 93

Church was a joyous celebration that last Sunday morning. Reverend Vander Zwaag recalled the perils of the voyage and how God protected them during the war and on this journey. Herve' said, "God heard my prayer, dad."

"Ja, boy, that he did" And he patted this son on the head. Herve' might be a handful for his mother but the lad was insightful.

The pastor read Psalm one hundred three. *"Bless the Lord, O my soul: and all that is within me bless his holy name. Bless the Lord, O my soul and forget none of His benefits. Who pardons your sins and heals your diseases. Who redeems your life and crowns you with loving-kindness."* And he continued a little farther with, *"Just as a father has compassion on his children so the Lord has compassion on those who fear him."*

He reminded them that they are only a day from their destination. It is time to be grateful and to thank the Lord for being there during those dark hours. He recalled when despair filled their hearts and encompassed their minds like the mist of the morning sea.

Tomorrow they will see the lights of their new Fatherland. The troubles and fears at sea will be a fading memory

All the people rejoiced, they broke out huge smiles and said, "Amen!"

Chapter 94

As the sun sank away into the horizon so did their hope of seeing land. Just after the sun dipped out of sight the last rays revealed silhouettes of sky scrapers. They stood like sentries guarding the horizon. As the sun light disappeared and darkness settled in new lights appear; millions of lights in the skyscrapers' windows and ferries.

The rails were lined with passengers looking west, watching these lights. For hours they kept watch, anxious to see land. Not just any land, this is going to be home, a new start in life and a great relief after fourteen days at sea.

The watchers cheered when they saw America. The cheer brought more passengers up on deck. Excitement surged as an electric charge. Many jumped in joy as the sky line revealed the city. Cameras clicked as they captured this sight, buildings that reached into the night sky.

Finally the crowd thinned as one by one the families returned to their cabins. With nervous excitement they cleaned their cabin and packed their bags. At peace with the world they slept confidant of the future.

The sky was dark, only a few stars peeked through the clouds. The dark water of the Atlantic was broken up only by the ice floes and the shimmering lights reflected across the water. This was fitting, the past darkness behind and the bright lights of the future before them.

The family stood in awe gaping at the awesome sights. Ferries sailed across the harbor; ships already docked have lights on the decks for loading or unloading.

In the center of the panorama was a statue of a woman dressed in a flowing robe. Her arm held high as she reached to the heavens. But she is not reaching to grasp the heavens, instead in her hand is a huge lantern; a lantern whose light gave direction to those seeking a new home.

"That is The Statue of Liberty; it is there to welcome

immigrants, like us, to a land of freedom." Jon pulled the boys close.

Herve' looked up at his father and watched the tears glistening on his cheeks. Tears of joy and hope, so Herve' cried too.

Herve' stayed a long time, ignoring his mother and father's call to come eat and get ready for bed. He grasped the rail tightly as he stared at the wonder before him. This was his new home. A home where there is plenty to eat, where there is sunshine more days than clouds and rain, a home where oranges grew. His heart swelled with hope and happiness. A home where he will no longer be afraid, no longer experience hunger.

America, America, as the name rang in his mind hope shone bright.

"Tomorrow I will be there," he thought as he is went to his cabin to sleep, sleep that will not come for a long time!

Herve' looked over his shoulder, taking one more look at this statue, he whispers, "I love you."

Chapter 95

At dawn the ship's deck was crowded with Dutchmen anxious to see New York. They glide past the Statue of Liberty and dock at Ellis Island.

The bags are packed and set by the door. The items in the hold will be shipped by freight to arrive at a later date.

Voices changed from hushed whispers to gasps. Excitement is in the air. Tug boats guided the Veendam past the Statue of Liberty to dock at Ellis Island. Her size and grandeur was stunning now that they are up close. Looking up, Herve' became giddy with happiness.

When the ship was tied off Jon and Nieske went down for the luggage, each boy carried one and dad and mom carried two.

The family waited their turn to disembark. They are in Steerage Class, thus the last in line. Nieske lifted Cornelia so she could see the city and watch the boats.

The immigrant's faces reflected a heavy dose of anxiety mixed with eager anticipation. Nieske was very nervous. Last night the family gathered at bedside to pray. Jon thanked God for save travel and made an earnest request that God would bless their new lives and new country.

It was the first time they had prayed for America.

Nieske reminded Jon, "Pray for the train trip too, Jon. We are not there yet. It would sure be nice if we could speak English."

The boys wiggled and jumped, anxious to get off the boat. They were ready for the next adventure. Herve' was besides himself with excitement, "Come on, let's go," he tugged at his dad's hand whenever the line moved a little bit.

"Do you have all the papers, Jon?"

"*Ja*, I have the passports, green cards and Dutch documents, we should be good."

On his knees, Jon looked his boys in the eye. "Do not say anything. When you are asked a question you must wait for me to say it is okay to reply." Then sternly, "Do not volunteer anything, you hear me?"

He had gone over the protocol of what would likely happen when they processed through Immigration and Customs. The health records would be checked and they would need to show the vaccination scars of the Small Pox. They might be asked to open their mouths and say "aah" by the health inspector. They might even be subject to body searches. But that would only happen if they were suspected of smuggling; he was not worried about that.

In a small cluster the family walks up to the Immigration Officer. They are not last but nearly so. The officer looked tired. He looked at the family, and then reached out for the passports and documents.

He checked each document, compared the faces to the photos smiled and handed them back. Only then did the young lady standing behind him speak.

"Welcome to America, you may take your bags and proceed to that counter for Customs," spoken in Dutch. She pointed to the row of Customs' officers.

The Customs officers also spoke Dutch. They selected Evert's bag to open and search. While one rummaged through the underwear, socks and change of clothing the other watched the faces of those waiting.

Jon figured that these men were experts at spotting nervous tics and could spot those who might be guilty of breaking the law. They have profiled thousands of immigrants and know what to look for. Jon smiled to himself, he had been interrogated by Germans who could take his life; compared to that this is a cake walk.

They opened Nieske's bag next. She blushed and became flustered when they went through her under garments. No one ever saw them except Jon. At home she had washed them in the evening or when the kids were in bed or at school and then dried them in her bedroom. Now these strange men were mauling them. She determined to wash them as soon as possible and certainly before she wore them again.

Jon asked them how to get to the train station, realizing this was the last time he would be able to ask a question in Dutch.

Chapter 96

They took the ferry and found a line of cabs.

Jon handed the top slip of paper to the cabbie. He read the note, "Train Station to California, please."

The cabbie nodded and loaded the bags into the trunk. He smiled to himself. He knew he could get a few extra dollars by taking a circuitous route, "This yokel will never know," he muttered to himself.

Jon used dollars for the first time when he paid the fare posted on the meter. The cabbie held out his hand for a tip, but Jon had counted blocks during the ride, Jon knew they had gone on scenic tour to benefit the cab.

"No," he said, shaking his finger.

"I may be new in this country but I am not stupid."

A porter met them as they entered the station. He was tall and slender with a big smile, he was also very black.

The boys slid behind their dad, not sure what to make of this. The only black person they had ever seen was Black Pete who came at *Sinterklaas* and they knew his face was covered with coal. This man did not look like he had coal on his face; his skin was black for real.

Jon showed him his next note, "I need a train to Fullerton, California."

"Come with me," he motioned for them to follow him. At the counter the porter said, "This fine family wants to go to California; imagine wanting to be in sunshine instead of this cold snowy place."

He stepped aside while Jon paid for the tickets, and then loaded the bags on his cart.

Tickets in hand, they followed the porter to a bench along the tracks. Pointing to his watch the porter indicated two hours then pointed at to four o'clock.

The family sat and watched trains come and go. At ten before four the porter came back. When the correct train stopped he motioned for them to come.

He loaded the suitcases into the luggage compartment and helped with the bags they carried on.

Jon brought out three dollars which he proffered to the porter. The porter smiled, showing off his bright white teeth, he took two dollars and motioned for Jon to keep the other one. Two dollars was the biggest tip he would get today. His wages were five dollars a day; he could not take more without feeling guilty for cheating a new immigrant.

Smiling, Jon reached out and shook the black man's hand. It is the first time he touched a black person. He had heard about Negroes; read about Negroes, he had even considered moving to South Africa. This was the first time to interact with a real person of color.

Settling into their seats Nieske looked at Jon. "He was really a nice man; were you afraid?"

"No, I was not afraid; it was written on his face that he is a great man. A man who helps others, and honest too, taking only two dollars." Then he added, "Not like that cabbie who tried to steal from us."

"Yeah, and he was a white guy! But not Dutch."

Looking patiently at his dear but naïve wife, Jon replied. "Not all Dutch are honest either; I hope that most Americans are honest, too."

Herve' watched all these things. It was a great introduction to race relationships.

"I am going to love America," he thought.

Chapter 97

February is cold in New York with far more snow than Holland. But spirits were high; in two more days they will be in California where it is warm. Palm trees and oranges grow there. The family snuggled in the warm train.

Noses are glued to windows; they are on the way to Chicago. Chicago, another new name, and a city they never heard of.

Herve' kept watch out the window thinking about America. As they pass from the city into the suburbs and then the country he saw how much snow there is. Snow piled high along the tracks, covered bushes and cars. "Wow, it is over a meter deep."

Nieske sat back, took out her yarn and needles and started to knit.

"Mittens, I am making mittens for the boys, they will need new ones," she said in response to Jon's question.

"It does not snow in California, or at least not in the part we are going to."

"If it snows somewhere in California it will be cold enough to need mittens."

"I think it snows in mountains, and they must be far away from where we are going because there are orange trees and they need sunshine."

"What are these mountains, honey, are they rocks or high mounds of dirt? What makes a mountain," asked Evert and Arie in unison?

"We flatlanders have no idea what a mountain is. We just know canals and dikes. Klaas says we will see lots of mountains from the train before we get to California."

Herve' listened to his parents talking and soaked it all in, contemplating the new things he will see and learn. His heart raced as his excitement grew. The future was going to be great!

When darkness settled in Nieske opened her bag. She doled out food she gathered while on ship. Jon called it scavenged food.

"Why not," asked Nieske as she rationalized her frugal and

Calvinistic ethic? "We were sick a long time and did not eat, what I saved is far less than what we skipped in meals."

They each had a raisin bun with cheese, and an apple. "Enjoy this cheese it will soon be gone and you will wish you had some good Gouda on your bread."

In the morning they are still in snow, not as deep but vast stretches of snow. They are passing through farm lands, no forests here, but snow as far as they can see. Farms covered with snow, beautiful white rolling land. Only fence posts protrude from the untouched snow. The further west they go the houses are great distances apart and towns are even farther apart. Not like Holland, where the next town is only a few miles away.

"Do you think these people get lonely so far from others?"

"I doubt it; they likely are very happy to be in a place that is not crowded. I think I could like this."

Herve' thinks he would love this wide open space. For him it spells freedom, freedom to roam and explore. Evert says he wants to be close to people. "Who would help us?" he asks.

Soon there are no fences and few trees, just lots of snow and a few cows searching for food. Jon had read about these reddish brown cattle with white faces. Herefords, he recalled. "Must not be good farm land or there would be more people and bigger towns," mussed Jon.

In the distance they had their first view of mountains, snow covered peaks reaching far into the sky. Unlike the buildings in New York, these are like a giant wall across the land. The tall peaks stay on the right side of the train as the train begins to climb higher and higher.

After the mountains came the desert. Jon tells his boys. "See, there are few trees, mostly open land with bushes and I think those over there, and he pointed, are cactus."

"I thought deserts were hot and dry and sand," said Arie.

"That is the desert in Africa, the Sahara."

"It is sand and does not have cactus," interrupts Evert.

~~~

For lunch the second day, Nieske gave everyone a half sandwich with Edam cheese and a pear. She looked at Jon and said, "Our food is almost gone, what shall we do?"

"I don't know? We can buy food on the train, but I do not know how much it costs or what to ask for."

"How long till we get there, oh, and did you let Klaas know when we will arrive?"

"Yes dear, I sent him a telegram from the train station; see here is a copy." He took out the yellow paper and hands it to her.

"*Angomst, helft elf*, Fullerton," (arrival half before eleven or 10:30)

"We are going to be hungry by then, hope he lives close to the station."

Around three that afternoon Cornelia began to fuss and cry from hunger. Nieske retrieved a small chunk of Pumpernickel from her bag, broke off a piece and gave it to her.

"*Dat is alles,*" she tells Jon. "*Der es nietmeer,*" (That is all there is, there is no more.)

An hour later the train stopped at Tucumcari, New Mexico. Most of the passengers got off to stretch their legs or shop at the curio stands. The Van Bemmels are the only souls staying on board. Jon wanted to get off too, maybe find some food. He figured he would watch what others do and get back on.

Nieske was too afraid. Don't you dare get off Jon! What if you miss getting back on? Then I am alone with the four kids and no idea what to do."

"Not alone with four kids, Nieske. I will take Herve' with me, he likes to explore too."

"That is even worse! He will wander so far you will never make it back, stay here! We have been hungry before; we can wait." Her eyes tear up.

There sits the whole family, six immigrants who speak no English. The boys dressed in knickers and knee socks, obviously not Americans.

The train whistled. The passengers filtered back into the car.

The last two are men. They are dressed in suits and ties, although the ties are loose and top shirt buttons are undone. They were carrying brown paper bags which they present to Nieske.

Nieske' mouth dropped open when she saw what was in those bags. She looked at the men and then at Jon. The men have foolish grins across their faces. They smiled with pleasure when they saw her timidity and obvious gratitude.

"For you and the kids," they indicated with a wave of their hands.

Tears well up in Nieske's eyes,"*Dank u, dank u,*" she exclaimed in awe and gratitude.

Jon clasped each man's hand pumping them and pouring out his gratitude in Dutch.

All three men are talking, but none of them understood a word of what was said. Yet, all understood kindness, compassion and the gratitude.

Nieske is in awe with the bounty of this gift. There were two loaves of bread, one white and one wheat, a carton of margarine, peach jam, peanut butter, cheese, a six apples and a half gallon of milk.

Herve' looked at his dad, "I am going to like America. They are not like Germans are they?"

"Yes, son, this is going to be good place. It is like God sent these men to welcome us to America."

"Are they angels, Dad?"

They ate their fill, there was plenty left for breakfast the last day. Yes, tomorrow would be the end of their journey.

They slept in peace and contentment, with great hopes for the future. When they woke up the two men are gone.

The train passed through some more mountains. The snow was replaced with trees.

"Thirty minutes to next stop, Fullerton," announced the conductor.

"Is this California," asked Arie?

"Yes, it is. Sure is beautiful. Look at the trees, the farms and nice houses."

"Oranges, Dad, oranges, look at all the oranges. The trees are full of them," shouted Herve'.

"Hush, do not talk so loud," cautions Nieske.

The other passengers smiled at the excitement and joy they saw on the faces of those four immigrant kids.

The train blew its whistle as it neared the station.

The entire family stood by the windows anxious to see their benefactor, Uncle Klaas, and to see where they will live.

They spot Uncle Klaas in the crowd on the platform. He is taller than most and has this wonderful smile.

Of course he has a wonderful smile; it expressed his kind heart.

Herve' knew he was going to love this uncle and his new home.

Epilogue

Fifty years later Herve' visited Ellis Island and the Statue of Liberty. Recalling the emotions of that wintery day in 1947 he penned this letter to the Grand Lady who welcomed him to America when he was just a little boy fleeing oppression.

"Yesterday I walked down memory lane. Fifty years ago I saw you standing here, welcoming me to America. There you were in all your glory with the message of welcome and hope for those who desire to make America home.

My family suffered under Nazi occupation and left the reconstruction of The Netherlands to begin a new life in California. Seeing you again with your torch held high brought back the emotions of that cold winter evening when we sailed into the harbor.

I was in awe of the beauty and splendor of this country. I had never seen so many lights and such tall buildings. America my new home! My heart still swells with the thrill and anticipation of what was to come.

At school I learned of Emma Lazarus' poem that is on the plague in your base. Those words described us so well. We yearned to be free. Our lives in Holland and on the voyage had been tempest tossed. You welcomed us to the Golden Door. Every time I read or hear those words, of Emma Lazarus, my eyes tear up because I recall that first time I saw you. Even now as I write my eyes are filled with tears as the emotions roll over me, remembering the joy and hope of arriving here.

Your welcome and your promise have been true. America is a great land with great opportunities. I have a blessed life. I thank you for giving me that gracious welcome to my new home. Freedom and Liberty!

I have since traveled to many places in Europe, Africa, South America and the South Pacific and no place is there a welcome that comes close to yours, "lifting your lamp besides the Golden Door."

Herve' Van Bemmel, 1997

Acknowledgements

A big thank you to Emmy Eleveld, Adriana Weeda, Alice Van Beek-Bouma; three great ladies, Ted and Tina Mejan, a wonderful new friend, and an old friend, Jack Van Kampen. Plus those who want to remain anonymous who all survived the Dutch Winter and war, immigrated to California and were kind enough to share stories and thoughts about growing up and living during the Nazi occupation. You have blessed my life and enriched this writing. Thank you for your kindness and support.

Author's Note

I am happy to hear from readers and attempt to respond to all. You should visit my website at www.albertvandesteeg.com for information on coming events, signings and future publications. I will not read any emails that have multiple addresses. When you send email do not send any attachments, as it will not be opened for fear of viruses.